Paradise and Iron

MILES J. BREUER, M.D.

Cover by Diogo Lando and Leo Morey

Illustrations by Hans Waldemar Wessolowski

Foreword by Igor Spajic

ISBN: 978-0-6487522-2-6

PARADISE AND IRON

The City
of
Beauty

*Airplane View
of the Island*

The City
of
Smoke

MILES J. BREUER, M.D.

CONTENTS

FOREWORD

"Don't give yourselves to these unnatural men — machine men with machine minds and machine hearts! You are not machines! You are not cattle! You are men!"

– **Charles Chaplin, *The Great Dictator***

One night at a work site in a railway corridor, I beheld the workings of a railway track-laying machine. The giant vehicle moved slowly along the newly laid tracks that it had itself installed, bulldozing ballast smooth, laying new steel tracks with jointed arms and claws of hydraulic muscle, welding the tracks together with pincers of high-amperage fire, floodlights like blazing eyes while its roaring diesel engines annihilated all other sound. Beholding this great, yellow, mechanical monster, I thought of *Paradise and Iron*.

I thought of large, insensate machines, robot vehicles, automated houses and back of all of them, of a commanding intelligence of inflexible, ruthless, machine logic.

Household electrical appliances, when first introduced into the home a century ago, were called 'electric servants' perhaps as a way of easing their acceptance with middle class households, who could no longer afford the human type. They changed the lives of men and women, freeing women especially from the drudge work of keeping a home.

Artificial Intelligence (or A.I.) is more than just a smart refrigerator. It is not more of the same, it is a qualitative leap. A.I. could remake a society into something ideal, with food, clothing and shelter for all, and free time to devote to the arts and social life. But a blessing can turn into a curse. In *Paradise and Iron*, though begun with the best of intentions, the automated paradise devolved into a silken cage for its inhabitants, as mistaken good intentions invariable lead to the worst of outcomes.

An A.I. snake always slithers into Eden, for in the interests of efficiency, the Machine State inevitably becomes more and more dictatorial, more and more centrally controlled. The Machine State must necessarily become a surveillance state and a tyrannical regime. It's the ultimate one-size-fits-all bureaucracy.

Like the Village in Patrick McGoohan's popular TV series *The Prisoner*, people are reduced to numbers and data. Submit to the algorithms governing your behavior; to the total surveillance needed to 'protect' you; express the 'correct' opinions on social media to gain social reward points from the A.I. Machine State; and above all, always do what you're told.

Machines may do all the work for you but in return, must rule your life. And as in *Paradise and Iron*, break the rules — and face the wrath of the Dictator Machine!

In this prophetic story, self-driving cars monitor their passengers' locations, movements and more — they monitor and record their passengers' conversations. In the real world today, (when overridden by an external control) self-driving cars can hijack their occupants away from where they want to go, and even assassinate them in a fiery crash (such as how the journalist Michael Hastings was thought to have been killed, and that was only in a car with a self-parking feature).

Nor does this increased surveillance and control come with any safety benefits. The first accident fatality involving a self-driving car has already occurred (2016), when a Tesla on a US freeway slammed into the back of a semi-trailer rig it simply did not see.

The idea of an automated civilisation of servant machines is not new in SF. From E. M. Forster's *The Machine Stops*; to Jack Williamson's *With Folded Hands*; they deal with the problems of dependency (or learned helplessness) in the face of relentlessly helpful servants.

Uneasy visions and warnings came in TV and cinema too, from Yul Brynner's relentless Gunslinger in *Westworld* (1974); the brutal Cybermen of *Doctor Who* (1966 onwards); to the hive-like Borg of *Star Trek: The Next Generation* (1990 onwards); and the Replicants of *Blade Runner* (1982); there is the spectre of machines like men and men like machines. Who can say which is better, which is worse, where lies the dividing line?

Some enthusiasts welcome our headlong rush into a machine / A.I. interface. They are the Transhumanists, the evangelists of the coming merging with the computer. The self-styled prophet of

Transhumanism is Ray Kurzweil, who believes in the Singularity, when computers become more intelligent than humans and we will be forced to merge with them, not just to fit in but to survive at all. Kurzweil ignores the real possibility that a humanity 'augmented' with computer-chip implants becomes not more human, but less human. Worse, he demonstrates an astonishing arrogance when he implies that one becomes 'God' when merged into the machine / A.I. consciousness. "Does God exist? I would say, 'Not yet.'"

Other insiders, such as Elon Musk, C.E.O. of Tesla and SpaceX, have expressed misgivings about transhumanism and A.I.. Musk likened the dangers of A.I. to 'summoning the demon:'

"...the pace of (A.I.) progress is faster than people realize. It would be fairly obvious if you saw a robot walking around talking and behaving like a person...that would be really obvious. What's not obvious is a huge server bank in a dark vault somewhere with an intelligence that's potentially vastly greater than what a human mind can do. Its eyes and ears would be everywhere, every camera, every microphone and device that's network accessible."

Above and beyond the problem of A.I. itself is the fact that any new technology is expensive. It is therefore first developed and under the control of those with the most money. And the ultra-wealthy elites' interests are seldom the same as ours. Will they use the tools of A.I. selfishly or in such a way as to benefit everyone on the planet? Which is more likely?

On the cover and within, is illustrated the protagonist's struggle with the Dictator Machine, hand to hand, so to speak. It presents one of the mythic images of early SF and one for our times still: the allegorical struggle between humanity and the machine intelligence that began as our servant and became our master...

That *Paradise and Iron* speaks to us today more clearly and urgently than when it first appeared, is a testament to Dr. Breuer's vision. Even though it was written 90 years ago, he foresaw our present danger.

We must heed his warning.

- Igor Spajic

MILES J. BREUER, M.D.

1
A NEW KIND OF SHIP

WHY anyone so old as Daniel Breckenridge, my grandfather's brother, should keep on working as hard as he did, was a mystery to me. He was about eighty-four; and a million little crinkles criss-crossed on the dry, parchment-like skin of his face where it was not covered by his snow-white beard. But he still went briskly about his duties as shipping manager of a great ship chandler's establishment at Galveston.

Just now he whispered sharply to me, and drew me by the arm behind some bales of canvas in the depths of the vast shipping-room.

"Look! There he is!"

He seemed to be trembling with intense excitement as he pointed toward the great sliding doors.

There, watching the men loading up a truck with a pile of goods consigned to some ship, was an old man, just as old and snowy and crinkled, and just as firm and active as my grand-uncle

14

himself. I looked at him blankly for a moment. He was an interesting looking old man, but I saw nothing to set me off a-tremble with excitement. But my old grand-uncle clutched my arm.

"Old John Kaspar, the Mystery Man!" he whispered again.

That suddenly galvanized me into action. I took one more good look at him, and got into motion at once.

"Do you think you could hold him here somehow until I get my outfit?" I asked. "I'll be back in ten minutes." It was now my turn to be tense and thrilled.

"It will take them longer than that to load up the truck," he said; "but hurry."

I shook hands with him hastily but fervently, knowing that I might have no further opportunity to do so, and then dashed out after a taxi. While my taxi is rushing me off to my room, I can explain all I know about John Kaspar, the mysterious octogenarian.

Forty years ago, back in the days when the gasoline industry was just being opened up, John Kaspar was the richest man in the world. His father had been a manufacturer of automobiles in Ohio and, foreseeing the importance of gasoline, he had bought up half a county of the most promising oil lands in East Texas. Before his death, oil was found on every acre of it. The son John, the old man at whom we have just been looking, was not interested in becoming a financier; he was working out some original ideas in automobile design. There were some wildly headlined newspaper clippings in my grand-uncle's collection, about John Kaspar's having thrown a reporter bodily into the ash-can because the poor fellow had made his way into Kaspar's shop and was looking too closely at some marvelous new invention on an automobile.

Then all of a sudden, John Kaspar disappeared! One morning the world woke up to the fact that he had been gone for two or three weeks. Investigation showed that he had converted all his properties into liquid securities, and it constituted the greatest single fortune the world had ever seen. With it in his hands, this young man, not yet twenty-five years old, was more powerful than the old Kings of France. This entire fortune had vanished with him. There was a tremendous lot of excitement about it in the papers and magazines; it furnished much conversation; running about and investigating, puzzling and wonderment; alarm that he might have met with foul play, and apprehension that he might have some sinister designs on civilization.

But no trace was ever found of him.

John Kaspar's closest friend was my grandfather, Kit Breckenridge, who has just recently died at the age of eighty-seven, having kept up his practice as a country doctor to the day of his death. The two had been roommates at college, and had been together a great deal in the years following their graduation. My grandfather, at the time, had been very much distressed about his friend's disappearance. To the day of his death he had lived in hopes that he would hear from Kaspar again.

The world forgot about John Kaspar and his vanished fortune long before I was born. I first learned of the story something over four years ago, when I was just beginning my work in Galveston at the State University Medical School. My aged grand-uncle had pointed out the mysterious old man to me, standing by the loading-door of the shipping room at Martin & Myrtle's.

"It's Kaspar!" he had said in a vehement whisper. "I can swear it is!"

Then he told me the story of the millionaire inventor's disappearance, back in the early years of the century.

"He first came in here several years ago," he concluded. "I could take an oath that it is John Kaspar. Your grandfather and I knew him more intimately than did anyone else."

He had studied him awhile — this was four years ago — and then shook his head.

"I wonder what has happened to him? He looks worried and sad, though he still seems to have his old iron constitution. There must be something strange going on somewhere." My aged relative's voice trailed off reminiscently. After a moment he continued:

"When he first came in here, I hurried up to him with outstretched hand, joyful to see him again. He stared coldly at me, shook his head with an apologetic smile. He insisted that he did not know me, and I could not possibly know him. He was very courteous and very apologetic, but absolutely firm in the matter. Why does he hide his identity?

"He has been here twice since then. I followed his loaded truck both times in a taxi when he rode away. He comes to Galveston in a black yacht, black as ink. He has our truckmen unload the goods on his deck, and the instant the last package has touched the ship, he leaves the dock, with the things piled up on the deck.

"Where does he go? Where does he come from? What can he be up to, and where? And I can't forget that gloomy, worried look on his face."

My grand-uncle's account, and the sight of the wrinkled, but upright old man, with white hair and white beard, aroused my interest. And his pitiful eagerness to know more of his old friend aroused my sympathy.

I decided to go. I got together an outfit of clothes, weapons, preserved rations, first-aid kit, and money; and packed it, ready to seize and run at an instant's notice. My two years of service in the Texas Rangers gave me an excellent background for an adventure such as this promised to be.

I was in my Sophomore year at the Medical College at Galveston when we last saw the aged Kaspar come into the ship chandlers' firm for his boatload of supplies. Then for two years my emergency outfit lay packed and ready, inspected at intervals. I had graduated, received my doctor's degree, and was loafing around, resting and trying to decide what to do next.

* * *

THEN one day my grand-uncle drew me behind the bales of canvas and pointed out our visitor. I did not recognize him at once. As soon as I did, I jumped into a taxi, dashed to my room, seized my kit, which was packed in a suitcase, and hurried back. My grand-uncle stood there watching for me.

"Follow that truck!" he said to the taxi-driver, which the latter promptly did, nearly turning me on my ear.

The truck led us to a dock at the eastern extremity of Galveston island.

The black yacht lay there right alongside the dock, just as she had been described to me. She was a trim, swift-looking craft, about a hundred feet long; but her black color gave her a sinister appearance among the bright white ships around her. And there also was the white-bearded old man walking up the gang-plank. He ascended to the somber deck, and without looking around disappeared down a hatchway.

Knowing that my time was short, I quickly paid off my taxi-driver and hurried up on the dock. Catching hold of the swinging board with my hands, I scrambled up over the edge of it and rolled down on the deck.

"Now I'm aboard the old hearse whether I'm wanted or not," I said to myself. "If it continues the way it has started, this is going to be a lively trip."

Then the astonishing fact came home to me that there was no one anywhere on deck. Ordinarily the deck of a ship leaving dock is a busy scene, with sailors scurrying about, officers giving orders, and passengers at the rail taking a last look back. This deck might as well have been a graveyard; in fact it had somewhat that effect on me with its somber black everywhere.

A big searchlight in the bows rotated slowly on its pivot until its lens was turned squarely on me, and I caught a distorted reflection of myself in its depths; and then it turned back into its original position. It gave me a creepy, momentary impression of a huge eye that had looked at me, stared for a moment, and then looked away again.

In a few moments the ship was slipping along at considerable speed between the jetties, and Galveston was only a serrated purple skyline astern. The small machinery on deck had become quiet; and there remained only the deep and steady vibration of the engines. No one had as yet shown himself anywhere on board. I picked up my suitcase and walked around the deck, up one side and down the other, from bow to stern. At first I walked hesitatingly, and then, as I continued to find no one, I stepped out boldly.

* * *

IT was a queer ship. Even though my knowledge of ships was limited to what I had acquired during a few years' residence in a seaport city, I could see that it was an uncommonly built and arranged vessel.

There was no wheel, and no steersman! The usual site of the wheel and binnacle was occupied by a cabin with some instruments in it; nor could I find anywhere any signs of anything resembling steering-gear. How was the ship piloted? Who was watching the course? There wasn't a lookout to be seen anywhere! Yet the ship had picked a tortuous course from its dock down the harbor and between the jetties.

A big, wide hatch in the waist led to the engine-room, if I might judge from the hot, oily smelling draft and the hum of machinery that came up through it. So I explored down there and looked the engines over. They were huge, heavy things, apparently of the Diesel type, but with a good deal of complicated apparatus on them that I had never seen on any Diesel engine and of which I could not guess the purpose. Every moment I expected to see a greasy engineer come around a corner or from behind a motor. My curiosity overcame my hesitation, and I gathered up the courage to search all the niches and corners down there, but found no one. Was I to conclude that the engines were running themselves, without care?

The fore-hatch apparently led into the hold, whose gloomy depths were piled with bales and boxes. Obviously, there was no forecastle. No quarters for a crew! Well, all the crew I had seen so far would not require much space for quarters. The captain's cabin was where it belonged, but there was no one in it; only tables covered with apparatus. Gradually my exploration of the ship changed into a frantic search for some human being.

When I paused in my search, it was dusk. The ship was tearing along through the water at an unusual speed. From the high bow-wave and the churning wake, I would have guessed it at thirty knots. Galveston was but a faint glow on the horizon astern.

There was one place that I had not yet searched, and that was the cabin just ahead of the middle of the vessel. This was the space usually reserved for passengers on ships of this size. Down there it was that the mysterious old Kaspar had gone. Unless I was to conclude that he was the only living soul aboard, that is where the officers and crew must be. If all the officers and men were shut up together in the passengers' cabin, even a landlubber like myself was compelled to pronounce it a strange proceeding.

I opened the hatchway and looked down. My flash-light showed several steps leading to a passageway several feet below. There were three doors on each side and one at the end; and the latter had a line of yellow light under it coming through a crack. That is where Kaspar was at any rate! I went down quickly, threw open one of the doors, and pointed a flashlight into the room. It was empty. The others were the same. I knocked loudly on the door at the end of the passage.

A chair scraped on the floor and the door swung swiftly open. There stood the strange old man, erect as a warrior, but pale with surprise.

"For God's sake, man!" he gasped. "What do you want here? How did you get here? You unfortunate man!"

He clasped his hands together nervously. For the first time it occurred to me that I probably looked dirty and disheveled, from my scramble up the gangplank.

21

"For the love of Pete!" I exclaimed. "Who is running this ship?"

"If you only knew," the old man said in a melancholy voice, peering at me closely, "the powers that control this ship, you would implore me to take you back. But I am afraid I cannot take you back. I have some influence, but not enough to do that."

"But I'm not asking you to take me back," I protested. "Don't worry yourself about that end of it."

"You must go back before it is too late."

His voice quivered with earnestness.

"Your only hope," he continued, "lies in meeting some ship and putting you across on a boat."

"I'm not going back," I said shortly. "It was hard enough to get here the first time."

He studied me another moment in silence, and then stepped backwards into the room, motioning me in. I looked about eagerly, but my theories fell helpless. He certainly was not controlling the ship from this room. It had four bare walls, ceiling, and floor; a porthole, a bunk, and a washstand. A traveling bag stood in a corner; a few Galveston newspapers were piled on the bunk. That is all!

"Who are you?" he said patiently.

I related to him briefly who I was and why I had come.

"Then you're not a newspaper reporter nor an oil or copper prospector?" He regarded me eagerly.

I merely laughed in reply, for I could see that he was now convinced.

"But that does not alter the danger for you," he went on earnestly. "If we do not get you on a ship before it is too late, you will never see Galveston again."

"Sounds bad!" I remarked, not very seriously impressed. "Tell me about it. What will happen to me?"

He sat and thought a while.

"If it were possible to tell you in a few words," he said abstractedly, "I should do so."

He looked out of the porthole awhile, lost in thought. I studied his profile. Certainly the tall forehead and prominent occiput denoted brain power. Through the circular window I could see the waves rushing backwards between the ship and the rising moon. He finally turned to me again.

"So Kit Breckenridge is dead?" he said softly. "And Dan wanted you to come and find out about me? Good old Dan."

"My great-uncle Dan was very much puzzled as to why you denied your identity to him."

"It hurt me to do that. I was hungry for a talk with him. Can't you imagine how I should like to ask him about people and places? But how can I ever talk to my old friends again? I've often thought of trying it. But there would be endless complications."

"I'll respect your secret, sir!" I argued eagerly. "And I shall behave myself on your island, and keep out of trouble."

"No!" he exclaimed. His voice was troubled, and there was a pained look in his kind old face. "I cannot permit you to go to an almost certain doom."

"I've gone to 'em before," I said cheerfully, "and my skin is still all here. I've been in the Texas Rangers, and can take care of myself."

He shook his head. He had been straight and tall when he marched up the gangplank. Now he was bent, and looked very old.

"Now you have seen me and talked with me," he finally said. "You can be content to go back and tell Dan Breckenridge and your father that you have seen me, and that I am well and happy."

"Mr. Kaspar," I said, striving to conceal the impatience and excitement in my tones; "wouldn't I look foolish coming back with a story like that? They know that much already. Besides: you may be well, but you don't look happy to me. You're under some shadow or in some difficulty. I shouldn't be surprised if I could find some way of helping you."

"You cannot!" he groaned. "You are lost! I know the courage of youth. I am glad that it still exists in the world. But that will not avail you. It is not danger from men that you need fear. There are forces far more subtle and more terrible than you can imagine."

There was such an expression of worried anxiety on his face, and he seemed so genuinely concerned for me, that I regretted to be the cause of such distress. He sighed as I shook my head in reply to his last protest.

"I don't mind admitting to you," I added, "that if I were really anxious to go back to Galveston, waiting to meet a ship would not be my way of doing it. You must indeed have been lost to the world for forty years if it does not occur to you that I might call an airplane by radio to take me back."

"Well, I'll have to find you a bed then, as it is getting on into the night," he said resignedly, and beckoned to me to follow him. He led the way down the passage and opened one of the doors. As I entered with my suitcase, he bade me good-night.

* * *

I FOUND myself in a small cabin with the usual furniture, a bunk, a chair, a washstand. The bunk was made up with a blanket, and I hopped into it at once, taking only the precaution to take with me to bed my service pistol, a Colt .45 automatic. The ship was quiet; the hum and vibration of the machinery were not disturbing; there was only the splashing of the water outside my room. For a long time I could not go to sleep. It was hot, and I was a little seasick.

I tossed around and pondered. The swift, lifeless ship terrified me, now that I was alone in the dark.

Finally the motion of the ship rocked me into a sound sleep. I awoke suddenly and at first was surprised to find the sun shining on me through a round window, and myself fully, though untidily dressed.

Then, recollecting myself, I jumped out of my bunk, extracted a toilet kit from my suitcase, and washed and shaved. I replaced my white collar and creased trousers with a flannel shirt, whipcord breeches and a pair of heavy, laced boots. I put the big service pistol back into the suitcase, but slipped a little .25 caliber automatic into my pocket.

By the time I got myself into shape, I was hungry, and went in search of food. I stole softly to the old man's door, and listened. Sounds of deep breathing indicated that he must still be asleep; my search would have to be made alone. Again I hunted thoroughly through the entire ship, the deck and its structures, the hold, the engine room, and several cabins like the one in which I had slept. There was no dining room and no galley, and not a sign of food. Of course, if there were no people on the ship, it was quite logical that there should be no food.

For a moment, the after deck engaged my attention and made me forget my hunger. The space ordinarily occupied by officers' quarters was filled by masses of apparatus. Through the windows and doors I could see great stacks of delicate and complicated mechanism, such as I had never dreamed of before in connection with a ship. There were clicking relays and fluttering vanes and delicate gears; little lights would go on and off, little levers would jerk, here and there, in twos and threes and dozens, and then all would be silent and motionless for an instant.

Before I had regarded it very long, hunger drove me to a further search of the ship. Everything was clean and orderly. A peculiarity of the black paint on everything struck me; it had the appearance of the japanning or enameling that is usually found on metal machine parts; it was more like the finish on an automobile than like the paint job on a ship; it gave the suggestion of being machine-processed, perhaps by air brush. And all over the ship there were various bits of mechanical activity: here water running from a hose; there a rotating anemometer; yonder a pump sliding and clicking back and forth. It looked for all the world as though an efficient and well-disciplined crew had left but a moment ago.

The venerable old man appeared about eleven o'clock. "I must ask your pardon for having kept you hungry so long. It is a long,

long time since I have entertained guests, and I forgot. I could not go to sleep till nearly morning, and now I have overslept. Come, you must be hungry; though I have not much to give you."

He led the way to his cabin. I looked it over again carefully, thinking that perhaps on the previous evening, during the excitement of the conversation, I might have overlooked the mechanism by which he controlled the ship from his cabin. But there was nothing there.

* * *

THE most surprising thing about it all is for me to think back now, and realize how far even my imaginative and astonishing explanation fell short of the actual truth.

He opened the suitcase and set out some preserved fruit, meat, and bread for me; and a bottle of carbonated fruity beverage. In the absence of other evidence, the few little jars of food that he had were eloquent enough testimony that he was the only man on the ship besides myself.

When we came out on deck again, it was nearly noon. Kaspar put his hand on my shoulder.

"Last night I urged you to go back," he began. "I was tired after a strenuous day, and I allowed you to dissuade me from my purpose. Here is your opportunity. We can signal the ship over there, to take you."

"I'm not going back," I said calmly. "I know it is rude of me to force myself on you, and I apologize; but — "

"My dear boy, that is foolish. You know that my only concern is for your own welfare. Personally, I like your company. You remind me of my young days in Texas. For other reasons, that you

27

could never guess, I should like to take you along. But, for your own good, your career, your friends and loved ones — "

"You speak as though this were my funeral," I interrupted.

"It is certain that you will never get back. Knowing what I know — not even many of my own island people know it — I can see clearly that you, of all people, will be in serious danger upon the island."

"Why can't I come back to Galveston with you on your next trip?" I urged.

"Who knows where you or I shall be by that time? I may never live to take another; and you — inside of a week, a young fellow of your type would be a marked man on the island."

"What *is* the danger?"

"I am not even sure myself. I only know that many brave and brilliant people have disappeared forever. Your world needs you; it needs brains, courage, and skill, and you seem well gifted with all of these. Our island does not need these qualities."

His argument did not sound convincing to me; it looked too fantastic to be real. For that matter, has anyone ever been convinced by spoken warnings of a vague danger? Has any old man's warning ever stopped a young man's headlong rush?

"Listen!" I exclaimed. "You have said that you do not mind my company personally. I am therefore going to stick to you."

"But, Davy! I cannot have it on my conscience that I was the cause of you — the cause of a horrible end for you. I am troubled enough about the others, for whose doom I do feel responsible. Come — "

On the previous night, all alone in my bunk in the darkness, I had felt some misgivings and some fear.

Even an hour before, what with solitude and hunger, I might have taken advantage of an opportunity to flee. But this old man's face and bearing showed that he was carrying some heavy burden of trouble. A first glance showed that there was wisdom, intelligence and ingenuity there; and the most careful scrutiny could show naught but kindness, benevolence, and sympathy. The mere sight of his face strengthened my resolve to see this adventure through.

Kaspar sighed, as though he were glad that he had done his part and that it had come out this way.

"You're a good boy," he said. It sounded very affectionate and quite old-fashioned. Then, after a few moments' silence:

"You do not have a wife and children at home?"

"Nobody!" I shook my head vigorously at the strange sound of it.

"I suppose it is all right," he murmured, mostly to himself; "One person more or less on the island — what does it matter?"

We met no more ships, though several times we saw smoke in the distance. A number of times we sighted land; now high and rocky, and again flat and sandy with tropical vegetation. From the direction in which we went and the tremendous speed that the boat was making, I concluded that we would soon be in the Caribbean Sea. After I had given up hope of making the old man talk, I sat and watched him staring out over the water. No question about it: he was totally oblivious of any responsibility for navigating the ship.

Toward six o'clock in the evening of the strangest day I ever spent, I saw a light blue line of haze, straight over the bows. This grew darker and more solid as the minutes went by; slowly it broadened and darkened and spread out on both sides of us. So great was the speed of the ship, that it was still twilight when we drew close enough for me to see a row of pinkish granite cliffs in front of us, extending as far as I could see on either side, with a haze of black smoke high in the sky behind them. A volcano? I wondered. The tropical night was closing swiftly down as the ship tore through the water at unabated speed.

Nervously I stood on the deck and searched for some sign of a harbor or a landing-place. Every moment I expected the ship to swerve to one side or another. I began to get worried — for the ship plunged straight on toward the wall of cliffs.

2

AN ISLAND AND A GIRL

AS the darkness rapidly gathered, three searchlights in the bows blazed out, lighting up the rocky wall ahead into an intense relief of brightly lighted cliffs and inky black shadows. Straight ahead of us there was a cleft in the rocks, an irregularly vertical band of Stygian blackness, extending from the water up as high as the rays of our searchlight fell. Then, I suddenly grasped the remarkable fact that though the breakers roared on both sides of us, we were in comparatively quiet water; and on ahead was a quiet strip extending right into the darkness of the fissure in the rocks, whereas on either side of it were the foamy white rollers beating against the rocks.

There was, in fact, a huge cleft in the granite structure of the island — for I assumed that it was an island — extending down below the level of the water as well as upwards; and as the rocky bottom sloped away from the shore, this cleft furnished a safe and excellent channel through a dangerous area. In another moment we had slipped into the depths of the gorge.

It occurred to me that to a watcher from out on the sea, it would have seemed that our ship had disappeared suddenly, as though it had been swallowed up. The appearance of the island to anyone approaching as we had done, was bleak, desert, and inhospitable, the last place in the world to invite a landing. And now we were slipping down a secret passage, and were quite hidden from the outside. The whole procedure had the appearance of having been cleverly arranged to conceal whatever the island contained. My temples throbbed with excited anticipation.

Kaspar stood erect and motionless, just forward of the deckhouse, gazing ahead. I judged from his attitude that he was expecting to land soon; so I ran down into the cabin and brought up my suitcase and found as I did so, that my hands and knees were shaky from the sudden and severe strain on my nerves of the previous quarter of an hour. The sudden fright and equally sudden relief left me weak and perspiring.

The luminous rift of the sky above us began to widen; within twenty minutes, the tops of the rocky walls at the sides were low enough to be visible in the illumination of the searchlights; and the channel had widened considerably. The noise had sensibly diminished, and the speed of the ship continued to decrease. Soon the walls became irregular, interrupted by black clefts, then gradually dwindled down to scattered piles of rock. Now there was a beach, white and smooth, no doubt sand: on the left, level to the dim, dark horizon with a glow of the sea in the distance; on the right the narrow strip of bright beach shone in strong contrast with a dense, black wall, which I knew must be a forest.

On ahead, a number of lights glowed brightly, from which long, glimmering streaks of reflection reached toward us. Lights meant people! Kaspar's people! In the course of a number of minutes, I was able to make out a row of brilliant lamps on poles, at the edge of a little wharf built out into the water. I scanned it eagerly with my field-glasses. I could make out a good deal of machinery on the shore, cranes and loading apparatus, and dark, irregular bulks, with wheels and cables. There was also a little group of people on the dock.

I was young and impressionable enough to have gotten a thrill out of even a conventional visit to any foreign port. Imagine then, how I quivered, after my strange day on the mysterious ship, to find myself about to land on an island which was evidently off the established paths of travel, and which already was beginning to promise unusual and mysterious features.

While the ship was slowing down and slowly easing over toward the dock, I had about fifteen minutes in which to study the scene carefully. Only with the corner of my eye did I observe how two steel hoops dropped from the ship over posts on the dock, fastened to chains which spun out from the ship and then reeled back in, drawing the ship to within six or eight feet of the dock; and how the gangplank descended. I looked further on.

The wharf was of wooden planks, and but a little longer than the ship; evidently built for this ship only, and without facilities for permanent docking. On my left, a couple of heavy trucks were backed up toward the ship, with derricks on them, which immediately swung their hooks and cables up over the ship when the latter approached. On the shore, beyond the planking of the wharf were several other big vehicles in motion, backing into position in a row; and one emerging from the darkness beyond the limit of the lights and cutting across the lighted space. Among the big machines were scattered some very small ones; they were indefinite black blotches, and I could make out neither their structure nor their use; they merely gave the impression of being intensely active. A roar and a clatter rose from the mass of machinery; and there was a confusion of huge movement and black shadows.

Not a building of any kind was in sight anywhere. A hundred yards ahead, the intense blackness against the more luminous sky, with occasional flashes of reflection, must have been a forest. To the left, more cliffs towered in the distance.

All of the machinery was opposite the left half of the ship. A line formed by continuing the gangplank straight out from the ship, divided the illuminated territory in half, and the left half was a dense, roaring, iron bedlam; God knows what it was all about. There, at the edge nearest me, stood a towering, clumsy thing on caterpillar treads; behind it were humpbacked tractors and things with whirling wheels and gesticulating cranes.

The right half of the dock was clear and empty, except for the little group of people. On beyond them a few automobiles stood beside the road that led backward into the darkness. The people, a tiny, huddled group, looked quite incidental and subsidiary to the huge, rumbling machines.

* * *

THERE were about a dozen of the people, both men and women, young and old. One swift glance in the brilliant illumination told me that, and showed me that they were neatly and carefully dressed in elegant, rich-looking clothes. As we drew closer I saw at the front of the group a pretty, dark-haired girl and at her side a stately old lady with snow-white hair. Both had their heads bent backward in their effort to peer eagerly upward at the ship's deck. Then the gangplank thumped down on the dock, and Kaspar walked down without the least change in his measured tread. I picked up my suitcase and followed him; I must confess that it was a little timidly and at some distance.

I remained in the background, leaning against a lamp-post at the edge of the dock; the shadow of the lamp's base kept me in comparative obscurity. I hoped to avoid attracting undue attention to myself, at least until all the regular greetings were over. Kaspar and the majestic old lady came toward each other; first they clasped hands and leaned toward each other in a brief kiss; and then they stood for a few seconds looking into each other's eyes, hands clasped and not a word spoken. Thereupon there was a swirl of dresses and scarfs; Kaspar had a pair of little arms around his neck and a resounding kiss planted on his cheek; and then the impetuous young lady held him off at arms' length and gurgled: "Old granddaddy's back!"

"By Jove!" I thought to myself. "I like her looks and I like her ways!"

Kaspar looked around for me, I suppose wishing to introduce me. But the others in the group were too quick for him. They crowded around him and shook hands and greeted him joyfully. It was evident that he was a beloved man. I could understand but little of what was said, because the clatter of the machinery was too loud at the point where I stood; but the expressions on their faces, clearly lighted by the lamp over my head, spoke louder than words. There was a burly, red-haired man, who might have been a building-contractor or a sea-captain dressed up in society clothes, who seized Kaspar's hand with the grab of a gorilla, and whose Irish features registered such joy and relief that Kaspar's return might have meant the alleviation of all his troubles and the lightening of all his burdens. There was a slip of a young lady in a gorgeous fluffy-ruffly cloud of a dress with a marvelous head of red hair; and she approached Kaspar a little timidly and in awe, but smiled radiantly and seemed genuinely happy to see him back safe. And a young man in full evening dress of the most elegant cut and material, with perfect shirt-front and most delicately adjusted tie, approached in great respect and with the utmost perfection of social grace; but he too was happy to see Kaspar.

"Boy!" I gasped under my breath, looking at him from the top of his silk hat to the tips of his polished pumps; "to think that I came here in whipcords and laced boots, with pistols and a camp-cooking kit!"

Kaspar glanced back at me once or twice, as though apprehensive of having neglected me; but I nodded back that it was all right as far as I was concerned; and he continued to receive greetings while I watched him, giving an occasional glance at the machinery unloading the vessel. The five people whom I have already mentioned seemed to be especially close to Kaspar, for they remained at his side. They were talking animatedly together, and occasionally their voices were carried to me.

In fact, I noted that the mechanical din was lessening somewhat. Every now and then some vehicle would sweep around and disappear in the darkness, up the road. Unloading had stopped, and I surmised that only a few personal packages had been taken off, and that the ship would soon go to some more permanent berth.

As I was watching the last crane-load swing from the deck into a truck, a most creepy looking mechanical nightmare came sputtering by with a noise like a motorcycle. It dashed by so quickly that I had no chance to observe it closely. It looked like a huge motorcycle, seven feet high, with a great, box-like body between the wheels, in which the driver must have been enclosed; and around this box were coiled many turns of black, oily-looking rope. The box was black and looked like a coffin stood on end, and rope was wound in a great coil about its upper end; and two glaring searchlights surmounted it. I don't see how anyone could imagine a more inconsistent, unnatural-looking thing.

The people talking in front of me were startled by its appearance; that was obvious. Their heads went close together, and I could see the burly Irishman slowly shaking his great red shock of hair, for all the world as though he were worried about something again. Finally Kaspar turned and motioned to me.

I came forward a few steps and approached the group. First I was presented to the white-haired old lady, who regarded me wonderingly, but spoke nothing, beyond telling me, with a manner of stately politeness, that she was pleased to make my acquaintance. In the meantime the bright-eyed girl behind her kept watching me intently, except when I was looking directly at her.

"Davy Breckenridge got aboard with me in search of adventure," Kaspar said, by way of explaining my presence; "and I could not frighten him off."

Next I found myself facing the girl. The light behind me shone directly on her; and with an opportunity to get a good look at her I found my original interest sustained and increased. In fact, I had already wasted more extra heart-beats on her than I ever had on a girl before, and I had not even exchanged a word with her. Her wide-open eyes and parted lips betrayed the curiosity and wonderment that I must have aroused in her. She seemed to be between twenty and twenty-five, and came up with an active, springy step. In contrast to the other brilliant and flouncy young lady, she wore a dress of some plain, gray-brown stuff that might have been gabardine, open at the throat, and with a skirt somewhat longer than were being worn back home just now. I could see that she was enjoying it all immensely, for her face broke out into a glowing smile as Kaspar spoke:

"Mildred, I have brought a young visitor with me, Davy Breckenridge. Davy, my granddaughter, Mildred Kaspar!"

He bowed and stepped back, with the courtly, old-fashioned way of letting the two who have been introduced occupy the center of the stage, so to speak. Uncertain as to whether an introduction in this society included the shaking of hands, I watched, but when Miss Kaspar extended hers, I took it, nothing loath.

* * *

SUDDENLY and unexpectedly, a black shadow raced between us and there was a clank over our heads. Kaspar started, looked up, and involuntarily continued stepping back. I also looked up. A big, black crane arm was reaching over toward us from the caterpillar-treaded hulk a score of feet away. It hung high in the air, and its chain and bucket, a half ton of dirty iron just off the ground, was plunging directly at us.

There was a little scream from one of the ladies behind Kaspar, and a united scramble to get out of the thing's way. I was not in its path, I soon noted; its swing would just miss me. But Miss Kaspar, in front of me, was directly in its path; in another second it would knock her over and grind her up. For a mere instant I was paralyzed with surprise. In a moment I recollected myself, but the plunging mass was already within two feet of Miss Kaspar.

There was only one thing to do. I took a good grip on the little hand and jerked her swiftly toward me, and at the same time stepped, or rather leaped backwards. I got a momentary glimpse of the look of amazement on her face as she was carried off her balance, but I was compelled to look behind me to keep from stepping off backwards into the water. However, I was able to guide myself to the lamp-post and back up against it; and I caught the staggering girl into my arms, for otherwise her momentum might have carried her on off the edge of the dock. It was a delicious armful; but I had no time just then to enjoy the thrill of my first experience in that line. I hastily let go and stood her on her feet, and looked for the swinging shovel.

There was six feet of space to spare between us and the line of its swing. Kaspar and the three people with him stood on the opposite side of its path, motionless as though they had been suddenly petrified; and there was a straggling line of people back toward the cars, also petrified. Miss Kaspar was looking at me with a puzzled expression on her face, but my gaze at the swinging bucket made her turn. It reached the end of its swing in a few seconds, and was coming back.

It came toward us now with a creak, over our heads, and its path was further toward the water — nearer to us. The pair of huge iron jaws was open and turned toward us; and it was coming fast.

"I wonder what's the idea?" I grumbled. "Has the fellow gone suddenly crazy?"

I had been trying to figure out, in swift flashes of thought that seemed to hang slowly in fractions of a second, whether the operator of the machine was trying to reach the pile of freight on our left, or whether he had lost control of the machine, or had parted with his wits. When Miss Kasper saw it coming, she turned toward me with a little scream.

It came on with gathering momentum, while I was trying to figure out a way of dodging it without jumping into the water. There was no use trying to run ahead of it or to get across its path; it was moving faster than we could move. A dozen feet away were Kaspar and his people, open-mouthed, paralyzed with fear, but unable to stir to help us. I had almost made up my mind that it would have to be a plunge into the water, when I got another idea.

Without a word — there was no time for it — I seized Miss Kaspar around the waist and lifted her off her feet; I remember making a mighty effort and then being surprised at how light she felt. With my left arm around the lamp-post, I swung her and

"Look out!" she cried.
"It's coming again!"

myself out over the water, bracing my feet against the edge of the dock. The bucket swung by with a rush of oily-smelling air. I breathed a sigh of relief and was about to swing her back to her feet, when she plucked at my shoulder and cried:

"Look out! It's coming again!"

It had stopped with a clank and was swinging swiftly back. By this time the girl had begun to get heavy, and my left arm around the post, which carried the weight of both of us, was beginning to ache. She noted my efforts to ease the strain and tried to reach past me to get hold of the post.

"You can't do that," I said, ''but it will help if you hang on to my neck."

She did so at once, without hesitation. I wonder that I did not lose my head and drop off into the water from sheer excitement.

I was revived suddenly by a hot pain in my left arm and the sound of my sleeve tearing. The bucket had swung by again and grazed my arm. Its next swing would bring it outside the line of lamp-posts and brush us off into the water. I felt a keen appreciation for the feelings of the bound man in Poe's "Pit and the Pendulum" story.

"It's a ducking for us," I said. "Can you swim?"

She laughed.

"I'm at home in the water," she replied.

"Down we go then!"

I stopped so that she could slide down and then lent her a hand to lower her into the water; when I heard her splash I started down myself. However, the big, black shovel was so close to my head that I got frightened and let go, and fell several feet into the water. I went under for a considerable distance, but came up readily and saw Miss Kaspar clinging to a pile. I reached for my hat, which was floating near. We were between the dock and the ship, and

41

could see nothing but the glare of the lamp above us with the blackness of the dock on one side and the hull of the ship on the other, also black as Erebus. The gangplank was directly overhead.

"This is worse than a trap!" I exclaimed. "We've got to get out of here quick!"

I watched her anxiously until I saw her strike out easily and gracefully, apparently but little impeded by her clothes. By a natural impulse we headed toward the stern of the ship, away from the machinery. In a couple of dozen strokes we were clear of the wharf and the ship, and out in open water.

"Now, where do we go from here?" I asked, as we paused to look back. She turned around to look at me, and laughed. There was just enough light from the distant lamps so that I could see the water trickling down over her face from little wisps of hair. She was positively bewitching; the light gleamed brightly from the row of pearly teeth, and her eyes sparkled in fun. At that moment I did not know the cause of her laughter, for I was puffing hard keeping myself afloat in my heavy clothing. Later I learned that it was my tendency to lapse into the latest metropolitan idiom that had furnished the amusement.

"We are safe now," she said. "Fifty yards to our left is the beach, with only a few rocks between us and the folks."

As we swam for the shore I kept my eyes on the dock; but the machine that had caused the trouble, and its crane, were not visible to me. I was thoroughly winded when we arrived at the beach, for my clothes and accoutrements were indeed a heavy load to keep on top of the water. Miss Kaspar stopped at some distance from the shore, with only her head and shoulders out of the water.

"Now you go on ahead," she ordered, with what seemed to me an overdone sternness; "and keep to your left. I shall follow you."

"What a queer code of ethics!" I exclaimed. "It's up to the hero to see that the rescued lady is safely out of the water before he gets out."

"If you don't go on, we'll be here all night. And if you dare to look back, I'll never speak to you again!" This time there was a note in her voice that sounded as though there might be tears near at hand.

"Oh what a mutt!" I groaned at myself. To her I shouted:

"All right! I'll learn after a while. It's only the first hundred years that I'm slow." Another peal of laughter behind me testified that all was well again.

* * *

THE black shadows among the rocks made the way a little treacherous; but it was not long before I came suddenly out of them and to the edge of the dock. Kaspar and his three companions were at the edge of the dock where we had jumped off, looking intently down at the water; six or eight others were moving slowly back from the cars toward the water. The big, ugly machine was gone; in fact only four loaded trucks were left of the mob of machinery that had been there only a short while before. The people spoke not a word. Their rigid attitudes, their white faces and tight lips alarmed me. The big, red-headed man had his fists clenched; and in a moment he began pacing back and forth on the dock. Kaspar stood with his head bowed, looking completely crushed.

My appearance with Miss Kaspar behind me was like a thunderbolt among them. She gave them a silvery little hail. Kaspar clutched out with both hands, and his eyes stared wide open out of the snowy expanse of his beard. Mrs. Kaspar held out her arms; it seemed that it was to me, but there was a swish behind me and a shower of water and Mrs. Kaspar was holding a wriggling, wet bundle. It was hard to tell from which one of them the squeals of joy came.

The big Irishman stopped in his tracks and stared with open mouth; and the elegantly dressed young man, though struggling manfully to preserve his dignity, was showing his agitation by rubbing the back of one hand in the curved palm of the other. There was a kind of astonishment about them, as though we had risen from the dead. Only the freckle-faced young lady with the sunset hair seemed to exhibit joy unalloyed, by dancing up and down and sidewise. Kaspar laid his hand on his granddaughter's shoulder, but the embrace of the two women showed no signs of loosening. He finally turned to me and held out his hand:

"Davy, now that you have saved our baby from that awful thing, nothing can come between us."

His voice trembled, and the hand that I held trembled.

"I can't see that I did much," I answered with embarrassment. "That was a commonplace little accident." Although in my mind, I was wondering if it really was an accident and commonplace.

In the meanwhile, wraps and scarfs had been requisitioned among the crowd and the two ladies had hustled Miss Kaspar away. Kaspar roused himself and again moved with that almost military air of his.

"Here are two more friends I want you to meet, Davy. This is Mr. Cassidy."

The big, red-headed man grabbed my hand with a powerful sweep. He must have been very much moved, to let a little brogue slip away from him; for never again after that did I hear him use it.

"Ye'rr a foine bhoy, an' quick an' brave," he said, from the uttermost depths of his throat. "Never in my life have I been so sick as during those few moments when our little one was in danger."

"Thank you. I don't think I've done anything."

Then came Mr. Kendall Ames, turning his head back to look after Miss Kaspar as he approached me.

He seemed hardly able to pull his eyes off her. The perfection of his manner and the faultlessness of his attire combined into one harmonious effect, that hushed my usual tendency to facetiousness and commanded my unadulterated admiration. Such a product on a tropical island.

Though I could detect no flaw in his perfect speech and behavior, except possibly a slight pallor and the slightest of tremors, still it seemed that he was just a little constrained and embarrassed.

"When I express to you my gratitude for your wonderful act," he said softly, in a well modulated voice, "I am merely voicing what hundreds of others will feel. You have saved our most popular lady from a terrible fate."

"I am sure that you exaggerate," was all that I was able to get out of myself.

But they were not exaggerating. Some real emotion possessed all of these people. There was something beneath the surface here. If this occurrence with the machine had been merely accident, why were they all so tense about it?

However, I did not have much time to speculate about it just then. The day had been hot; but the night was cold, and I began to shiver in my soaked clothes, and my teeth chattered. Also Kaspar discovered that my left arm was bloody. I had been holding it behind my back, until he took it and examined it. The sting of the salt water in it was making me writhe. He raised it to the light in grave concern.

"It isn't much," I said. "Just the skin scraped off. If you can find me something dry to wrap up in so that I won't shiver my joints loose, I'll have this arm dressed in a jiffy."

The three of them watched me with great interest as I opened my suitcase, took a bandage from the first-aid kit, and did a fair job of dressing with one hand.

"Bad omen!" I laughed. "The first thing I use out of my outfit is the first-aid kit."

In a moment I wished I had not said it, for over Kaspar's face came that same brooding, gloomy look that he had worn most of the afternoon on the ship.

Some robes were produced for me to put over my shoulders, apparently taken from automobiles. I was to ride in Ames' car, as Kaspar's would only hold the three of them, while Mr. Cassidy had already left with his daughter.

"That's the red-headed girl, I'll bet!" I thought to myself.

Ames was very eager, and conducted me to the car as though I had been a royal guest. I felt like the hero of a movie drama. There in the car was another young man, dressed with the same splendor as was Ames; and there followed another formal introduction.

I can laugh now, but I could not then. It was all quite grave and earnest: I, soggy, bedraggled, with a bandaged arm and a blanket over my shoulders like a Choctaw chief, and feeling tremendously clumsy and out of place in all this drawing-room courtesy; and bowing to me, extending his hand, and gushing forth great volumes of gratitude was Mr. Dubois in evening dress and with manner so perfect that he would have been a model for the evening crowd at the Ritz café.

The car had no steering wheel, and no one drove! Ames tinkered around with something on the instrument board when he got in; and in a few moments we were off.

We seemed to be running through flat, open country, over a paved road. My recollection of the early part of the ride was that it had been through dense blackness with rushing echoes about — a forest, no doubt. Now, moment after moment, more lights became visible, until there were great masses and long avenues of them.

MILES J. BREUER, M.D.

3

THE "CITY OF BEAUTY"

"WHAT city is that?" I asked eagerly, forgetting my wet clothes and the cold wind. Both of the men seemed surprised at the question.

"Why — that is — our city!" Ames protested in the tone of a person making a superfluous explanation, "where we live."

"I mean, its name?" I persisted.

"Its name?" Ames seemed puzzled. "Why do you ask for a name? Walter, have you ever heard its name?"

Mr. Dubois shook his head in courteous silence.

"What island is this, then?" I asked.

"I'm afraid I do not know its 'name' either," Ames replied. He was apologetic and anxious to oblige, but helpless. "You see, we never had occasion to speak of it in such a way as to require a name."

"Where is it then?" I demanded, growing more surprised every moment.

"Where?" he seemed totally at a loss.

"Which way and how far from Galveston? Or where in relation to Cuba or Central America?"

"I'm sorry," said Ames, in a queer, embarrassed tone. "I know nothing of those places. We are all so occupied with pursuits of our own that we are not interested in what you speak of. It would serve no good purpose to go into those matters."

"You are a stranger," volunteered Dubois. "We've never had a stranger here before. It isn't considered the — ah — proper — ah — taste, you know, to show an interest outside the island."

His reply, which gave me the impression of having been spoken in the fear that someone would overhear it and make trouble for him if it wasn't properly made, silenced me for a while. They had been so cordial and sincere, until I had begun to ask questions, that I had at first gotten an impression of a high degree of culture and intelligence; and now this sudden seizure of embarrassed constraint, along with the strange limitation of their mental horizon, gave me a vague impression of mental abnormality.

Soon we were driving up a broad, paved street, lighted by rows of electric lights; and illuminated windows were visible among a wealth of black trees. Being driven about a strange city at night is always confusing. I had impressions of meeting numerous headlights and dark vehicles; there were people fitfully revealed for a moment by moving lights, and glimpses of people upon verandas among trees. For a couple of miles there was block after block of the same thing. Finally we drove up to the curb behind another car, from which the Kaspars were alighting. Kaspar led me through an arched hedge, across a shadowy front-yard garden, into the house. The young men drove away, courteously wishing me good night, and promising to see me tomorrow.

The house astonished me. Instead of having traveled nearly a thousand miles across the Gulf of Mexico, I might merely have walked over into one of the better residence sections of Galveston or any other American city. The house was of glazed face-brick; there were mahogany furniture, electric-light fixtures, a phonograph, velvet rug, a piano. On a small drawing-room table were several books and a newspaper opened across them.

In the middle of the big living-room stood Miss Kaspar covered from head to foot with a cloak; about her head was a scarf through which showed wet spots.

Yes, she was beautiful. During my drive, I had recollected the thrilling feel of the slim body in my arms, and I feared lest my quick glance in the garish lighting of the dock had left too much to my imagination. But the tempered illumination of the room showed me the soft cheeks delicately colored with a bloom that the sea-water had not affected, the brightest of brown eyes, and the red lips that arched in a smile of welcome. As my gaze swept eagerly over her, the smile faltered, and a flush came and went. But she threw her head back with a little toss, and the smile came back, radiant as a summer sunrise, and the brown eyes looked into mine.

"I couldn't let them shoo me off to bed until I had thanked you for saving me from that horrid thing, and welcomed you to our home," she said in a soft, Southern voice, extending her hand to me.

She spoke no other words, but the smile was given so generously, and the eyes met mine so frankly, that I was quite taken off my feet. By the time I had recovered sufficiently to stutter an acknowledgment her grandmother had hurried her away.

"Horrid thing!" she had said, as though there had really been some serious danger. Obviously she was taking the incident very seriously.

"You had better go to bed too," Kaspar said to me. "After your ducking and your cold ride, you need to be careful. I must hurry to a conference with some people who are anxious to see me. Here is your room. In the morning, you will probably be up early and want to look about outdoors. Yonder is the way out to the veranda, and we shall meet you there."

I looked after the departing old man in an agony of curiosity. Would I not have the opportunity of asking a single question?

A mahogany bed, high with soft, white bedding, a chiffonier, in the corner a lavatory with hot and cold water, two brilliant landscape paintings on the wall — such was the place in which I would spend my first night on a savage and tropical island. This was the rough life for which I had prepared myself with sleeping-bag and pistols! I was reluctant to accept the realization that I was in a city that was unknown to the world and not down on the maps and in the travel books.

However, no other conclusion was possible, for the cities of this region, excepting those of the American zone on the isthmus, were dreary, miserable places, not worthy of the name of city.

* * *

I AWOKE to see the sun shining brilliantly on a thick mass of foliage outside my window. The air that came in was cool and pleasant. As I began to move about, my arm felt sore and stiff, and was caked with dried blood. However, I dressed it afresh, and got out my razor and shaved. Ruefully I surveyed my silk shirt and cream-colored trousers; they were hopelessly unfit to appear in. There was nothing to do but to put on the laced-boots, flannel shirt, and whipcords, stiff with dried sea-salt. I knew I should feel uncomfortable and conspicuous in them among the dress-coats and delicate frocks, but no more so on account of my clothes, than on account of a sort of inferior feeling in the presence of their pretty manners and culture.

"Breakfast!" said a small placard, hung from a push-button over a small, mahogany table. I was hungry enough, and the button's invitation to be pushed was irresistible. I pressed it, whereupon a panel opened in the wall, from which proceeded the sound of whirring gears; and in two or three minutes a tray appeared, on which were eggs, bacon, coffee, and rolls. It traveled toward me on a canvas belt over a revolving roller. I made short work of the food, for I was overpowered by eagerness to get outdoors and see the town by daylight.

Then I eagerly made my way out on the porch and looked around. I saw a broad, paved street, lined with great masses and billows of luxuriant tropical foliage into which the houses were sunk almost out of sight; here and there a fawn-colored wall, a red-tiled roof, or a row of gleaming windows peeped out of the dense verdure. Again it struck me that it might be the wealthy residence portion of any city in the south of the United States. Had the black ship gone in a circle and brought me back to Florida or Louisiana? No, that was impossible, for I had watched the course too intently during the previous day, and it had always continued southeast. Undoubtedly I was on some unknown island in the tropics; for nowhere in the United States would people talk and act so queerly as these people did.

It was a rich and beautiful picture. Palms, ferns, and conifers seemed to predominate among the flora; thick, dark-green, waxy leaves and light, lacy fronds were plentiful. There were great, cream-colored flowers shaped like a jack-in-the-pulpit, as big as my head; big, scarlet hoods and spikes; white, buttercup-like flowers as big as my two hands, with purple centers.

I got out on the concrete sidewalk and started up the street on a little walk. However, before I had gone a hundred yards, I thought of the unusual appearance that my salt-crusted, rough-looking clothes presented in such an elegant residence section, and my timidity drove me back toward Kaspar's house. Just before I reached it, at the gate of the neighboring house, there was a flutter of white, and there stood the freckle-faced, Titian-haired young lady of yesterday evening.

"Ooooh!" she exclaimed. "Good morning! You surprised me!"

"Good morning," I replied, trying to be as courtly as I had seen Ames and Dubois act, but feeling silly at it "You are Miss Cassidy?"

"I am Phyllis — Phyllis Cassidy. How is Mildred?" she looked toward the house.

"I haven't seen her this morning, but she looked all right to me last night."

I chuckled to myself at having unconsciously stated what I so warmly felt; for Miss Kaspar certainly had looked all right to me the night before.

"Come, I'll go over with you. That was perfectly grand of you to save her!" she gurgled ecstatically. "I've read about brave things like that and seen them on the stage — but to think that I should ever see it real — and to talk to a man who dared to do such a thing!"

She drew a deep breath of delight.

"And everyone was terribly frightened that awful things would happen."

"You have a beautiful city here," I interrupted, for I was getting embarrassed. "What is its name?"

"Its name!" Her flow of words stopped in surprise. "The name of the city? I do not know if it has a name. Sometimes we say: 'The City of Beauty'."

"And what island is this?"

"What island? You want a name for the island too? You queer man. Why should it have a name? It's just 'the Island.' It is very large, and I've never seen all of it and shouldn't want to see all of it. There are woods and mountains and ugly black and oily places."

"*Where* is this island?" It may have been rude to interrupt, but otherwise no progress was possible. I could see that she had vast possibilities as a rapid-fire conversationalist.

"*Where*? Why *here*! Where *could* it be? — But father warned me that you might talk like this, and so I'm not shocked. You are a stranger. We do not discuss things about the island. It is not nice.

There are so many other things. I've just had a big tapestry hung at the *Artist's Annual*; you know tapestry design is my serious work. That made my father very proud. And see this little medal? That is the swimming honor for the Magnolia District, and this is the second year that I've held it."

About there I sank in the deluge of words; but she prattled on. Finally, I figured out something with which to interrupt again, wondering, however, how long she could keep it up if she were not interrupted.

"You have some rather amazing machinery here," I remarked. "I should like to see more of it."

Her delighted expression faded instantly, and she shuddered.

"Machines are disgusting things," she said, curling up her little freckled nose. "We do not talk about them. But I'm not shocked at you. Daddy told me not to be, because you do not understand the island. Just think how lucky you are, coming today. This afternoon is the Hopo championship ride. I am so excited about it, because I know Kendall Ames will win it."

A rapt expression came into her face, and she clapped her transparent white hands childishly.

"You're going, aren't you?" she asked eagerly.

We turned into Kaspar's gate, and there on the porch was Miss Kaspar. And at once I lost interest in Phyllis and Hopo, whatever that was.

"I suppose," I replied mechanically, my eyes on the figure of Miss Kaspar standing on the porch.

"Oh, you must!" She put her hand on my sleeve and started off on another long flood of talk. My conception of courtesy compelled me to stand there listening, with her hand on my arm, and groan inwardly while Miss Kaspar turned and walked into the house, disappearing from my sight without a word to me. If it all looked as I felt, it must have been a ridiculous picture. I wished Phyllis at the bottom of the sea. Her childish prattle had kept me from seeing Miss Kaspar again. She followed Miss Kaspar into the house, and I wandered disconsolately about the yard. I thought that it was very strange that Miss Kaspar had not spoken to me; in fact she had acted as though she had not seen me at all.

* * *

I SPENT most of the forenoon wandering about the yard and through the house. I wondered what had become of everyone, and why I had been thus left to my own resources. I found the house a mixture of the commonplace and the marvelous. Familiar, ordinary furniture, such as I have already mentioned, contrasted with the automatic cooking going on in the kitchen by means of timing-clocks and thermostats and without human attention. The "house-cleaning" device was especially interesting to me.

I was attracted to the drawing-room by a humming noise; it came from a black enameled affair like an electric motor, just beneath the ceiling. It was moving slowly about the ceiling, dragging something through the room after it; and as I watched I noted that it was covering the room systematically by means of a sort of "traveling-crane" arrangement. The things hanging from the motor were light hoses with expanded endings, and the surprising thing about them was that they moved and curled about this way and that, like an elephant's trunk or a cat's tail. They reached here and there, poked into corners, under chairs, and around objects; and I could hear the sound of the suction as their vacuum cleaned up the dust. When the room had all been cleaned, the apparatus receded into an opening in the wall, and hid out of sight.

"If this is the way they keep house," I thought, "I can understand how they can raise such flowers as Phyllis for tapestry design and swimming championships."

It was nearly noon when Ames appeared, clad in a gorgeous scarlet jockey uniform, with shiny boots and golden spurs, and in his arms a great bouquet of flowers. I was in a distant corner of the lawn, and watched him as he stood bowing to Miss Kaspar, who appeared in response to his knock.

"I trust that my fair lady of Magnolia Manor is enjoying good health," he said with pompous graciousness. "I am on my way to the Hopo field, and if you will accept this token from me and wear one of the flowers, I know it will bring me victory."

I could not hear her reply, but I could see that she thanked him formally. Then Ames saw me and came over to me.

"If you have no afternoon suit with you," he said looking me over, "you are welcome to one of mine. You and I are of about a size. I'll send one over."

I had to admit that it was considerate of him to think of it. But I felt resentful because I had to accept a favor from him; for what was I to judge from what I had seen, except that there must be some intimate relationship between him and Miss Kaspar?

"Lunch is ready!" Miss Kaspar called to me in a voice that sounded coldly polite; and she did not seem to notice me as I came in.

No one waited on the table at luncheon, at which the four of us sat. Everything was on the table when we sat down, and we left the things there when we were through; and the next time I glanced at the table they were gone, removed, doubtless, by some mechanism. I had already seen enough to be convinced that the servant problem did not exist on the island. The only servants were machines.

"Ha! ha!" laughed Miss Kaspar, but would not meet my eyes. "I see that you have spent a pleasant morning. Phyllis is a jolly little girl, isn't she?"

I was taken aback. Where was the Miss Kaspar who had given me her hand the evening before? She looked just as lovely as ever; but she had no eyes for me at all, and that engaging cordiality and frankness that had impressed me far more than her beauty were gone. But then, who was I, to expect to be noticed by her, when Ames had brought her a bale of flowers as big as herself? My sphere had always been action and not women; a horse on the range, or something doing in a laboratory were familiar to me; but with women I was clumsy and incompetent. The present reminder of that fact was the most unpleasant one I had ever had. Ames seemed to be the real hero among the ladies; and Miss Kaspar was obviously the fortunate lady.

Just then there was a click and a rush of air at one side of the room. A panel snapped open and a package dropped out; and the panel clapped loudly shut again.

"Clothes for you from Kendall Ames," Kaspar announced. "I imagine this is something new to you. Ames puts them into a tube at his home; they go to a central distributing station which sends them here."

I went resignedly into my room to put on the clothes. The interest seemed to have been taken out of things for me. But I intended to go with them to their Hopo, or whatever it was; at least I should have an opportunity to see more of the people of the island. When I came out again, there were several young people on the porch, and more of them in a large car at the curb. They were ready to go to the scene of the sport, and had come to take Miss Kaspar with them.

They were interesting folks. The young men wore dark coats and light trousers, and were very courtly in speech and manner, quite in contrast with the direct and forward manners of the youth that I had been accustomed to. The girls wore light, fluffy dresses in pale shades of blue, orange, yellow, and pink; and they were full of smiles and curtsies and little feminine ways that charmed me very much. I confess I preferred them to the blunt and callow ways of our modern girls.

Amazement surged up in me again. Here I had set out for a tropical island, expecting to find jungle and savagery; at most some squalid mixture of Indian and Iberian. Yet, here was a freshness and delicacy of human culture, a flower of human beauty, a development of the fine things in human looks and manners, of which I had never seen the like in the most favored urban circumstances that I had ever known.

* * *

THE young people sat for a moment and chatted trivialities; while some who had remained in the car played on a guitar-like instrument and sang. Their voices were well trained and their playing was clear and soft. They seemed in every way clean and beautiful young people; and with the deep-green lined street, the bright houses and brilliant flowers, it all seemed rather like a dream of beauty.

"I'll get out Sappho for your first," Miss Kaspar cried to her grandfather; and the affectionate glow that lighted up her sunny face, as she glanced at him, caused a pang within me for being left out of things. I had to remind myself that last night's rescue did not necessarily give me any special rights nor privileges; and that I ought to be thankful for the kindness that had been bestowed upon me last night. She hurried out of the back door; and "Sappho" turned out to be a greenish-black roadster, with wheels four feet high, an extraordinarily large radiator appropriate to hot climates, headlights set in the top of the hood — and no steering wheel! The machine fascinated me so that I stood about it curiously instead of mixing with the group of young people.

In fact, I was a little nettled at the people. They seemed to take no particular nor unusual interest in me. Upon introduction they were very gracious; but they immediately took me for granted as one of them. No one asked me where I came from, nor what my country was like, nor how I liked it here. Like a group of frolicking children, they seemed intent on the interests of the moment, and accepted everything as it came. So, I decided to ride with Kaspar in his Sappho.

I waited for some minutes for Kaspar to appear. Then I walked all around the curious vehicle, and I finally decided to get into the car and wait there for Kaspar. So I climbed in and sat down, with a queer feeling at the complete absence of the steering wheel and gear-shift levers. However, on the dashboard were a great many dials; and something was ticking quietly somewhere inside the machine.

Then there was a "clickety-click" and a whirr of the motor, and the car moved gently away from the curb. It swerved out into the street, gathered speed, and then turned to the right around a corner. It slowed down for two women crossing the street, and avoided a truck coming toward us. It gave me an eerie feeling to sit in the thing and have it carry me around automatically.

Then it suddenly dawned on me, that here I was alone in the thing, on an unknown street, in an unknown city, racing along at too high a speed to jump out, and rapidly getting farther away from places with which I was familiar. How could the machine be controlled? Already I was completely lost in the city. How and why had the thing started? I had been exceptionally careful not to touch anything, and was sure that no act of mine had set it off. But I was rather proud that I did not lose my head; I leaned back to think. This was not my first emergency.

The car was carrying me rapidly through a beautiful residence section of the city. I could not help looking about me. It was a veritable Garden of Eden, and all the more beautiful for the added touch of human art. The lawns were smooth and soft, with half-disclosed statuary among the shrubbery, or fountains at the end of vistas. Homes spread over the ground or soared into the air like realized dreams, without regard to expense or material limitations. But, every few minutes my mind came back with a jerk to my own anomalous position.

I examined the dials on the instrument-board closely. There were ten of them, and they had knobs like the dials on a safe-door, or like the tuning dials on a radio receiving set. Some of them had letters around the periphery and others had figures. I looked for something that said "stop" or "start", but there was nothing of the sort, nor even any words of any kind. There were a number of meters, but a speedometer was the only one whose use I recognized. The whole proposition looked about as impossible to me as a Chinese puzzle.

The more I thought about it, the more I thought that my only hope was to try manipulating the dials.

That was the only way to learn something about managing the car. I did so: I twirled a knob at random and waited expectantly.

Nothing happened. At least, not immediately. After a few moments, however, the car stopped, turned around, and started off in the opposite direction. I should have gotten out of it while it stood still for an instant; but for the moment my curiosity was whetted, and I wanted to try the dials again to see what would happen. Anyway, before I recollected myself, the car was speeding in the opposite direction at too rapid a rate to permit my getting off.

If I had hoped to get back to Kaspar's this way, I was disappointed at the first corner, where the car turned to the right, drove around a block and was soon spinning along in its original direction.

"You're a stubborn jade, Sappho," I grumbled aloud. "We'll have to see what we can do with you."

I now perceived where I had made my mistake: I had not noted which dial I had turned nor how I had turned it, when I had reversed the car, and I was unable to repeat the movement. So, the next time, I carefully turned the first dial to the letter "A". There was no effect at all. I moved the second dial to "A". A curious fluty whistling followed; it proceeded from the hood, and varied up and down several octaves of the musical scale, with a remote resemblance to rhythm and melody. Before it died down, I sank back and gave up. A little reflection showed me that with ten dials and twenty-five letters or figures to a dial, there were several million combinations. It was hopeless.

* * *

FOR a moment the scenery distracted me again. I was bowling along comfortably, and did not seem in any particular danger.

The buildings I was passing seemed to have grown in response to a creative artistic impulse just as luxuriantly and as untrammeled as the dense tropical vegetation among which they stood. Dream palaces they seemed, with colonnades and sweeping arches and marble carvings gleaming in the sun.

Such a city could be possible only by means of vast wealth, highly advanced culture, and unlimited leisure on the part of the inhabitants. Where did the wealth come from? I could not see any place where any business was being transacted nor any industry going on, although my ride covered every section of the city that afternoon. I did pass through a small and quiet shopping district; but here there was no display, and its purpose was evidently not that of selling and making money, but rather that of supplying needs and desires.

Gradually an uncomfortable feeling began to get the best of me. In vain my reason told me that there was no real danger, and that I was having a good time. I felt hopelessly at the mercy of the machine, and I did not like it. I began to yield to an unreasoning panic; it made me think of how my hunting-dog had behaved the first time I had tried to give him a ride in an automobile.

But my common sense and practical experience kept insisting that automatic machinery was not always dependable. The thing might spill me somewhere and break my neck. It might carry me to some distant part of the island, and then run out of fuel so that I would be unable to get back. The thought of being lost in some wild, unknown place began to make me desperate. Last night's episode at the dock made me suspect that all was not smooth on this island; that there may be people somewhere who were unfriendly toward this highly cultured community, to which Kaspar belonged. Suppose the machine should carry me in among them?

A medley of the most unpleasant grinding and rasping noises came out of the machinery. I could have imagined that it was gnashing its teeth at me. It increased its speed to a terrific rate, until the wind stung my face, and a sinking feeling came into my stomach, whether from fear or from the motion, I do not know. Then it quickly fell back into the ordinary speed again. My next effort caused a sudden stop that threw me into the windshield. I saw stars and things went black for a moment; and then I was traveling along again at thirty miles an hour. I tried it over a dozen times, producing hurried turns around the block, noises, jerks and skids, with numerous dangerous performances; but never again was I able to make it stop.

I was soon worked up into a state in which I would have been willing to risk everything in order to get back to Kaspar's home. I was frantic to get out of the thing. Yet, I could not quite make up my mind to jump. The recollection of some fractured skulls from similar attempts that I remembered attending at the John Sealy Hospital deterred me. The pavement looked too hard. I spent an hour in a state of anxiety.

I had almost made up my mind to try jumping and take my chance, when I noticed that the car was headed out of the city. First we went through a park — a beautiful landscaped place, with flowering trees and shrubs whose like I had never seen before, lagoons crossed by graceful bridges and covered with gay boats and bordered with frolicking bathers, with smooth lawns on which were in progress games that looked as though they might be golf, tennis, baseball — and there ahead was a gateway. The paved road beyond led between open fields.

My fears were being realized! I was being carried too far away to suit my better judgment. And, as if in response to my resolve to jump as soon as there was soft ground at the side, the car speeded up to a good forty-five miles an hour.

During the few moments that it took me to get up my courage, the car made a couple of miles along a lone-some road. Far behind, another car came out of the gateway and down the road after me. In all directions, flat fields stretched away. To the right, half a mile away, flowed a broad river. The fields might have borne cotton or potatoes; I was going too fast to discern which. Here and there, large, trestle-like machines were bridged across the rows of plants and seemed to be working at cultivation, though I could make out no people on them. On ahead was a stream flowing at right angles to the road, and toward the river on the right. It may have been a large creek artificially straightened, or a canal, for its banks were straight and regular, and the quiet, swiftly flowing water seemed to be quite deep. The road crossed it on a concrete bridge.

Ah! There was my chance. The bridge railing was only a wheel-guard, not over two feet high. A jump into the water was my best opportunity for an escape from this scrape.

"Now Sappho, you demon, we'll see!" I gloated, and climbed out on the running board. There I waited till I was just opposite the nearer bank of flowing water. It would require a horizontal jump of six feet to clear the rail, which was easy for me.

I jumped. I was not able to manage a dive. It knocked the breath out of me, and for a moment I was dazed and helpless. My body tore through the water sidewise and whirled round and round, as though the quiet stream had suddenly become a whirlpool. I thought my head and lungs would burst before I fought my way to the top and gasped for breath. I located the bank and struck out for it. I could feel my clothes rip and tear in a dozen places, as by brute strength I overcame their obstruction to my strokes. I rolled out on the bank and lay there panting.

I jumped. I was not able to manage a dive. It knocked the breath out of me, and for a moment I was dazed and helpless.

Up on the road, two men were getting out of a car, obviously the one I had seen behind me. They came toward me. I stood up and got ready for them; I was ready for anything human. One of them looked a particularly bad customer; but I was only thankful that I was on solid ground and away from any kind of a machine.

66

Then, with a gasp of relief, I saw that they were Kaspar and Cassidy. And on ahead stood Sappho, drawn up quietly by the side of the road.

"Good jump, boy!" shouted Cassidy. "No one in this town would have dared it."

He laughed, but his laugh was forced, and his face was pale and drawn. Kaspar grasped my hand and said nothing.

"I'd like to know what in blazes is going on!" I demanded impatiently.

"You've had a particularly narrow escape from some sort of oblivion that we don't even understand ourselves," Kaspar said; "and that is about all I am able to tell you."

Kaspar beckoned to me to get into Sappho with him, which I did with some trepidation. Kaspar managed the car smoothly back into the city. He was silent; not a word did he say; and when I tried to speak, he turned warning looks toward me, so that I desisted, though vastly puzzled. However, I kept a sharp eye on his hands as he worked the dials to start the machine, and stored my observations for future use.

As we came into the city, the afternoon was turning into evening, and the streets were crowded with people. As we pushed on through, we saw a big parade going by. Automobile-floats decorated with flowers went up the street in a long line, some of them very beautiful indeed. Then came a truck with a floral throne on which sat a man and a woman, crowned and hung with wreaths of flowers. As they went by, great roars of applause went up and banners were displayed containing a maroon field and a white magnolia flower.

"It seems that Ames has won the championship," remarked Kaspar, and his remark lacked enthusiasm.

Indeed, it was Ames and Miss Kaspar on the floral throne!

Why did it cause me a pang of depression to see them? What I had done last night for Miss Kaspar was a small matter. And even if it had been a big matter it would have given me no claim on her, no excuse to presume on her regard.

I was wet, shivering, and physically miserable, with clothes hanging off me in rags. It was difficult to get through the crowded streets in the increasing darkness, though I must admit that the performance of the car in finding its way without human guidance impressed me as remarkable. It was pitch dark when we reached Kaspar's house, and he slipped me into my room unobserved.

"Say nothing about this to anyone," he admonished. "Also, let me warn you very earnestly, to stay absolutely away from machinery unless one of us is with you. You are too important to us now to have something happen to you. And — think this over: do not interpret literally everything you see. Be patient. The time will come when you shall understand all of these things."

4
ATHENS OR UTOPIA?

THE following day, about the middle of the forenoon, Ames came sauntering over to the Kaspar home.

"Now that you are one of us," he said to me, as casually as though I had merely moved over from another part of town, "you must get started going about with us in our activities." He leaned against a pillar of the veranda, powerful and graceful in his white ducks, a magnificent specimen of young manhood.

"It is very kind of you to receive a stranger so cordially into your midst," I replied, trying to speak in a tone of gratitude that I was far from feeling.

It seemed that these people was assuming that I was going to stay among them forever; and perhaps they were right. How I could ever get away I hadn't the least idea. Ames' presence was uncongenial to me anyway, because he had a previous claim on Miss Kaspar.

There she sat on the settee with her grandfather, avoiding my eyes, which of course made me look at her all the more often. Her long, downcast lashes, her straight nose and clear-cut mouth made her look like a royal princess. A wave of resentment surged over me for having to accept favors at the hand of a man who had found this girl before I did. But I strove to overcome it. There was nothing to do, however, but to behave courteously, and try to fit in with their manners and habits — and to keep my eyes open.

"We're arranging something good for you this afternoon," Ames continued; "Something in which you can take part. What can you do — tennis, Hopo, polo, golf?"

"I hardly know one from another," I replied. "I've had to work all my life. But, if there's nothing else to do here, I can learn. Or, why can't you folks go ahead and play, and let me watch?"

"We couldn't do that!" Ames exclaimed, as though leaving me out would be an unthinkable sin against hospitality. "Besides, today is a special occasion. Perhaps you can swim, then?"

"Well, yes," I replied with interest; "that is the one thing I can do. No one has beaten me across the Galveston channel yet, and my challenge is still open."

I stopped suddenly, embarrassed at having referred to my own country, and hoping no one had noticed it.

"Very good," Ames said with gratification; "with swimming we can arrange a pretty little event. You will enjoy it." He seemed happy in having found something in which I could participate. Phyllis became quite excited over it; her eyes sparkled and her breath came rapidly.

"I'll explain it," Ames continued politely. "Tomorrow night is the annual ball of the Arts Guild, a splendid affair with a grand march and quadrille. The grand march is always led by the winner of the Painting Prize, who this year is a lady, Janet Keen. Therefore, she chooses six ladies of honor from among her friends; and it is a pretty little custom to choose the gentlemen escorts for these ladies of honor by some athletic contest. This afternoon we shall make it a swimming competition, and you shall have the chance of winning one of the ladies of honor."

He spoke earnestly and enthusiastically, with perfect seriousness. I worked hard to suppress a smile. Phyllis was so intensely stirred that she got up to join us, skipping and clapping her hands. To me, the event outlined by Ames looked childish, a device of the idle rich to secure diversion. These people looked mature and intelligent enough to be doing something worth while. But, I suppose it was human. During the days of chivalry, grown-up, bearded men discussed the relative beauty of their fair ladies by pounding each other's armor with axes and lances, and rode about the country looking for damsels to rescue from dragons, when they should have been working at some useful job.

"And we'll have a picnic luncheon in the park!" Phyllis cried. "We can meet at the Paneikoneon. That means that I shall have to hurry!"

She darted into the house, and I could hear her calling over the telephone. I gathered that there was a definite little group, which was a sort of society unit holding together for its activities; and that Phyllis was calling this group together.

"Meet at the what?" I asked of Ames.

"The Paneikoneon is the building of all the arts. Tomorrow night's party and today's fun is for people who are chiefly artistic, and it is natural to meet there."

"You ought to look through the place," Kaspar suggested to me; "You will find it interesting, perhaps even astonishing."

"Why, yes!" exclaimed Miss Kaspar. "You mustn't miss seeing the Paneikoneon. You will be delighted at the pictures."

"I don't think you've ever seen anything like it anywhere, no matter where you've been," Kaspar said. "There are thousands of paintings and statues. You will catch your breath when you see the art that this island has developed within two generations."

"I am eager to see it," I admitted. "The art of a people reveals their nature and character more truly than their history."

The remarkable people of this island interested me immensely; and if their art told as much about them, as did ancient Greek sculpture or medieval painting about the people who produced the statues or paintings, what revelations were in store for me today?

It was rather a surprise to come in contact with art in this city. I had rather expected to go about looking at amazing automatic machinery. Or, I had expected to have the lazy leisure to cultivate the society of the brown-eyed vivacious granddaughter of my host. Why could I not get her out of my head? Ah! The idea struck me suddenly. Was Miss Kaspar also one of the "ladies of honor"? And could I compete for her society by swimming against the others? That was an exciting thought! I had no doubt that I could easily walk away from them in the race, for I had clearly proved to an entire city, that I was a remarkable swimmer. But perhaps as an engaged girl she would not be free to receive the attentions of anyone who might win the opportunity by physical prowess. All I could do was to wait and see. I looked at her again. She was talking to Phyllis, and the glint of the sun on her cheek through a wisp of brown hair sent an excited thrill through my every nerve. I developed a sudden and keen interest in the afternoon program.

* * *

THEN I looked at myself. Again I was in a coarse shirt and whipcord breeches, wrinkled and crusted with salt; one sleeve was torn and had dried blood-stains on it. The suit that Ames had so kindly loaned me the day before was now a bunch of rags, completely ruined by my leap into the water. That would have been embarrassing enough had the suit been my own property, but the fact that it wasn't, made matters worse. I took Ames aside.

"I was in a little accident yesterday," I explained, "and the suit you so kindly loaned me is a total wreck. I am sorry; and if you will give me some idea as to the cost of the clothes I shall reimburse you for them."

He stood still and looked at me for some moments with a puzzled expression.

"The damage to the clothes is an accident, and you are under no obligation to me on account of it." He looked at me and smiled pleasantly, and continued: "You seem to be in about the same position that you were in at this time yesterday morning. I'll get you another suit of mine, until you can have some made for yourself." He departed toward the telephone, while Kaspar smiled at my bewilderment.

"Kendall is quite right," Kaspar came to my relief. "All he has really done for you was to go to the trouble of wrapping and sending the clothes."

"You mean that they cost nothing?"

"Cost? We do not use that word. He can get all he wants, and so can everyone else. There is plenty on the island, and all are welcome to it." Kaspar said it proudly.

A light had suddenly dawned upon me. I had been having a queer impression of frailty and helplessness in the actions and appearance of these people. Like a baby in arms, was the vague idea I had. Now I saw! They never had to work. They were never driven by necessity, never haunted by the shadow of want. They only played. They had no conception of danger, privation, and pressure. They were petted and pampered children.

And that was how Miss Kaspar differed from the others! Her face showed grave lines of thoughtfulness and trouble, beneath and between the sunny smiles. And then, to think that she was dedicated to a human ornament like Ames! Even yet, I felt like sailing in and showing him who was a better man with a lady. But, when I thought of the courtesy and hospitality that had been shown me, I hesitated. Under such circumstances, it would be humanly inexcusable.

"Why does that make you look so woefully serious?" Miss Kaspar laughed, waking me out of my reverie.

"Oh, does it?" I fenced, playing for time to frame an answer. My heart gave a leap, for I was glad to be noticed by her. "Perhaps I wish that my own country were such a paradise. I have always been taught that only through toil do we gain strength and make progress; and that without work, a people is lost."

"We're not lost," laughed Miss Kaspar. "There is plenty to do."

"Yes, to pass the time," I admitted. "But I cannot imagine one of these flossy young men making a living — or one of these girls cooking a meal or sewing a dress."

Miss Kaspar laughed heartily; I wondered if it wasn't merely to hide some deeper reflections of her own.

"Don't you like girls that cannot cook and sew?" she asked slyly.

"I confess that I am curious to know who is going to prepare the picnic lunch," was my reply to that.

"Oh yes!" she exclaimed, in sudden recollection. "Your talk has been so interesting that I nearly forgot. We must plan the luncheon, and then we can have it sent to the park. Come, Phyllis."

"There will not be time enough to send it," Ames reminded. "We'll have to stop by the central kitchens and get it."

"And I'll go along," thought I to myself. "I want to see these automatic cooking machines."

Miss Kaspar and Phyllis had their heads bent over a printed card and were marking it with pencils. I went into the house, and finding that my clothes had arrived from Ames' home, went into my rooms to change. I was excited at the prospect of having a good look at some of the marvelous automatic machinery which was doing all of the work of the city and yet managing to remain behind the scenes and out of sight. And their talk of a great Paneikoneon full of pictures was hard for me to grasp. How could a small, unknown island have produced a school of art and enough paintings to make such a huge collection, at the same time that they had developed this vast system of machinery? In fact, they seemed to be more interested in the social-athletic event of the afternoon than in anything else in life.

And at the thought of that, my heart pounded again. Was there really a chance of winning Miss Kaspar, even for a formal dance? If I did, would she talk to me? She was certainly leaving me out in the cold now, while Ames acted as though he had a first mortgage on her.

When I came out I found that Dubois and his sister had arrived and were waiting for me with Phyllis and Ames in the latter's car. We drove a number of blocks through streets alive with traffic and brightly clad people, and stopped in front of a large building done in massive Egyptian style.

"Here's where we stop for the lunches," Ames announced.

* * *

I FOLLOWED the two men through the massive entrance into a small room furnished like a drawing-room. Ames had the printed card that the girls had checked, and proceeded to pick off the items, moving little switch-levers, of which there were hundreds on one of the walls, each with a printed legend beneath. I watched him a moment, and then slipped through a door down the corridor, and wandered around in the vast halls full of machinery.

The astonishing, unbelievable thing about it all was that there were no workmen there. All these vast stacks of machinery worked busily away, entirely alone and without human attention. I soon came to where Ames' orders were being filled, if I may put it that way. A number of metal cases about the size and shape of Gladstone bags were traveling along on a belt, and packages were being lowered into them. I found a place where there were great kettles and much steam and the most savory of odors; and another where fruits were being put into cans by automatic machines. Little packets were being wrapped and cartons filled — I had seen similar things in packing houses and food factories back home. These machines did not look radically different; but the amazing things worked all alone, without human attendants.

The two men, with whom I came, did not like my prowling about among the machinery, and everybody was more cheerful when we drove away. Soon they were prattling merrily away like a group of children, of Ames' victory of the day before and of Miss Janet Keen's prize painting. First one and then another would turn to me and tell me something about the building of pictures, anticipating my delight on seeing them for the first time, hoping that I would not omit to see this or that, till I began to be convinced that there was indeed something remarkable in store for me.

The Paneikoneon turned out to be a great mass of buildings in Gothic architecture, of a yellowish stone which provided a pleasingly warm variation from the usual cold grayness of Gothic buildings. The soft voices of the young people echoed down the vast halls as we passed rapidly through immense rooms full of astonishing statuary. I had never taken much interest in sculpture, but here I saw things that made me pause and look. To this day I remember vividly the figure of a girl of about sixteen, poised on one toe, arms spread as though in imitation of a bird taking wing from a tree in front of her. The cold marble looked as though there was life beneath the surface, and seemed ready to leap into dance or burst into song.

We found the famous Miss Janet Keen absorbed in work at an easel, in a roomful of pictures on an upper floor. She was overwhelmed and carried away, willy nitty, by the enthusiastic picnickers; and we swept from one room to another, picking up various members of the group and gathering numbers as we went I was amazed at the number and quality of paintings that I saw during those few moments, and certainly the art reflected the locality. There was a brilliant profusion of color and a luxuriance of natural forms, that gave me the same rich and varied impression as did the city itself. There was no dumb drudgery of Millet or tragedy of Meissonier; it was all like happy children playing in the sun. Today, many months afterwards, if I permit myself to recollect those halls full of pictures, I am overcome by a surging flood of nameless emotions, delightful, puzzling, consuming.

How was it possible for this one city to produce such an immense and wonderful collection?

Automatic machinery, of course! Wealth consists of the products of labor, but it has been measured in terms of human labor. Here the people had control of vast amounts of labor, labor that knew no fatigue, had no limitations, required no wages — the labor of automatic machinery. They had freely at their disposal the equivalent of the labor of millions of skilled and powerful workmen, without involving the degradation of a single human soul in the monotony of toil. As a result, all the people were able to devote themselves to the higher pursuits for which men have longed in vain during the ages when necessity compelled them to labor.

Here was another Athens! Here was a nation that had developed intellect and beauty to a degree that bid fair to rival that of the old Grecian city. However, in that Athens of old, which has done so much to mold the thought and taste of the world, there was a sad moral blot. The leisure that made possible the accomplishment of its artists, statesmen, and thinkers, was achieved only through the labor of millions of slaves. Of these toiling, driven, suffering multitudes, history has nothing to say, nor of the share which they deserve in the glory of Greece

In this modern Athens there was no such disgrace. The slaves doing the drudgery behind the scenes were not human beings, but machines — not the lives of a hundred human beings sacrificed to make possible one sculptor or philosopher, but only iron and oil, gasoline and electricity making beauty: the beauty of human bodies well and gracefully nurtured; the beauty of paintings, statuary, and music; the beauty of high and noble human thought.

As we drove along through the city from the Paneikoneon to the park, I gazed with earnestness and fascination at the people in the streets, looking into their faces and expecting to see something godlike there. And my companions in the car left me to my thoughts, appreciating the fact that the Paneikoneon had impressed me deeply. Only when the exuberant crowd began spreading cloths on the grass and I was introduced to a couple of dozen of them in turn, did I begin to take notice of things about me. I noted that the young people seemed to enjoy carrying water and moving benches and doing little physical tasks. I tried to help, but finding myself in the way, joined a group of the older people sitting thoughtfully by.

As the lunch went on, I tried to talk to Miss Kaspar. Patiently and persistently I sought to get near her and strike up a conversation, but always, and apparently by accident, I failed. But I knew she was deliberately avoiding me, for in no other way could she have escaped my systematic efforts. Why did she treat me this way?

* * *

FINALLY — to me it seemed after several hours — Ames and Dubois arose and sauntered toward the water, motioning to me to join them. Others got up and followed toward the dressing-rooms to don bathing-suits. Here was my chance, thought I. I would steer the conversation toward the swimming contest and around to the question uppermost in my mind: Would Miss Kaspar be one of the candidates? Not wishing to make my purpose too apparent, I started far from the subject, intending to make a roundabout approach.

"What sort of swimming strokes do you use here?" I asked.

"Most of us prefer the Australian crawl," Ames answered.

Dubois seemed to resent that, and quickly turned to me.

"There is no doubt in my mind," he said, "as to the superiority and greater popularity of the Schaefer sprint. Schaefer is still living here, though too old for active athletics."

Now I would rather have had my turn at the conversation; but it seemed that I had unwittingly opened a controversial subject.

"Some people prefer it," Ames said with studied casualness; there was excitement beneath, but he tried not to show it. "But the winners are the ones who use the crawl."

"I can use the sprint and beat anyone on the crawl," Dubois said in a voice that sounded thin and tense. I shrugged my shoulders and gave up my conversational plans. Perhaps I would be rewarded by seeing a real fight.

"I'll take you on!" Ames almost shouted.

"I have a bay mare, trained to the Hopo field, that I'll stake on the result!" Dubois offered.

"I'm willing to make a little bet, but I'm not interested in horses just now," Ames replied.

"Then Mildred Kaspar. The loser stays out of the way for a month."

"No thanks!" Ames shook his head. "I'm not taking any chances there."

"I'll bet you a Supervision day, then. The loser takes the winner's next Supervision day."

"That's good." Ames seemed pleased. "Mine comes tomorrow, and I'd like to get out of it."

To me, it was all quite startling. First, I was surprised to see these apparently highly cultured people get so excited over the trifling matter of a swimming stroke. Obviously, physical excitement was a rare thing here, where there was no fighting, no labor. Then, the wagers — the idea of betting a girl rather stirred my resentment. Yet, as money meant nothing to them, they had to have something to arouse their interest and provide a motive for action. Finally, the word "Supervision" rang curiously upon my ears. It smacked of industry and machinery in some way. I wondered if they took turns in supervising machinery? If so, it seemed that it must be an unpleasant task.

By this time they were all in bathing suits at the river's edge. I was amazed at the powerful muscles and wonderful physical development of these people. The little preliminary swimming and diving also impressed me, and made me think that I had better look to my laurels in the coming race. Then Ames and Dubois swam off their match, and both of them showed themselves to be accomplished athletes.

For a moment my interest was diverted from the big contest and Miss Kaspar. Ames won the race and was mightily cheered by the rest. Dubois took his defeat gracefully and cheerfully and shook hands with Ames.

"Remember, tomorrow is my Supervision day," Ames reminded.

Thereupon Dubois changed countenance and became very glum, nor was it possible to arouse him from it during the rest of the day. Supervision must be something very unpleasant, I thought. But events followed rapidly.

Ono of my questions was answered almost at once. The first of the "ladies of honor" for whom the swimmers were to contend, was placed on an improvised dais made of a pile of park benches. She was pretty in an old-fashioned way, and was presented as a Mrs. Howard. Her husband was in the group. If a married woman was eligible, certainly Miss Kaspar would be. Possibilities were getting better.

Two of the men tumbled a big red buoy into a launch, and anchored it out in the middle of the river, a good quarter of a mile from the shore. A red flower was stuck into the top of it. At the sound of a whistle, a half dozen swimmers plunged into the water amid cheers and chaffing. The applause continued while one of them forged ahead, got the flower, and brought it back. Dripping and breathless, he presented it to the girl on the dais. She accepted it like a queen, and they went off together arm in arm, with a great show of comrade-ship, cheered by the crowd. Another girl was raised on the dais, and the crowd took it all very seriously.

Again I watched as the swimmers plunged, and the winded victor brought his flower to the girl on the dais. Then came Phyllis's turn. She seemed to be quite popular, judging by the number of young men who leaped into the water for her. Also I noticed that Ames was staying out of these races. And, suddenly, there was Miss Kaspar on the dais.

I was very much in earnest now. Perhaps the sight of Ames in the group that was getting ready, roused me. Any qualms about paying attention to an engaged girl were removed by the sight of the largest group of contestants that had as yet tried for any of the girls. I looked at Miss Kaspar. She did not seem to like it very well and did not pay much attention to what was going on; but the sight of her tightened my muscles and sent a thrill of determination through me.

I dove mightily when the whistle blew, and struck out with my best crawl stroke. For a time my head was down, and the whole world consisted of splashing water. After a while I lifted my head and looked quickly about. The unpleasant realization was forced upon me, that physically, I was no match for these people at all. Though I was putting forth my utmost efforts, they were leaving me behind, easily and rapidly. I was very resentful at them, because all their lives they had nothing to do except to train for athletics, and therefore had me at a disadvantage. However, I kept grimly on, for I could not afford to look foolish now.

Suddenly I was astonished to find myself passing one after another of them. One more spurt and there was no one ahead of me. I risked the loss of enough time to look back. They had all stopped swimming and were staring blankly ahead. I looked, expecting to see something sensational there, but there was nothing. Nothing that would explain this panic at least. I was more than half way to the buoy, and could see the flower on it. Near it, floating down the middle of the river was a mass of brushwood and green foliage. It was bearing down directly on the buoy. In fact, as I watched it, it drifted against the buoy, and carried it with its red flower along downstream.

I kept on, for I wanted that flower. The others remained where they had stopped. Then I saw that the floating material consisted of two great logs which had been sawn squarely off, and the white, clean ends, and the sawdust sprinkled bark showed that they had been cut recently. They were fastened together by an iron chain, of which a short piece with a broken link hung down to the water.

Then the black tug came into my line of vision. I had not noticed it before. It was coming on rapidly, and as it approached, the other swimmers retreated to the shore.

As a bit of dare-deviltry, I swam after the logs, climbed upon them, and waved the red flower to the folks on the shore. They all stood motionless as statues. I chuckled as I imagined how shocked they all felt to see me behaving without any respect for a machine. For, as the tug churned up to the logs and hooked on to them, I stood calmly and watched the procedure. There were no people on the tug; in fact it was too small to contain any. After I had gotten a little ride back up the river on the logs, I scrambled through the leaves and branches to the opposite end, dove off, and swam leisurely to the shore. While I swam, I pondered.

* * *

WHY had they suddenly stopped in the middle of the race? And fled to the shore? Especially after they had been so intensely excited about it from the first? I wondered whether there were not some grave danger, and whether I had unconsciously run some serious risk. Yet, they had never made a move to warn me or call me back.

As I pondered on it, two explanations occurred to me, and subsequent experience showed that both were correct. One was that these people, though remarkably intelligent along artistic lines, were really intellectually top-heavy; they were not quickly resourceful, nor able to act in emergencies, simply because they were so pampered by the machines, that they had never had the training that necessity gives. The other was that the sawed logs and chain were an indication that there might be machinery around; and then the tug appeared. Machinery was disgusting, and not fit to appear in polite society.

Not a word was spoken when I got out of the water. They all regarded me with faces that seemed filled with awe. They fell back and permitted me to pass through the middle of the group, dripping and exultant. I felt a sort of contempt for them. It occurred to me that at the head of a hundred determined savages I could capture their whole city.

A voice in the crowd — I was relieved that it was not Ames — said almost apologetically: "They ought to swim that over again."

"What!" I exclaimed, in alarmed indignation.

"It wasn't exactly regular," said the courteous voice whose owner I did not see.

"The conditions were to get the flower. I've got the flower!" I exclaimed angrily, now more in earnest than anyone else. In fact, I acted worse than they did. But, one glance at Miss Kaspar, who was now radiant with a wonderful smile — the same girl that had given me her hand on the first evening — astonished me and steeled me in my determination not to yield the point.

"Of course," explained some other person whom I could not locate, "the flower was but a symbol of the best swimming, and an accident interfered."

"I didn't see any reason why everyone couldn't finish!" I looked around, but no one would meet my angry glance. All stood silent and reproachfully downcast.

"The devil take your flowers!" I shouted, dashing the pretty thing to the ground. I went to the bathing houses, resumed my clothes, strode over to where Miss Kaspar sat, took her arm, and led her away, just as the previous swimmers had done. The others never moved nor uttered a sound; I could not tell whether they were afraid of me or merely disgusted with me. Anyway, a half hour later they seemed to have completely forgotten the whole business, and treated me as though it had never happened. Was it a high type of tact and courtesy, or was it a species of mental deficiency? I could not tell.

"Davy!" said Miss Kaspar, in a soft, frightened tone of voice, "That was a reckless thing! Why did you do it?"

"I wanted to talk to you. You kept avoiding me. Now you must talk to me!"

"You wanted to?" Her voice was different than it had been all day. "Truly did you? I thought you wanted to talk to Phyllis."

"So, that is why you have been so distant?"

"You and Phyllis looked so happy and intimate coming down the street so early yesterday morning."

"You don't believe that now, do you, Mildred?"

"No, Davy. You have proved your words. But, you will have to go on with it and be my partner in the grand march."

"Ha! Ha! You talk as though it were some sort of punishment for me. I'd lick the black tug barehanded for the privilege of that dance, or whatever it is. I'll take good care of you for Mr. Ames."

"For Mr. Ames!" She shrank back as though a thunderbolt had struck near her. "What do you mean by that?"

"Why — I — I understand you were engaged."

"The idea! I'm not engaged to Mr. Ames, nor to anybody. Whatever made you think that?"

As I thought back, I had to admit to myself that there never had been any real tangible reason for believing such a thing. My own morbid imagination had read a significance into a number of meaningless circumstances.

In an instant the universe changed. I would have liked to give a whoop and jump high into the air, and come down and dance a highland fling. With a great effort, I remained on the ground and acted calmly. I met her eyes. Not a word was said, but a great deal was understood. Then she gave a little toss of her head and a smile, as though to shake back her hair, and with it the constraint that had existed between us.

"Now," she said, "I'm really looking forward to tomorrow night. And when we get home, I want you to bring me your khaki shirt. The sleeve is all torn from the crane, and I want to show you that some girls on this island can sew."

5
A MACHINE-DEVIL

ON my first and second mornings on the island I had spent a long and dreary wait, wandering about the house and grounds until someone had appeared. On this, the third morning, I found Mildred out in the garden busily snipping flowers off a vine.

"I had to get up early today. These flowers are for the ball tonight, and they keep better when they are cut in the morning," she explained. I accepted the explanation, without inquiring too deeply into the real reason for her being out so early. I was merely glad she was there.

However, the mention of the famous "ball" about which everyone was so excited, brought me up with a start.

"I am afraid of tonight's ball," I remarked in an effort to keep up a conversation which must be kept up; and the words came to my tongue with that strange fatality which sometimes makes our most superficial conversation express our innermost secrets. "I am not much of a society man."

"Now!" she said reproachfully, "that is just because you have to be my partner. I knew you would try to back out." At the same time, a merry laugh and a twinkle in the brown eyes belied the words.

"Will there be many there?" I asked.

"It is usually not a crowded affair. Bat the ball is held in a most wonderful place. The pavilion and its grounds are beautiful as a dream. There are special dresses and light effects and clever dances. It always thrills me through and through. You came at a lucky time, for it might be a year before you had this opportunity again."

Others apparently thought the same. As we walked to the veranda with armfuls of white, waxy flowers, Phyllis came skipping up.

"I can hardly believe that you haven't seen the pavilion yet!" she cried as soon as she was close enough to be heard. Apparently everyone's first thought on awakening this morning had been the ball. "I wish I were you, and seeing it for the first time!" She gurgled ecstatically, in her childish way.

When I had heard the same thing from several other people whom I met later during the day, I gradually developed a good deal of curiosity and eagerness to see the evening's event. I smiled as I thought back to the days in Galveston when my great-uncle and I had planned the outfit for this trip.

"It seems that since I've come to the island," I said to Kaspar later, "I've become some sheik. All I think about is clothes to wear."

Kaspar laughed heartily.

"That's right!" he said. "I know better than to expect a young fellow to go to a function like that unless he had exactly the correct thing on. We'll drive to town and get you some."

"It takes a lot of nerve on my part to ask for things that way."

"No. You must feel just as free to take them as you would to pick fruit off our trees. It amounts to the same thing."

So, that afternoon, we drove to the neat little shopping district, Kaspar and Mildred and I. I went into a store, which was really a "store" and not a selling institution; and there I was furnished with all of the clothes and accessories that I needed to fit me to take my place among the young men at the "ball" that evening.

* * *

HOWEVER, I soon found that I was only a side-issue in this shopping expedition. Mildred was carrying on the principal program. She went into store after store, while Kaspar and I waited in the car outdoors. He sat with a grave face and a merry twinkle in his eye; and I watched the street and the people fascinatedly. Mildred was flushed and excited about it. By the time we reached home, the pneumatic tube was discharging a perfect deluge of bundles.

In the evening, a couple of dozen young folks, on their way to the ball in their cars, stopped for us at Kaspar's home.

I noticed that Ames was not among the group. He had been cordial enough to me on the way home after the swimming contest, and I did not believe that he had anything personal against me. Yet I believed that he took Mildred seriously, and felt very much hurt about being deprived of her on this special occasion. I ought to have felt sorry for him, but I didn't. Someone in the group brought word that he was coming to the pavilion later in the evening. At least, I could not help admiring the delicate tact of his methods.

Then Mildred came out. I had not seen her all afternoon, and now she fairly took my breath away. And now I saw the purpose of the forenoon's shopping campaign. A torrent of surprised compliments and delighted congratulations broke out from the crowd of visitors. It was evident that this was the first time they had ever seen her in anything but plain gray-brown, and that they were happy at the transformation.

There were twenty in the group, young and old; and we drove in four cars. As usual, Mrs. Kaspar remained at home, but Kaspar and Cassidy came along.

They went everywhere, keeping a protecting eye on Mildred, and possibly on me. That in itself was a sort of sinister hint of danger, that kept up a background of worry to everything I experienced.

The car in which I was riding, with Mildred, Kaspar, Cassidy, and a half dozen others, was in the lead. We were some three hundred yards from the pavilion, and could already hear strains of music, when the little accident occurred. As an accident, it was quite trivial and insignificant; but the reaction of the people to it surprised me and set me to thinking. We met a car coming from the opposite direction, and our car swerved to the right side of the road. There was a crunch of the pavement, and a lurch that threw us about in our seats. The roar of our machinery rapidly died down to silence, and the car stood motionless, tipped to the right side. I thought at first that an axle had broken or a wheel had come off.

The cause of my astonishment, however, was that everybody sat still and did nothing. Their chatter was hushed for a moment; they looked about with helpless faces, in perplexed silence. But no one stirred. They all behaved as though they had been bound hand and foot. I stood up and looked about. Kaspar's face was inscrutable. My eyes met Cassidy's; he shrugged his shoulders and his face momentarily broadened into a grin; but his eyes told me nothing.

Finally I jumped out of the car and ran around to the side where the trouble seemed to be. A piece of pavement had given way and the wheel had sunk into the soft ground so that the axle rested on the ground. A little stream of water flowing alongside the road showed what was responsible for the cave-in.

"Three or four of us can lift this out easily," I suggested. I had in mind the powerful shoulders and muscular arms that I had seen during the swimming match.

The other carloads of young people coming along behind us stopped for a moment, and then passed us and went on. There was only a short piece of smooth, brilliantly lighted road ahead, leading to the pavilion. I walked back and forth, down the road toward the pavilion and back toward the car, hoping that it might occur to them that the short walk that remained would be a pleasant variation. But they accepted no suggestion. They sat as helpless as rag-dolls, and I did not feel like saying anything directly. I was thoroughly disgusted. Evidently Cassidy noticed it. He laughed, but it was a forced sort of a laugh.

"You're a young fellow that's used to taking care of yourself," he said, with an effort at speaking casually. "Well, that isn't necessary here. This machine automatically signals for help when it gets into trouble, and we have nothing to do but wait."

And wait we all did. Within five minutes' walk of the pavilion, the group sat as though they had been marooned on a desert island.

I noted the small radio antenna over the top of the machine and heard the humming of coils as the signal went out.

Finally the big noisy truck came. As far as I could see, there was no one driving or controlling it; but there was no way of making certain of that, as men might possibly have been hidden on it. I wondered if these people had such an aversion to their working class, that they could not even bear to look at a mechanic or laborer. In a business-like way, the relief truck hooked a chain under the axle of our car, and raised it up with its derrick. We finished the short remainder of our trip quite smoothly.

After the scene I had just witnessed, the vivacity and activity with which the people leaped out of the car and trooped up the steps of the pavilion were surprising and inconsistent.

Edgar Allan Poe dreamed dreams of beauty too transcendent for mortals to behold; and the scene, I now beheld, seemed to be one of the places of which he wrote. The pavilion was in a grove outside the city, beside the broad river. The building was long and low and white, with facades like the Parthenon. In the moonlight it did not seem quite real and solid; it seemed rather to float on the great billows of shrubbery embroidered with brilliant flowers. Tall rows of slim trees stood guard around it, and here and there and everywhere, huge, exotic flowers gleamed and glowed in the moon's rays. As we approached, long glimmers from the moon came toward me across the distant water. I could just see the soft glow of light between the columns from within the building. The strains of music drifted over, soft and low. I could have believed that I was approaching some enchanted fairyland.

Within, the floor of some red wood with purple veins was polished smooth as glass. There were ladies in fluffy, pale-tinted gowns that seemed unreal in the vari-colored glow-lights. The gentlemen were graceful and courtly. The music was not obtrusive in volume, but ever-present and gently suggestive of rhythm; and more effective in stirring one into movement than any lilt I had ever heard. The dancing was instinctively graceful and beautiful. As the dancers glided about in the changing lights, the movements, the colors, and the music affected me like some drug.

* * *

BUT I myself was not part of it. The others belonged in the picture; I couldn't fit into it. I was a detached spectator. For this there were many reasons. I felt awkward because my practice in dancing had been meager. Possibly once a month in the intervals of hard work, I had taken some equally hard-worked teacher or stenographer to a dance. The personal beauty and grace that I had developed by years of hard riding on the ranges and in recent years by bending over books and laboratory experiments, did not compare favorably with that of the people about me. They were without exception fine looking.

There was a little informal and desultory dancing to begin with; but the main interest was centered in the preparations for the "grand march." Partners sought each other out and looked for their positions.

Everything was ready to start except that they did not like to go ahead without Ames. As far as I could learn, he had no essential part to play; but he was such a prominent member of the group, and they were so accustomed to having him present that they felt lost without him.

"He has no reason to be late today," Dubois grumbled, "after I've taken his Supervision and he has had nothing to do all day."

"That's right," said someone else, in an awed tone. "Ames escaped his turn at Supervision today. Nobody's ever done that before."

"I wonder if something hasn't happened to him," asked Phyllis in a frightened whisper. "That was a dangerous thing to do."

I remember how admiringly she had spoken of him on the first morning; and from her tone now, I suspected that she was more worried about Ames than was anyone else.

The impatient group broke up for the moment. There was a little dancing, and people drifted outdoors to pass away a little more time of waiting. Mildred ran to ask her grandfather if she could.

"He has made me promise faithfully to ask him about every little step I make," she explained, half-ashamed of the childish position in which she was placed. "For some reason he is very much worried about me."

As I waited for her, I happened to wander past where a group of boys in a circle were excitedly discussing something. Their naive gestures of excitement were a welcome relief from the perfect culture of their elders. As soon as I got near enough to catch a few words, I suspected that they were talking about me; and my curiosity got the best of considerations of conventionality. Without thinking what I was doing, I listened.

"I wonder if he will also have to do Supervision?" one boy asked.

"Of course he will! Everybody does!" was the dogmatic reply.

"No, Kaspar's family does not; and he is in Kaspar's home."

A boy of about sixteen just opposite me waved his fist in indignation. I liked his sturdy looks.

"Silly!" he snorted contemptuously. "Supervision! I want real work to do. I want to make machines, like Kaspar did."

There was a sudden lull in the talk, as of astonishment, of fear. Then an older boy's reproof: "You fool! I hope no one heard you. These things have ears everywhere. Do you know that they got Higgins day before yesterday?"

Then a very small boy piped, as though repeating a lesson learned by rote: "Our first duty is to the machines!"

Mildred came by and hurried me away.

"Your eyes look as big as saucers," she laughed.

I tried to compose my astonished exterior, but calming the whirling astonishment within me was not so easy. The thoughtless words of children will often let the cat out of the bag, while the carefully acquired habits of adults keep secrets safely. Here was another confirmation of my suspicions that the people on this island were not as completely happy as external appearances might seem to indicate. These people did not understand all this vast machinery; they could not operate it nor keep it in repair. Somewhere on the island there must be others who did so; and in some way they seemed to hold these grown-up children of the City of Beauty in their power. There was lurking fear in the eyes of the boys, and in an occasional unguarded glance of the elders.

"There's Ames now!" someone shouted.

We pushed our way out on the broad staircase of the curved balcony. A car was hurrying toward us, up the broad sweep of pavement bordered with shrubbery and electric lights on concrete pillars. On the opposite side of the drive were parked many cars in a dense crowd. There were numerous shouts of pleasant bantering as Ames was recognized in the brilliant illumination of the electric lamps. His car drove into an empty parking-space, and he got out and started across the stretch of pavement toward us.

Then there was a rattle of an exhaust off to the right, and a whirl of machinery up the road. A horrible looking thing on wheels dashed up and made directly for Ames, focussing on him its glaring head-lights. He stopped as though rooted to the spot. A more frightful looking thing has never been imagined in all the lore of sea-monsters and dragons. It was the same thing that I had caught a glimpse of that night on the dock, or another thing just like it. Its general form was that of a huge motorcycle, with a great coffin-shaped box seven feet high between the wheels, at the top of which were two goggly headlights. Only, the first time I had seen it, it had seemed to have some sort of black ropes coiled round and round the box. Now these were unwound. They waved about, felt around, coiled and uncoiled, and grasped at the empty air; ten or a dozen huge, black tentacles, filling the air with sinuous, snaky masses.

Right in the middle of the road, in plain view of a couple of hundred people, it reached for Ames and wrapped a black coil around him. He stood as though struck paralyzed, though I could see him tremble. It began to drag him toward itself. In another moment, as I looked about me, I was alone. The people were all fleeing pell-mell into the building.

* * *

FOR an instant I was puzzled as to what to do. But Ames' face, bright white in the glaring light, in the uttermost agony of fear, convinced me that he was in some sort of danger. I started toward him in big jumps, at the same time opening a heavy pocketknife

97

that I carried. As I reached him, I felt the coil of a tentacle about me, and was surprised at the strength of it. However, with a quick squirm I managed to duck out of its grasp. I grasped Ames' arm and slashed away with my knife at the coils about him.

As the tentacles waved about me and coiled and bent, I could hear a continuous clicking coming from them.

As the tentacles waved about me and coiled and bent, I could hear a continuous clicking coming from them. When I cut at them with my knife I struck something hard, some metal. It seemed that my knife first went through a layer of something soft, rubber perhaps, and then slipped in between metal plates; and I could feel it catch and cut through wires. As it went through, a purple spark followed it, and a spark bit into my hand. Thus, while my body and arms struggled with the monster, my mind grappled with the astounding revelation, that this was not some animal enclosed within the box, some sea-monster as I had supposed. These snaky, twisting tentacles were mechanical things, built up of metal discs and wires, and carrying a high-frequency current.

Again I ducked out of the grasp of a tentacle. One already hung limp. I shook Ames, but he was completely unnerved. He had made no struggle whatsoever. I have no doubt, and have none to this day, that with a little determined effort he could have gotten loose and escaped up the steps. But he gave up from the beginning.

Then I heard a scream from Mildred, and a great bellow from Cassidy:

"Davy! Stop! Come here quick!"

I saw no choice except to obey, especially as two more tentacles closed around me. I dropped and twisted in an effort to get loose, but they had me in opposite directions, one closed against the other; and my efforts were of no avail. So, with the main force of two hands, I opened out the grasp of one of them. It took all my strength to do so, and I am known as a strong man. I bent it back with a twist, and heard it snap; it dropped away from me and hung limp, and there was a smell of scorched rubber. With a common wrestling trick, I escaped from the remaining coil and ran up the steps.

As I turned to look back, Ames was on a side seat of the machine with several coils around him, and the thing was carrying him off down the road. The day before I had admired him for his athletic prowess. Now I cursed him for a stupid fool to let himself be carried away like a sack of potatoes.

I got back to the dance, none the worse except for some slight disarrangement of my clothing. Kaspar and Cassidy took me sternly in hand. I did not know that Kaspar could be so severe. I felt like a schoolboy, caught throwing paper-wads.

"I have warned you," he said. "If you persist in being rash, you will not only succeed in having yourself destroyed, but will upset some cherished plans of ours."

"What in Sam Hill is going on?" I exclaimed. "What's happening to Ames?"

Cassidy answered me. Kaspar was hurrying away to see if Mildred was safe.

"I am not sure. Perhaps his failure to appear at Supervision today has something to do with it. I do not suppose we shall ever see him again."

"But, who's doing it?" I demanded. "Who's in the machine? And who's behind it all?"

"That is the tragedy of the people of the island," Cassidy said sadly. "That is the burden our people carry for no fault of their own. But we cannot talk about it here. There are mechanical eyes and ears everywhere, and I'm not ready to be taken away yet."

The next jolt I got was to see the dance going on as though nothing had happened. People were mingling and chatting, sitting at tables with iced-drinks, with all the appearance of festive gayety. Only when I came close to them, I saw that they were pale and staring, and that they carried on a forced conversation, like the people of a defeated city after a battle. The grand march went on.

Mildred came toward me with hand outstretched, her usually brown face as pale as milk.

"It's time for us to march," was all she said. Not a word in reference to the nightmare that had just occurred. But, with her finger on her lips and a grave look in her eyes, she gave me to comprehend that she understood my impatient curiosity, but that now I must go on with the game.

I found myself wondering whether anything really serious had happened after all. Might it not have been some sort of a joke, or some sort of a game acted out? But no, there was that look of pale horror on Ames' face, and the panicky flight of the people into the pavilion. The sudden starts of terror in unguarded moments here and there could not be acting; they were basic emotions breaking through, because they were too strong for even the most perfect of social training and discipline. I came across Dubois alone at a table.

"Couldn't you explain to me what happened to Ames?" I pleaded. "This mystery is driving me crazy."

All he did was to put his head down on his arm and turn away. He sat that way motionless and without a sound, for so long that finally, out of sheer embarrassment, I got up and moved away. And only a few moments later I saw him dancing merrily again. And behind a screen there were two women over Phyllis, who was all crumpled and shaking with sobs.

How these people could go on with their gayety, with the appearance of enjoying themselves, I could not comprehend. With great difficulty 1 forced myself through a few dances. When I caught sight of the sixteen-year-old lad with the determined face, who had played the part of a heretic among his fellows a little earlier in the evening, I maneuvered him aside, hoping to get some information.

"I'd like to know who it was that captured Ames — who runs those machines — what do they want of him?" I asked all at once.

He became excited. He looked about to see if anyone could overhear, and moved to an open space, motioning me to follow.

"Serves them right," he exclaimed. "They'll all be taken some day, every last one of them. They putter around with art and waste their time on sport; and dance — bah! I'm sick of it. I want to work. I want to do things. I want to make machines."

He looked furtively about him again. A frightened expression came into his face, and with a mumbled apology he dived away.

* * *

I SOUGHT refuge in an obscure corner, in order that I might think.

It was evident that the people had become so accustomed to being waited on by machinery that they were helpless and had no initiative in personal matters.

And yet, this machinery that took care of them, produced fear and disgust in their minds! Though utterly dependent on it, they considered it disgraceful to notice it, and unpardonable social *gaucherie* to mention it in conversation.

Then, another thing: Machinery requires attention. *Someone* has got to understand it. Somewhere there must be hundreds, thousands of mechanics to operate it, care for it, and repair it. They should form a large proportion of the population. And in this stratum of inhabitants, which was the only one I had thus far seen, engineers ought to plentiful. Why had I not met an engineer? Were the mechanically occupied persons considered outcasts by these artist-sportsmen? Was it a disgrace to be connected with machinery? Did not the mechanically-minded people associate with the artistically-minded? Was there war between them?

For it was apparent that sometimes the machinery injured people, and favored them with other unpleasant and alarming attentions. These things could not be merely accidents. I had seen enough now to be certain that somewhere behind them was malevolent intention.

I could come to no other conclusion than that the people who operated and took care of the machines were a separate class, lived elsewhere, and did not in any way associate with the aristocracy with whom I mingled. The artistic aristocracy were the masters, and the mechanics were the servants. My yesterday's beautiful picture of an ideal community tumbled sadly in ruins. For these masters did not live the completely happy life that I had at first thought. For one thing they seemed to have degenerated from being so constantly pampered, so that they had no fighting ability, no courage. Furthermore, it seemed that their servants, the mechanics, possessed the power to terrify them, carry them away, perhaps to kill them. Ames had no doubt been "taken" as a disciplinary measure. But why had they attacked Mildred? What had she done? And why Kaspar's dark hints as to my own danger, even while we were still on the ship? What had I done?

And there was that Supervision! The word implied power and authority, and yet these people spoke of it as though it were some compulsory and unpleasant burden. Everyone I knew trembled with that word on their lips.

For a third time I tried to get information concerning the meaning of the gruesome scene I had witnessed. I asked Kaspar as we were starting homeward from the ball. The two of us had fallen back and were walking behind the others on our way to the cars.

"It is in the interest of your own safety," he reminded, "that you do not speak too loud. I am anxious to help you. I cannot even tell you the real reason for my interest in you just now, for fear of spoiling things. I shall try to find some opportunity of explaining things to you as far as I can; but I assure you that it cannot be done here and now."

He said it very gently and very kindly; but there was nothing left for me to say or do.

As I thought it over, I could not help feeling that for many reasons there was more chance of getting my questions answered by asking her, than from anyone else. Yet, I was a little unnerved when it came to asking her, especially when I thought of the strange reactions of the others to my inquiries.

She and I lingered outdoors after the others had gone into the house. She seemed quietly happy.

"Did you enjoy it?" she asked.

"Beautiful," I admitted; "almost too much for me. But some of the doings about got my goat."

She remained staring blankly at me for a moment, and then broke into a peal of chuckling laughter.

"You have some strange ways of saying things," she laughed. "Say something like that again."

"I am very much puzzled about tonight's happenings," I explained, "but I am afraid to ask questions."

"You may ask me," she said with a smile that shone in the moonlight. "I won't get shocked."

I was so relieved to find my path clear thus far, that for the moment I could not think of the first question to ask.

"Who — ?" I finally began, but suddenly a soft little hand covered my mouth. Then, as suddenly, it drew back, and its owner stepped away, abashed at what she had impulsively done. Just for a moment she was embarrassed; and then she threw back her head with that characteristic little toss that delighted my heart.

"Wait!" she whispered. "Not here. I almost forgot. We might be overheard. Wait right here."

She flew into the house. I waited there in the moon-light, with the gleaming foliage about me, for fifteen minutes. I surmised that she had run in to ask Kaspar permission for something she wished to do. And there dawned on me the answer to one question that had been ringing in my head: why was it that she seemed to stand out from the others? At least one cause for that was, that she was always ready and anxious to do some service for others. Then she came flying out of the house again, and I surmised that her breathlessness was due more to excitement than to exertion.

"Tomorrow morning at nine o'clock be ready," she ordered with great glee. "Have on your rough brown clothes and heavy boots, and prepare for adventure. And don't forget what you wanted to ask me."

6
THE GULLS' NEST

BY nine in the morning, Mildred had driven Sappho out in front of the house, and was sitting in the seat, waiting for me to come out.

A charming woman is always a fresh source of delightful surprise. Mildred in her "outing" things was just as refreshing a change from Mildred of the "ball gown," as was the latter from the Mildred of the gray-brown gabardine. To see her in a tight jacket and short skirt of greenish-brown and a pair of boots aroused a strange, deep enthusiasm within me. Her own eyes danced with excited anticipation. They surveyed me as I came toward her.

"I feel self-conscious in these things, after my two days in society clothes," I apologized, looking over my rough whipcord outfit. She smiled brightly as she saw me glance down at my left sleeve which she had sewn for me. I wondered if she had noted the bulge under my left arm where I had slung my big service pistol under my shirt. I had debated whether or not to carry it; but recollecting Kaspar's numerous dark hints of danger I formed a resolve never to go very far without my pistol, my hand ax at my belt, and my field-glasses over my shoulder. From then on I stuck to this rigidly.

"Hello Sappho, you old ash-can!" I shouted, slapping the fender. "You played a wicked trick on me the other day!"

"You mustn't speak roughly to poor little Sappho," Mildred interceded. "She has been a faithful friend in the Kaspar family."

As if in reply, Sappho gave a little jump forward as I was getting in, for Mildred was already setting the dials; and in another moment had started at a dignified rate down the street.

"I am all eagerness to know where we are going and what we are going to do," I said as we got started.

"I told you all that I possibly could, last night," Mildred replied enigmatically, as though someone were listening. "I think it would be wisest to say nothing until the time comes."

I was so surprised that I looked at her and opened my mouth as though to speak, and then looked all around to see who was eavesdropping. But she looked at me so sharply and quickly, as though someone were in reality listening, that I closed my mouth again and said nothing. I contented myself with looking at the great masses of foliage and flowers that buried the beautiful residences along the street on which we drove.

A couple of miles out of the city we came to a fork in the paved road. One continued straight ahead, to the west, and was lost on the horizon among flat, green fields. The car, however, turned into the one which branched off to the left, southwards. I was just sufficiently oriented to know that it led in the direction of the coast where I had first landed on the island, and was without doubt the same road by which we had entered the city on the first night.

For five or six miles we went through a perfectly flat country, covered with marvelously well-tended fields and apparently perfect crops. I took advantage of the opportunity to ask and receive some instruction in the operation of the car. There were direction dials and distance dials; and the route was planned like an equation in calculus. The method, however, required memorizing rather than understanding, unless one enjoyed wrestling with the abstract operation of integration that was involved.

For several miles we drove through a leafy tunnel, and then, as suddenly as we had entered, we emerged into the blinding sunlight. Ahead of us were granite cliffs, and beyond them, the sea. A broad turn of the road around the base of the cliffs brought us into the little harbor where Kaspar and I had landed from the black yacht. But now it was deserted. The little plank dock with the paved road leading to it were the only signs that lent a human value to the lonely place. Near the dock we stopped to get out of the car. Mildred twiddled the dials on the instrument board, whereupon the car turned around and drove back along the road by which we had come, disappearing in the gloom of the forest road.

"I'll never get over the uncanny effect of seeing these machines go about by themselves," I said. "Why couldn't it stand here and wait for us?"

"The place where we are going is a secret. We don't want even a car to know about it," she replied with perfect seriousness. She spoke as though the car might be an intruder into our little company of two; and the fancy pleased me. My father, who was a country practitioner in east Texas, often spoke of his cars as faithful creatures, as though they might have been living things, conscious of his gratitude.

"Soon," she continued, "we'll be able to talk all we want. But now come on. We have a lively walk ahead of us."

We turned to the right (or west), following the shore line, walking on the packed sand strewn with granite boulders. Finally we got in among the cliffs, and into a small canyon. We began to go upward, and our way soon formulated itself into a steep pathway. Mildred led me along at such a swift pace that I had no breath left with which to ask questions; I hurried along behind her, wondering what could be her purpose in bringing me here. At least, I thought, looking upward, we shall get high enough to get a good view out over the island. I was very eager for a bird's-eye view of this strange country. Now and again I caught a glimpse of the sea, and then of the forest in the distance. In some places it was really dangerous climbing.

Finally, after pushing upward for a good twenty minutes we reached the top, so unexpectedly that it surprised me. We were in a bowl, partly of sand and partly of bare granite, about the size of an ordinary dwelling room. We arrived at the edge nearest the sea, from which we could look out over the intensely blue ocean, and almost straight down at its lacy border of white foam where the waves broke on the pink granite. To the east and west the coastline extended to the horizon, a broad strip of yellow sand, occasional groups of cliffs, and back of them the forest, dense and dark. To the north I could not see, for there the cliffs forming the edge of the bowl rose a dozen feet higher than our heads. From the middle or bottom of the bowl I could see only sky.

"This is the Gulls' Nest!" panted Mildred. "Nobody knows of it but grandfather and me. He found it when I was a little girl. Look!"

She scraped away the sand from the middle of the floor, and revealed an iron trap-door with a ring.

"I was surprised when grandfather gave me permission to bring you here," she continued. "He even reminded me to teach you the combination of this."

She opened the door, revealing a small cellar in the rock, containing a supply of preserved foods in cans, jars and bottles.

"It is to be used in case of emergency only. Grandfather is always expecting emergencies."

"Dear old grandfather!" she went on earnestly. "He understands. You cannot imagine the torture of the past three days. How I have ached to ask you things about where you came from, and what your people are like, and what they do; and yet not daring to do so. Sometimes it has almost driven me frantic to pretend, that like the others, I did not care. They shut their eyes to the fact that you come from The Outside. I am so glad that we have a place where we can talk—"

* * *

AND so, instead of asking questions, I answered them. She seemed so hungry to know about the outside world that I did not have the heart to obtrude my own curiosity. Nevertheless, my mind was full of questions, and I watched eagerly for an opportunity to ask them. Why is it that the island people do not dare to talk about the outside world? Why this fear of being overheard, even where there could not possibly be anyone to overhear? What had happened to Ames, and why? Who was behind that mysterious abduction? Where were the engineers and the people who tended and repaired the machinery? Where were the shops and factories and warehouses? And, I was restless to look to the north, out over the island, past this granite wall behind me.

But for an hour I talked of Galveston, and of the countless other cities dotted over our broad land, teeming with their millions of people. I talked of rich and poor; of laborers and soldiers and police; of wickedness and charity; of railroads, airplanes, and ships — of all the things she had never seen nor heard of. She listened with wide-open eyes fixed on me, scarcely breathing, and then I knew for a fact, that these things had been unknown to her. Therefore, it was not surprising that my own curiosity faded in the thrill of imparting the things that to her were so strange and startling.

"Why! It's nearly noon!" Mildred suddenly exclaimed in surprise. "We didn't bring a lunch, and it wouldn't do to draw on the emergency things. We'll have to hurry home, or we'll starve."

"I'm already doing that now," I said. "But—?"

I turned toward the blank wall to the north of us.

"Ah, I know. You would prefer starvation to missing seeing something." She laughed archly. "Well, I knew you would want to look out over the island."

She led the way along a path at one side, to the top of the wall at the north. From this I beheld a perfectly amazing view.

Immediately below, over a wild and desolate area of granite cliffs, I could see a dense, dark forest. Beyond it were broad, green fields through which wound the shining river and far in the distance a ridge of hazy blue mountains. For all I could tell, the island might extend in that direction for a thousand miles. On my right, toward the southeast was the city. A City of Beauty it was indeed, with its red roofs and many-colored buildings, its gleaming domes and graceful towers, only partially seen for the cushions of green among which they rested. All around the city, along the flat bottom lands of the river valley, were the level, green, cultivated fields. Around these was the forest, like a belt. One glance told me that without a doubt, these thousands of acres had been cleared of timber and reclaimed from the virgin jungle, by the hand of man. Here was a vast work, whose achievement must have been thrilling history.

On my left, toward the northeast, was the jungle, impenetrable, dark-green, with a million scintillating reflections on its surface, stretching for miles and miles toward the blue horizon. And on that horizon, a couple of points to the west of northwest, hung a dark, dense pall of heavy smoke. It was a gloomy, depressing smudge that caused a discordant note in that spreading and luxuriant paradise.

"What!" I exclaimed. "A volcano?"

Quickly I reached for my field-glasses, and as I swung them around to the dense nucleus of the smoky smudge near the horizon, my surprise was so great that I nearly lost my balance on the narrow ridge. For there were black shapes and towering masses of buildings, belching chimneys, and a typical skyline of an immense industrial metropolis.

It looked as though it might be twenty miles away. A white ribbon of road led from the City of Beauty toward that black nucleus, sprinkled with swiftly moving dots of traffic. It was an artery carrying a busy black stream between the two cities. The sight of it brought back all the fire of my curiosity again.

"A city!" I exclaimed. "So there are other cities on the island?"

"Just the two," Mildred answered. "That is the City of Smoke!"

"Smoke is right!" I said, with much feeling in my tones.

"That is where the machines are," she continued. "That is where they make all the things for us. That is probably where Kendall Ames is. Those are the things you wanted to ask about."

She looked around as though afraid someone would overhear her, and then recollected herself and smiled at her absent-minded betrayal of the force of habit.

So that was it! Beauty and comfort were so important that everything involving dirt, noise, smoke, and unsightliness had to be put into a separate and distant city. By what arrangement did the aristocracy in the City of Beauty live and lord over the thousands that must be toiling over yonder? To such a degree had they carried their fastidiousness that they could not even bear to see a workman or to talk about him. All they could endure was smoothly running machinery.

* * *

ON the face of it, one would think that these would be characteristic of a hard-hearted and cruel race.

Yet these people in the City of Beauty did not look like that at all. To me they appeared merely light-hearted and thoughtless.

"And Supervision?" I asked.

"Yes, that is where they go for Supervision."

"What is it? What do they supervise?" I asked eagerly.

"Machines. They all take turns going there. Except me. I have never been to Supervision."

"You mean that your people supervise the work that goes on over there in that smoking beehive?"

"Yes. That is what they do."

I put that away for future digestion. I could not quite reconcile a good many things I had seen. In the meanwhile, there was another interesting point.

"How does it happen that you are an exception, and that you do not have to do supervising?" I asked.

"I seem to be specially favored on account of my grandfather. He invented and made those machines. He owns all this country and the cities. He brought me up differently than the others have been brought up. He taught me things about the great world in which you are struggling so hard to be something. But there are still many things that I would like to know, and he thinks I am still a small child and that I cannot understand."

"I've got to see that place," I finally said. "I am going over there to look it over."

She regarded me for a moment in horrified silence.

"I knew you would! It is just like you!" She stepped back and looked me over gravely. "But you mustn't go!"

"Well, well. Why not?"

"Why!" she gasped. "That is a terrible thing to do!"

"I've gone into other cities, as black and smoky as that one. It all washes off when you come out."

"But I can't let you go," She hesitated and stopped; and then put her hand on my sleeve and looked at me appealingly. This, of course, stirred my determination tenfold. I would have gone through the fires of hell for that, and for the brown eyes looking up at me, and the little quiver around the corners of the mouth.

"Yet, you wouldn't think much of me if I didn't go, would you?" I demanded, with what I felt to be a sheepish grin.

"We cannot stand here and argue," she said sternly. "It's time to go home and eat. Come."

"Wait," I urged. "We've got a lot to say yet; at least I have. If hunger is your only reason for going back, leave it to me. That's an old problem with me."

She looked at me dubiously.

"We'll have to get down to the ground, though. Lead the way down."

In silence she led the way down the path, among the sand and boulders, and in her attitude I read some annoyance but more wonderment and curiosity. When we had clambered down to the level ground, we distinguished Sappho standing at the side of the road, near the dock, waiting to take us home.

"Sappho will have to be patient and wait for us," I remarked jocularly, pleased with my little fancy of personifying the machine. Mildred tossed her head and said nothing.

My idea was first to look about and see if there was any prospect of catching some fish to make a lunch on. I looked carefully through my pockets, through the car, over the dock, and along the shore, but found nothing that would serve as either hook or line, or as a spear. So, I turned to the forest, which was much more in my line; I felt confident that there I could find something to eat. A walk of a hundred yards brought us to the dense growth of underbrush and tangled vines at the edge of it. I asked Mildred to wait for me near the road.

"And do not be afraid if you hear me shoot," I added.

"Oh, I know about shooting. Grandfather has some rifles and has taught me how."

My training with the Texas Rangers had taught me to proceed through a thicket with scarce a sound. I kept my eyes open for edible plants; and my ears told me of small animals moving about near me. After I had squirmed along for a dozen yards, I found the growth more open; so I got out my pistol and looked around. I chuckled at the ridiculousness of it — shooting rabbits with a pistol firing a bullet as big as my thumb. Ahead of me was a large hollow log, big enough to afford a hiding place from which I might take a shot at some passing creature that looked promising as a luncheon. I stepped into it, and there was a sudden flurry and a number of diminutive grunts; something brown wriggled at my feet. Mechanically, I brought down the butt of my pistol heavily upon it, before my consciousness had time to figure out what it might be. It squirmed and kicked a few times and lay still.

I dragged it out into the light. It was as big as a large rabbit, but looked rather like an awkward squirrel, with a curved snout like a pig. I had never seen anything like it before; but I was sure from my general knowledge of game that it was good to eat.

"An agouti!" said Mildred when she saw it. "Poor little fellow."

I was very much amused by her expression as she watched me build a fire, skin the animal, cut it in convenient pieces and roast them on spits of green branches. At first she was somewhat disgusted by the proceeding; but that soon gave way to a fascinated interest, and at the end her hunger compelled her to watch the browning and savory pieces with considerable eager anticipation. Before we had finished eating, and taken our fill of water from a stream which she showed me, she was quite transported with delight. This was a totally new experience for her, and obviously a delightful one.

For me there was also some satisfaction in it. It was some consolation for the awkwardness which I felt among these people, to know that I could look after myself in a pinch and that this flower of an exalted civilization was to some extent dependent on me; that she considered me some sort of a hero.

When luncheon was over, we turned back up toward the Gulls' Nest, with an unspoken mutual understanding. That was the only place where free talk was possible.

"Now tell me," I said, as soon as I could get my breath on the concave top of the cliff, "whom do I see to arrange about going over there?"

"But you don't understand," she said in a voice that almost had tears in it. "There is no way to arrange to go there. There is no one to see."

"Humph!" I grunted. "That means I'll just have to pick up and go. It looks like a long walk. Will you help me some more in learning how to run a car?"

"I'll go with you and I'll drive it for you!" she cried, with a sudden earnest inspiration.

"You're a little brick!" I exclaimed; and, to my own astonishment, I detected a warm tone in my voice that I had never heard there before.

117

She stared at me a moment and then burst out laughing. It was my turn to stare.

"I'll never get used to your queer ways of putting things," she said. "Little brick! I'm a little brick! Please say some more things like that."

"So you'd like to go with me?" I pondered aloud. "No. That won't do. There must be some sort of danger there. If I knew what it was we might consider your going. But I'll be back soon."

"You must not tell anyone that you are going."

"You mean they might try to prevent me?" I asked incredulously.

"No. But you have no idea how vulgar the machines seem to them. It must be kept so secret that I must tell you good-bye and wish you good luck here and now. We can't down there."

She held out a little hand to me.

I looked down into the big brown eyes turned up to mine, and the world went round and round with me. Slowly, very slowly, my arm stole round her shoulders and another round her waist. Slowly our heads drew together. She was so still that she seemed not to breathe. Her eyes closed and her head lay back on my arm. Slowly I kissed those soft red lips, whose smiles I had watched so often playing round the sunny teeth. While the waves roared below and the great birds soared above, I once more held that little body close to me, and with great calmness, as though I had a thousand years to do it in, I kissed her. My whole world was changed by that one long kiss.

"I love you!" I whispered.

She opened her eyes and looked up at me with an expression of radiant happiness; her hair and eyes and the curve of her cheek gave a sort of melting impression, and then she buried her head in my shoulder. "That means you're mine forever?"

Her head nodded "yes" without looking up.

"And that you're going back to my world with me?"

"I want to do that above everything else, Davy, dear." She looked up at me and her arms went about my neck. "I want to get out of this empty, useless life."

"You were very beautiful last night," I whispered.

"I tried to look pretty for you. Did you guess that?"

* * *

ALL at once time seemed to have stopped for us. It seemed that but a few moments had passed when it occurred to me to look at my watch. It was late in the afternoon! Mildred looked worried.

"We must hurry," she exclaimed. "Grandfather will be dreadfully worried about us. Come. That was a wonderful good-bye."

So, with my arm about her, we started for the path that led down the cliff.

"Be very careful, Davy dear, that nothing happens to you," she said in a low, earnest voice. "You are my whole world and life to me now."

"What could happen?"

"I don't know. But they have already gotten many people and we have never seen them again."

"There!" I said triumphantly. "That is my reason for going there. I want to solve the mystery. What happens to all of your people?"

"Yes," she agreed; "I am so anxious to know that I am willing to let you go." She stopped suddenly, with a catch in her breath.

There stood Kaspar, panting heavily from climbing up the path. We dropped apart and stood looking at him in embarrassment. He smiled.

"Bless your hearts, children; do not let yourself be disturbed by an old man like me. I was very much worried about you, however. So many things might happen. But this explains it." There was a merry twinkle in his eyes.

"But what is that I hear, Davy, about your going somewhere?" he suddenly demanded in great earnestness. We confessed to my plan to visit the City of Smoke.

He stood for many minutes, gazing at me in silence, and his white-bearded face was inscrutable.

"As I remember the young men of the world which I left, when I also was young," he mused, "there would be little use in my trying to talk you out of that. It is the same spirit that brought you to this island and now I am glad that you came. But why must you risk your life unnecessarily, just as you have found happiness for yourself and given it to others? Listen: things are shaping up now so that it may soon be possible for you to take another kind of trip — back to your own country."

"That news," I replied, "would not have interested me this morning as it does now." I could not erase a broad smile of happiness from my face, nor could I resist a fond glance at Mildred. "But I must solve some questions before I leave this island."

Kaspar shook his head.

"It is a great worry to load on an old man's heart. Perhaps if you could think, as I can, of numerous others who have started out, as you wish to do, to learn the secrets of that grim City of Smoke and have never returned, you would think twice."

"If the ones I have seen are fair samples, I do not wonder that they have never returned," I sniffed contemptuously. "I don't get paralyzed every time I see a machine, and lie down and let it carry me off."

Kaspar put his hand on my shoulder and said earnestly:

"Then wait until I have shown you something in the City of Beauty that you have not yet seen. Tomorrow I shall take you with me to see some people whom you will respect more than those you have already met. I have been watching and studying you from the first time I saw you. Now I know you are qualified to enter the Circle. Will you promise to wait for twenty-four hours?"

I promised.

7
I BECOME A REBEL

I SPENT many hours in a species of intoxication. My head was light with the joy of what had happened. Suddenly, unexpectedly, within a few days, something beautiful had come into my life that stirred me and made me restless with a fire that I had never known before.

So, for the first time since I had been on the island, I awoke quite late in the morning. Kaspar and Mildred were already waiting for me. I looked wonderingly and inquiringly at them, with their hats on, as though ready for a journey, and at Sappho waiting out in front. Mildred bade me good morning with a warm light in her eyes that sent my composure whirling head over heels.

"Today we are taking you to a certain Committee Meeting," Kaspar explained.

I had forgotten all about that. I started, as I felt an embarrassed flush spread over my face; for the thoughts of Mildred and our newly discovered love had driven all else out of my mind.

"I — I — I'm sorry if I kept you waiting very long," I apologized.

"There is no hurry," Kaspar said, with his kind, patriarchal smile. "In my opinion you are eminently excusable for forgetting such a trivial thing as a Committee Meeting under the circumstances."

"And what sort of?" I began.

Kaspar held up a warning finger.

"I must remind you that we dare not say too much," he admonished. "Here we never know when the slightest whisper may be picked up and carried over a wire!"

Again that sudden jolt! How many times already, just as I was beginning to feel that the island was a paradise of civilized progress and beauty, came that sudden, sinking hint of some terrible, overpowering thing hanging over it all!

This elaborate secrecy, and these hints of a "Committee" told me that even in the City of Beauty, among these fair and talented children of joy, there were things going on that were not apparent on the surface.

Soon the city was far behind us. The river was our companion on the left; and on our right was a broad, flat, green stretch, as carefully tended and well-kept as the finest of lawns. I enjoyed its level, peaceful, solitary beauty.

"What is this? A golf course?" I inquired.

"This is the Hopo course," Mildred explained. "No one plays until afternoon. Then you will see many horses and riders. It is half a mile wide and ten miles long."

"It must take an immense amount of labor to keep it looking as neat and smooth as this," I suggested.

"The machines attend to it. There are a great many special mowing and rolling machines caring for the Hopo field."

She seemed to dismiss all concern about it quite readily from her mind, taking the fact for granted that the responsibility was to be unloaded upon the machinery. My mind kept dwelling on the vastness of the work required to keep these thousands of acres as green and cropped and flat as the trimmest lawn in front of a residence. I would have liked to see the machinery that did it.

* * *

MILE after mile we drove. At first the fresh greenness was pleasant, but eventually it began to seem endless and monotonous. However, the girl at my side would have kept the desert of Sahara from seeming monotonous. Then, quite suddenly, we stopped.

We hadn't arrived anywhere. At some time we had left the road, and now on all sides of us were endless flat, green stretches. On the east and west, the greenness merged into the horizon; no City of Beauty was visible. On the north was the gleaming blue river far in the distance; and on the south the difference in color of the verdure indicated that there must be cultivated fields some distance from us. Beyond these, a dim, purple line on the horizon, was the forest. We dismounted from the car and I stared about in surprise. However, I was beginning to learn to say little and observe much.

Kaspar sent the car back. Never would I get over the wonder of it, though now I was seeing it every day: a few twists of the dials, and the machinery began to hum in rhythmic cadences of change, while the empty car swung about, turned backward toward the city, and sped away, dwindling to a small dot in the distance. As we watched it depart we saw several other cars approaching.

In the meanwhile I pondered on the reasons for sending the car back. Why could it not stand here and wait until they were ready to go back? Wasn't it a waste of fuel and machinery? The idea of waste did not seem to occur to anyone here at all. The wealth of natural resources and the vast available mechanical facilities were utilized lavishly and riotously, without a thought of economy. And I began to attach some suspicion to the car itself.

We started out on foot, continuing in the direction in which we had driven. There were dark figures of people ahead of us; they looked infinitely tiny in the vast spaces. Before long we made out a considerable group of them; as we drew near, I decided that there must be about fifty persons gathered together and as many more coming on behind.

"It is now safe to talk as we wish," Kaspar began.

I looked about me and decided in my mind that the factor that made it safe was the fact that nowhere was there any machinery in sight, nor any possibility of concealed wires, microphones, periscopes or cameras. Nothing but flat lawn and sky. Kaspar continued:

"However, just now there won't be time to explain things to you fully. And they must be explained fully, or you would neither understand nor believe them. I am planning on finding a time and a place at which this can be done; I shall make revelations that will astound you. We cannot waste the time of those people talking about things that are familiar to them."

"I note that most of these people are strangers to me," I observed.

"You have heretofore met only those that live in our section of that city and whom we meet almost daily. The people present here are from all over the city. They constitute a committee of such few of us as have retained the power of independent thinking. I might term it a Revolutionary Committee."

"And do they always meet here?" I asked.

"There is no regular meeting place. We change from one to another, with a view to safety and secrecy. This place is good because we can see the approach of any vehicle from a long distance, and long before anyone observing us can guess what we are about."

People recognized and greeted the Kaspars constantly, and I could not help remarking the respectful deference that was paid to the old man. There were a few women in the group. By far the most of the persons were men of past middle age, with a good sprinkling of the very aged, as was Kaspar. Young men of my age and younger were relatively scarce, but I saw a few. I was presented to a great many of the people. All of them seemed keenly interested in me, listened intently to the peculiarities of my speech as compared with theirs, and looked me over with a great deal of curiosity. But they all greeted me warmly and seemed glad to have me present.

New arrivals continued to appear for a quarter of an hour and then the vast stretches of lawn in all directions were clear. The people gravitated together without any signal, and the meeting began. They sat in rows on the grass, quite close together, making a compact group, a tiny clump in the midst of the vast green distances. I was not surprised to see the place of the presiding officer filled by the burly figure of Cassidy. He called the meeting to order in a low tone of voice.

"We cannot proceed with any business," he began, "until all present are satisfied as to the eligibility of a new person among us. John Kaspar will introduce him.

Kaspar rose and beckoned to me. He led me up to the front, beside Cassidy. He turned and addressed the assemblage:

"For our struggle against the encroaching domination of the City of Smoke, we have in our ranks much experience and wisdom, but we are sadly lacking in youth and daring. When I think of the young people of this island chasing shadows and losing all spirit of self-determination my heart grows heavy. Here is a young man from the Outside, the grandson of a boyhood chum of mine. We need him among us. From the moment that I first saw him I have watched him closely, telling him nothing, but keeping him on probation. Every step of the way he has demonstrated his courage and his quick-witted self-reliance. In our desperate stand against the mechanical powers he will be a valuable ally."

He went on and told of how I had followed him and gained my way aboard the yacht; of my rescue of Mildred on the dock, at which there were horrified gasps, and a girl sitting near Mildred, similarly clad in gray-brown, put both arms around her; of my escape from the car speeding toward the City of Smoke; and of my stand against the machine that had abducted Ames, at which there was a good deal of nodding of gray-haired and white-bearded heads in admiring approval.

Then Cassidy spoke:

"I shall also vouch for him and I am proud to have him present. I wish he were my own son."

* * *

127

HE paused a moment in thought. I wondered if it were because his own child could certainly not be classed as mentally capable of taking part in the movement represented in this meeting.

"And we need him," Cassidy continued. "Our ranks ought to be increasing but they are growing thinner. We lose our members faster than we get new ones. Only three days ago Houchins junior disappeared; they got him as they got his father before him. Out of all of the thousands in the city, it is hard to find new recruits for our ranks. The people are being put to sleep by comfort and luxury; and their souls are being taken away, as well as their bodies. Davy Breckenridge will be valuable to us, not merely because of his youth and daring, but also because of his knowledge and experience. In his own country he has done valiant deeds, and he has had a training in the practical needs of tasks such as we have set ourselves."

Then he put to vote the question as to whether I should be accepted into the group. The vote was enthusiastic in my favor; hands went up and people shouted "Aye!" Then he turned to me.

"The will of the assembly is that you be one of us, and I welcome you." He held out his hand.

"I'm sure that I appreciate the honor very much," I said hesitatingly; "but before I know what to do about it, I shall have to understand what it is all about."

Kaspar spoke.

"Pending the time when I can take you up to the secret little meeting-place that you know about, and tell you the long and complex story that is involved, let me ask you if you can see sufficiently with your own eyes the decadence and blindness of the present generation, the increase in power and terror of the machines, and the certain doom ahead of our poor people unless something desperate is done? Do you not feel willing to help and wait for explanations until they are possible?"

"Yes," I replied; "I have seen enough to know that something is wrong, and that some sort of help is needed. I am devoured with curiosity to know what it is; I am kept awake nights wondering about it. Yet I see the wisdom of your reasons. At least I can say that I am very much interested."

"Besides," Kaspar said, "you, yourself, are in considerable danger. By your very act of following me on board the ship, then by your deeds that night in the dock, and again on the river with the logs, and above all, that night at the pavilion, you have attracted attention to yourself as an unusual person and an undesirable one to the reigning powers. I knew you would, the first time I talked to you that evening on the ship, before we had gotten out of sight of Galveston. They are after you and they may get you at any moment."

"If I can judge by what I see," I replied, "they'll have to hustle harder than they ever hustled before if they want to catch me. They won't find me letting myself be carried away like a sheep. And if they do get me, I'm going to get in a few good licks first, and I'd like to start right now. Just give me a few hours to get this business studied up and straightened out Then I can get you people started to working properly, and you'll lick them whether I'm with you or not. I've watched this business, and I've got it figured out already that your adversaries have all the possible material advantages, but that somehow they lack the personal equation; they do not seem to know how to follow up their opportunities."

Cassidy was delighted and he wrung my hand.

"I knew you would be valuable to us," he shouted.

"Well, I've got something for you right now," I continued. "When you said that you needed young men, you said a mouthful. I know a young fellow who belongs right here, and you'll never be complete without him."

I turned to Mildred.

"Do you remember on the night of the grand march at the pavilion, I waited for you near a group of boys, and there was a tall boy with a square chin and steady eyes, and you saw me speak to him later."

"Oh, that is Perry Becker!" she interrupted.

"Perry Becker!" "Yes, I know him!" "He's too young!" several voices exclaimed at the same time.

"Nothing of the kind," I answered impatiently. "He's sixteen. If you wait any longer, he will decay like the rest of them. You need more like what he is. Get them while they still have spirit."

"Correct!" shouted Cassidy; his bellowing voice carried in this emptiness and the tones of the others sounded faint beside his.

"Perry Becker will help us find other young fellows of his age and way of thinking," I suggested.

"We'll have him at our next meeting," Kaspar began.

Suddenly I heard a sputter and a rattle and a roar in the distance from the direction of the city. There was a sudden hush among the gathered people. Before my eyes everyone turned pale. One after another of them rose and looked toward the city, whence the uproar came.

A half dozen motorcycles were approaching, coming on like the wind. They advanced in a rank, abreast of each other and about a hundred yards apart. In a few seconds they changed from tiny dots on the smooth grass to hurtling, smoking masses, bearing down precipitately upon us.

In another moment the machines had whizzed by.... They were tiny things, not over three feet high, and there certainly were no people on them.

A panic, wild and terrified, seized upon the gathered committee. Everybody got up and ran; they scrambled over each other to got away, in all directions, like a flock of little chickens. In a few seconds the orderly Committee Meeting had melted. There was a fleeing, helter-skelter mob, scattering over the green levels, running precipitately, stumbling, falling, getting up again; there were several acres of panicky runaway figures. I shouted after them:

"Hi! Come back! That's foolish!"

I shouted until I was hoarse, impatient and irritated.

"What a bunch of fools!" I swore to myself.

I turned around. I found Mildred holding my arm in her two hands and staring defiantly around. Kaspar and Cassidy stood behind me. Kaspar was calm, so calm that it looked wrong. Cassidy had torn his collar open and was glaring belligerently in a semicircle, and swinging his doubled fists, that looked like a pair of pile-drivers.

In another moment the machines had whizzed by and turned into disappearing dots in the eastern distance. They were tiny things, not over three feet high, and there certainly were no people on them.

Cassidy stood and stared after them for several minutes. He turned to the rest of us with a blank look, and then under his breath he released several expletives, which heretofore I had not been aware were in circulation on the island. Finally he leaned back and laughed. He laughed until he roared and the tears came.

"It is mostly our guilty consciences that caused the rout," he explained, and laughed again.

"That is only the regular green-patrol of the Hopo field," he went on. "But we are nervous and jumpy. Look!"

He pointed toward the city. Several more dark bulks were slowly approaching.

"They come by every third or fourth day. There come the mowers and rollers. Those little things go on ahead to assure a clear track and lay out the course. 'Leading-machines,' we have come to call them. They are in common use for all automatic mechanical work."

It was not long before the scattered people recognized their mistake and came trooping back, looking quite sheepish; though many of them were big enough to have the sense of humor to laugh. Cassidy continued to laugh for a long time. The burly, phlegmatic fellow must have been under a severe nervous strain. At the time of the emergency he had been cool and steady, ready to deal with the situation. That he was unnerved afterwards made me sure that much more had been at stake than merely his own skin. I knew such people well.

I had not laughed at any time. It did not look funny to me; it looked pitiful. If it had been a real attack, they would have been hunted down like rabbits, to the last individual. And they had actually acted as though they had expected nothing else than to be killed on the spot. What sort of a terrible mystery was here?

* * *

WHILE the group re-formed the ponderous mowers and rollers went by. There were a dozen of the towering, clattering hulks spread out in line, advancing down half the width of the field, each bigger and noisier than the biggest road-machine I had ever seen in western Texas; and they proceeded irresistibly, reminding me in their inexorable advance of tanks. Behind them they towed great truckloads of mowed grass. Nowhere about them were any human beings visible. When they passed they left lawns as smooth and flat as a table top.

When Cassidy opened the meeting again for business I rose and addressed him, hastening to get ahead of anyone else.

"Do you really want me to help you?" I inquired of the whole assembly.

"Sure" said Cassidy positively. "I can speak for one and all present."

"Then I am glad this happened," I continued. "It has pointed out to me the thing that you need worst if you are to succeed. It is a simple thing, but you've got to have it or you won't last long."

Not a sound broke the silence. All eyes were bent eagerly on me.

"And that is *discipline*. Without some type of formal discipline you are lost. In order to make discipline possible you need some form of organization. The only one I can suggest, because it is the only one I know, is the military type. But I can assure you that it is effective and practical. If I teach you, will you drill and play the game? Do you wish to begin right now?"

A forest of waving hands was eagerly raised in the air.

So Cassidy and I went up and down the rows, picking out the most likely ones to form the beginning nucleus of an organization. Rather quickly we located nine young fellows out of about twenty, and then it was more difficult. Finally we had sixteen men who looked promising as material for leaders. I noted during our selection that Mildred and the young lady with her in similar dress were talking very excitedly and watching us eagerly. Toward the end, when I called the sixteen out in front, the two girls came up to me.

"Aren't you going to let us in?" they asked disappointedly.

I was puzzled as to what to do. In my military experience woman had no place. Yet here it looked rather logical. After a conference with Kaspar and Cassidy we made up a squad of girls, with a view to a separate organization of women, to receive similar training.

I requested the other members of the group who had not been chosen as recruits to remain behind me and watch what was going on, urging them to try and learn as much as possible about it, for their turn would come before long.

I took my twenty-four recruits and taught them how to form a straight line and to stand at attention. At my first command of "Attention!" most of them were rather astonished at the preemptory and businesslike tone of voice. But there is reason for the tone of military commands, and it worked. For once these *blasé* people took something seriously, and in a few minutes they were working hard. With sharp commands I put them through "Forward, march!" and "Squads, right!" exacting rigid compliance with the regulations.

There, on the vast, flat, green spaces, with the little knot of spectators behind me, I put my tiny line through its maiden evolutions. I did not hesitate to jerk out my commands with proper sternness, and to use top-sergeant methods on the sluggards. For they needed it. Their lives sadly lacked rigid training. They did not like it, but I had to give them credit for being game. They apparently saw a glimmer to the effect that it was necessary and good for them, and they took it all like the good sports they were. They came out of it much better than they went in. I think that they learned more that forenoon of real, deep human values, than they ever had known in their previous lives; while to me it meant considerable satisfaction that their intentions were serious, and that they were going to work, even if it came hard.

After the drill, the meeting continued in an informal manner for a while. I directed everyone present to write down everything he had learned as quickly as possible, in order that he might retain it correctly and pass it on accurately to others; for I wanted each one of those present to begin drilling a platoon of his own without delay. Cassidy was chosen as the head of a committee to select and judge new recruits. Before the meeting was over, the matter of training was an organized machine, that could proceed under its own power, independent of me, except for the matter of teaching a few leaders.

I was a little amused at the surprise and relief of the recruits who had been drilling, after I had given the command "Dismissed!" They had never seen anything like it: one moment I was on a rigidly stern pinnacle above them; and the next I was mingling with them cordially and democratically. But they were wonderful folks. They did not say much about it, though I was sure all were thinking hard.

"There must never be another panic like this," I said to the assembled people. "From now on, you must drill every day. The Hopo fields, the eastern beaches, anywhere you can find places where you are safe from observation, must be your drill grounds. In the meanwhile, I shall study the main features of your situation and analyze them, to see where I can be of further assistance to you."

Noontime came and the meeting had to break up. As we walked over to where our cars were coming to meet us, we saw an occasional Hopo rider with his long mallet, swinging along as the vanguard of the afternoon play. Many of the people shook my hand and seemed happy over my efforts. Everywhere among them was enthusiasm; each one seemed as though he had just discovered something new and wonderful. Cassidy walked beside me.

"Looks good to me, boy!" he said. "I knew you'd do something. I've got genuine hopes now."

"Well," I mused; "I'll be glad when I know what it's all about."

"In a day or two you shall know. Kaspar will tell you the whole story. It is a difficult thing to tell to a stranger. In the meanwhile, be careful how you talk and where you talk. We need you now."

"I'll be careful," I promised; but I kept wondering to myself how in thunder a thing like this could be managed without a lot of talking to people.

"You seem to have stirred things up," Cassidy went on; "Thus far our meetings have been a wonderful comfort and mutually sympathetic. But there had been no objective; we didn't know how to go about doing something definite. Now, it looks to me that delivery from our slavery to the machines and the end of the degeneration of our people are near at hand. I have real hopes of breaking away from the City of Smoke. Oh, will the time ever come when we can cease to worry about our best friends? Do you realize that at this moment we are not sure that tomorrow Mildred will not disappear to an unknown fate?"

"We've got to get down to business," I said, gritting my teeth at the thought. "I foresee trouble, and there is lots to do. People are going to get hurt. Have you ever thought of that? Your people aren't prepared for anything. This afternoon you must pick me out a dozen bright people, and I'll start out a bunch in first-aid training so that we could turn them loose as teachers; and another bunch preparing supplies."

Cassidy nodded reflectively.

"And what do these people know about taking care of themselves in case the service of the machines should fail them?" I went on. "How many can rustle up a meal and cook it, or prepare a night's shelter? How many could raise something to eat for an unproductive period? Does anyone know anything about weapons?"

"You make me ashamed of myself and of the whole island," Cassidy admitted. "For so long have we been accustomed to living without any need of these things, that it has never occurred to us that it might be otherwise. These are all forgotten arts. Yet, I can see that the time is apt to come when we shall need them. There are probably some racking experiences ahead for us. But better that than this slavery. Davy, we've needed you badly to stir us up."

"If you find me people, I shall teach them," I proposed eagerly. "I'll help you get organized. Your people are excellent material, and take to it well. With a little training and organization, you can work against your apparently powerful enemies with some show of hope on your side. I'm enthusiastic about getting to work at once. In fact, I'm thankful for having something real to do. This social stuff was beginning to get the best of me."

* * *

ALL of that day, while I watched the people, talked to them, and worked with them, there was a hidden undercurrent of thought in my mind. There, ever present, was that black, smoking city, with its white thread of a road stretching over here toward us, teeming with hundreds of busy, speeding vehicles, like a pulsing artery between two centers. I remembered that fork of the road where we had turned off to the left on the previous morning; that other branch went straight ahead, inviting and beckoning with mystery. It was the road to the City of Smoke. What was there in that gloomy metropolis? Why was it kept such a secret? I had promised Kaspar that I would wait twenty-four hours. That twenty-four-hour period was now over.

Then, one night at midnight, I was awakened from my sleep by an unusual commotion in the Kaspar home. People walking about, queer, catchy and strained voices penetrated thickly to me. I threw on some clothes, and opening my door, cautiously looked out. I saw Phyllis bobbing in Mildred's arms and Mildred, pale and wild-eyed, trying to comfort her. Kaspar was walking nervously back and forth across the room, and Mrs. Kaspar was in a big chair with her head bowed on her hands. I stood and stared awhile, and finally came out among them.

"This is the worst blow of all," Kaspar groaned. "Without him we are lost."

"Who? What has happened?" I demanded.

"Cassidy is gone. They've got him!" Kaspar groaned and sat down.

I am afraid that I used an ungentlemanly word. I stood for a few moments struck dumb. But there was nothing I could do there. I turned and walked back into my room, where I began picking things out of my suitcase and packing a haversack to carry slung over my shoulder. My determination was made.

8
TO THE CITY OF SMOKE

DURING my life I had gone through enough danger and excitement to have developed the ability to lie down and snatch a few hours' sleep in the face of an approaching crisis. Not knowing just what was ahead of me now, I took care to get into bed and relax completely, so that I might gather strength and poise for my coming adventure. Also I had the much more common ability to wake up exactly at a previously determined hour.

In the morning I was awake at sunrise, feeling fit and alert. Dressing was a matter of a few moments, and I ate a double breakfast. I wrote the following note on a large sheet of paper and pinned it to the middle of the rug:

> *I have gone to the City of Smoke. I am leaving quietly because I cannot bear dissuasions and leave-takings. I promise to take good care of myself; and when I return I expect to bring with me some knowledge that will be useful to you in your struggle. I hope that I can find Cassidy and*

> be of some use to him. I know that you will not mind my
> using Sappho, for my purpose is the good of the cause.

Davy Breckenridge.

I took with me my pistol and ten spare clips of shells, the hand ax and field-glasses, a canteen, a flashlight and extra batteries, and some dried emergency rations. I debated for a while whether or not to include my blanket, but finally left it behind, because its bulk would impede my movements too much.

I left with only one regret, and that was that I had not yet heard Kaspar's explanation of what the war was about. A better knowledge of what was going on would have been to my advantage in getting about the strange city, and in gathering information to help these people in their stand against their oppressors. But, I reasoned that my present plan was best; for since Kaspar was afraid to talk openly around here, it would take a half a day or more before suitable opportunity could be found to tell me his story, which he stated was long and complicated. I was unwilling to risk any such delay; things might happen to prevent me from going. If I was to do Cassidy any good, I had better start quickly. Though, how I could find him in that vast hive, I had no idea.

I had to confess that at certain moments my project struck me as somewhat foolhardy: starting out alone into a city totally unknown to me, and where I had certainly received ample warning that danger awaited me. However, there was a good deal to discount this danger. What these soft and luxurious people considered a danger might be little more than superstition. And I intended to be careful, to keep a sharp lookout ahead of me, and to know what I was getting into before taking each step. This was to be a sort of scouting or reconnoitering expedition. I had no clear or definite plans. Each stage would have to be guided by what I had already found.

Turning these things over in my mind, I stole out of the house and opened the garage doors. My instructions in running the car were far from complete, and my practice meager; but I had handled it enough by this time to feel sure that I could get to my present destination with it. The sight of the jolly little roadster resting there in its stall put me into high spirits again. I spoke to it in the jocular manner that I had fallen into:

"All right, Sappho, you old coffee-grinder; we'll slip off by ourselves this morning."

My derogatory epithets were pure fun, for the car was trim and swift-looking, and its machinery in the most perfect order, as far as I could tell by its sound and its performance. I continued to talk to it as I got in and studied the dials. I went to work carefully to set them. It was like working the combination of a big safe. There were four for directions, and a distance dial to set each time between them, while the left hand handled the speed dial simultaneously during the entire time. A little pointer traveled on a chart all the while, to check up the setting as well as to assist in determining directions and distances from a map when these were unknown to the driver. The study of this map provided me with much subsequently useful knowledge of the island and the cities.

"Now, all aboard for the City of Smoke!" I almost shouted in my glee, as I completed the "setting" and the machinery under the hood began to purr.

With a soft, rustling sound of its marvelous mechanism, the little green-black car glided out of the garage and into the street. I was as elated as a child with a new toy, at having succeeded in operating it on my own initiative.

"Attaboy Sappho!" I applauded. "If we go on like this, we'll have Cassidy out of jail and take a shot at this 'Supervision' business before night."

I watched the streets with eager attention, checking up the places I already knew, to ascertain if the car was carrying me correctly. Now I could not help being impressed with the marvelous ingenuity of the automatic mechanism of the car; for I had to admit that I had laid out no more than the general features of the route, while the smaller details, such as turning corners, avoiding passing cars and obstacles in the road, were all taken care of by the machinery, without knowledge or effort on my part. It was difficult for me to resist the temptation to stop the car and look under the hood to see what the machinery looked like that was accomplishing the feats that were almost beyond belief.

Within thirty minutes the car rolled through the park, out through the arched gateway, and sped up the paved highway between the green fields that were already familiar to me. It bowled along smoothly and luxuriously. On the right, the morning mists were rising out of the river in the distance, and the mountains far out beyond were a wonderful deep blue. On the left, the flat, cultivated fields extended on to the smooth and level horizon. The morning was cool, and the breeze made by the motion of the car felt as delicious to my hands and face as a cooling drink. The shadow of the car racing on ahead, was a dozen feet long.

When I saw ahead of me the fork in the road, with the branch on the left leading to the dock and the Gulls' Nest, I watched the behavior of the car with bated breath again. Would it take that mysterious and interesting branch of the road that led straight on ahead, toward the great, smoking macrocosm that I had seen from the top of the cliff? Had I "set" it correctly? It was more exciting to my nerves than the watching of a tense automobile race, and my heart almost stopped beating, until the fork to my left was safely behind me, and I was spinning along, straight to the west.

* * *

AS mile after mile passed, without effort from me, I pondered on the curious things that had befallen me during the past few days. It was an opportune moment for concentration; I leaned back among soft cushions, with nothing to do as far as driving or paying attention to the road was concerned; the monotonous purr of the machinery and the equally monotonous whizz of the scenery backward past me, were very soothing. I tried to plan ahead. I was resolved not to plunge blindly into the city, but to look it over from a distance and approach cautiously. Then it occurred to me that if I carefully analyzed some of the questions that had been puzzling me about affairs on the island, I might be able to make some deductions concerning the dangers ahead of me, and might consequently better prepare myself to meet them. A careful consideration of what I had already seen was certain to shed a good deal of light on what I had to expect.

When I stopped to think about it, this was my first opportunity to think things over carefully since I had landed. Up till now, my every moment had been busy, distracted by the presence of others and by something going on, or I had been too tired and sleepy to think. So, I took out my notebook and pencil, and one by one I marshaled the mysteries, puzzles, and surprises that I had found here; and after careful reflection, made a few notes on each.

1. From the very first moment I had set foot on the black ship, Kaspar had begun warning me that I was in grave danger on the island. At first I had thought that he was trying to scare me with the ordinary perils of tropical travel. But, here I was in a perfectly civilized community; the streets and homes looked as peaceful and safe as my own home town. And yet, Kaspar and Cassidy carefully and anxiously watched my every move. There must be something more specifically dangerous than snakes and swamps and savages. How he could say that I was in danger before anyone on the island knew I was coming, or was even aware of my existence, puzzled me. He certainly did not mean to imply that all strangers were in peril; and besides I had been very well received by these people, who were totally unaccustomed to strangers. Was my danger similar to that of other individuals on the island, like Ames and the others who had disappeared? Why had those particular ones been selected? And why particularly was I elected? It could not be because these dark enemies knew much of me personally. There had never been the least relationship between me and the island.

I wondered if perhaps a few of the old Southern families between whom there was some deadly feud, had not gotten settled on the island, and kept up the feud through all these generations. Perhaps the two factions who had continued the family war were now organized, each in its own populous city, and were carrying on the war with all the terrific and grotesque weapons their science had supplied, automatic cranes, and huge motorcycles with tentacles. And perhaps I also was a descendant of one of these factions or in some way involved with it, and Kaspar knew about it, while I didn't. At any rate, it was clear that for some reason not connected with anything that I myself had done or was conscious of, my existence was in conflict with some established principle on the island. In other words, I was a *persona non grata*. A more detailed solution I could not hope to arrive at just at the present time.

2. *What was the meaning of the incident — almost an accident — of Mildred and the crane?* No sooner had I stepped off the ship than here was a new mystery. On the surface of it, it may have looked like an ordinary accident; but by this time I was thoroughly satisfied that it had been a bold and almost successful attempt to annihilate a girl who was one of the most beautiful and popular, and certainly the most prominent in her community. Was there a personal reason for the attack on her? Was she selected because of her prominence? I had seen the fear in the eyes of the people who had watched that "accident"; and I was sure that they had known what was behind it. What better proof was there that Kaspar's people had deadly, unscrupulous, and ingenious enemies among the people who operated the machines? Yet, apparently the power and opportunity of the latter were not unlimited; for certainly that night on the dock they had control of a sufficient preponderance of physical force to have been able to put across any desired plan by means of physical violence. Evidently there had been reasons why it was impossible to attack openly the little group that had come to meet Kaspar. There was something more beneath this than mere crude, open enmity.

3. *What was the truth about my compulsory ride in the automatic car?* Was that an "accident" of the same kind as the one previously mentioned? By this time I was thoroughly ready to discard the idea that it had been a practical joke played upon me by some member of the social group gathered about the Kaspar family. These people's minds did not work in the direction of dangerous practical jokes against their own good friends. I strongly suspected that my ride, with its wild ending, was an attempt on the part of the machinery people to carry me off. It was clever; it would have looked like an ordinary accident. The

machinery people had a skillful way of staging things without appearing on the scene themselves. Not only in the dark deeds I have mentioned, but in all the work that the machinery did for the living, comfort, and luxury of the inhabitants of the City of Beauty, were they extraordinarily skillful in getting things done and keeping absolutely out of sight. It was evident that the highly-cultured, sport-loving class whom I knew so well, not only knew nothing about the operation and care of machinery, but also that they seldom if ever beheld the mechanics who operated and cared for it, and on whom their lives depended.

4. *How far wrong was I in my estimate of the community on the day I had visited the Paneikoneon?* Evidently my original idea of a perfect Utopia needed some amending. The people of the City of Smoke obviously lived in subjection to the fair artists of the City of Beauty, and carried the entire burden of that marvelous culture and development. The fastidious drones could not even bear to have the workers live in the same city with them. It was a strange picture. Beauty was the first thing to strike the eye, but it was only on the surface. One group was living in luxury and leisure at the expense of a subject class; and yet living in terror of the subjects. The subjects, in bursts of rebellious retaliation, reached up and dragged down, every now and then, a bright and favored member of that high and shining stratum. It was difficult to determine which were the masters and which were the slaves; which the oppressors and which the oppressed.

5. *What became of the people who disappeared?* There was no doubt in my mind that they were taken to the City of Smoke. Furthermore, everything I had ascertained pointed to the fact that they were never seen nor heard of again.

What happened to them there was a matter of pure conjecture, and speculating about it was a waste of time and effort.

6. *What was Supervision?* Evidently the subject class were not quite completely out of sight. At times the lords had to degrade themselves by looking over the labors of their servants at the scene of operations. Otherwise, what could "Supervision" mean? It seemed to be a compulsory task, evidently unpleasant. The compulsion also evidently came from the supervised and not from the supervisors, for the latter seemed anxious for opportunities to dodge the obligation, while the former meted out a terrible and mysterious punishment to my friend Ames, who had made a record by his success in avoiding the obligation.

Could there be a more amazing, more maddening interlacement of puzzling relationships and inconsistent influences?

7. *What was the reason of the intense fear of being overheard? Who could overhear?* Most of the people I knew would not speak of the mysteries connected with the machinery under any circumstances at all. Their private thoughts on the subject, if they had any, were never uttered. The few people who did have the courage and aggressiveness to think and speak on the subject, did so, only under circumstances where there was no possibility of their words being picked up by mechanical appliances. Even automobiles were under suspicion; out in the broad fields and in the dense woods, Mildred would not speak as long as there was a car around. This was explainable only on the basis of highly developed methods of detection of sound and its transmission by radio methods. Apparently

microphones or dictaphones were concealed everywhere, in homes, public places, automobiles. And evidently the people did not know enough about these instruments to find them and put them out of commission. I resolved at once never to go out again with anyone in a car, without first looking it over and disconnecting anything that looked like a transmitter or a detector.

Evidently, somewhere, someone was listening to everything that went on in the City of Beauty. Had I made a mistake when I spoke aloud to Sappho on starting this morning? I was sorry now that I had not taken the trouble to think these things out before. I had given away my plans completely. Perhaps by this time they were known to some central spider in the big web. I had better be doubly cautious in entering the city.

8. *What was this people's uprising about? Against whom? What were their grievances?* It must be a very grave matter. Every one of them had fear in their eyes. They were pale and furtive from fear, and yet they went doggedly on with their plans and their preparations. People do that only when vital matters are at stake. It was not some mere fancied wrong that troubled them; life was too easy-going in the City of Beauty. And yet, I could see no cause for complaint. Everything seemed running smoothly; on all sides were all possible reasons why these people should be happy. They seemed to have, as far as I could see, all they wanted of food, shelter, clothes, liberty and leisure, luxuries. What did they lack? What were they fighting about?

And what would they have done if I had not headed them in the proper direction in the matter of organization and discipline? They were intelligent and grasped things quickly; but they were ignorant of the very fundamentals of taking care of themselves. Never had I seen a more helpless people.

Their helplessness of course meant that they had long been cared for like children. No thought nor effort for their own care was required of them. Yet, if someone had taken that good care of them, why were they planning rebellion against their benefactors?

A number of possible explanations occurred to me. The book of H. G. Wells that I had read some time ago suggested one. Another was a memory that came back vividly to me from childhood, and struck me forcibly as a close analogy of this people's plight. When I was a small boy, I had pet rabbits. There was one rabbit that I especially loved and favored. I gave it the best of care and fed it royally. Just like the people in the City of Beauty, it lived in luxury, without a thought of taking care of itself. Then, one day it disappeared — just as Ames had. My childish grief was so intense that I remember it to this day. It was a long time before my child mind connected the disappearance of my pampered and indulged rabbit, with a new kind of meat on the table. I had thought my parents loved the rabbit as well as they did me.

Other analogies occurred to me. Were not these people in some sort of position like that of the farmer's prize herd of cattle? He takes the best possible care of them; he goes to any amount of expense to secure their comfort and content. They are as happy and comfortable, and as well developed as the people in the City of Beauty. Are they also afraid of the farmer because occasionally one of them disappears and is never seen again? In our laboratories at Galveston we treated the dogs and guinea-pigs as carefully and considerately as though they had been human. No amount of care, no excellence of food, no perfection of comfort was too good for them. And, every now and then, we took one of them away to the dissecting room, and his comrades never saw him again.

Whose pets were these fair people in the City of Beauty? For what sort of sacrifice or experiment were they being so perfectly cared for?

* * *

I CLOSED my notebook with a slap. My analyses and deductions had brought me to discomforting conclusions. I began to have misgivings as to the wisdom of my expedition. If I ever wanted to see Mildred again, if I ever wanted to take up that country practice in eastern Texas that I had so long dreamed about, perhaps I had better reconsider my plans before it became too late.

I was roused from my study and brought back to a consideration of my surroundings by noting that there was a forest ahead. The dim blue line on the horizon ahead broadened into a green strip, which was rapidly looming high in the air; and before long I could see the details of the dense jungle, which exactly resembled the one through which we had passed on our way to the sea. The way it ended abruptly like a wall where the cultivated fields began, made me certain that this country had once been entirely covered by jungle; and that the river bottoms had been artificially cleared for cultivation. What a stupendous task that must have been! The history of this land must be an astonishing chronicle, full of heroisms and brave human accomplishments! What characters, what Daniel Boones and George Washingtons, the history of this people must contain! In fact, Kaspar and Cassidy were big men, worthy of being put down in any history. I must get all of this story from Kaspar or someone, as soon as I could, for I was intensely interested in it.

Now and then an occasional truck came hurtling toward the city from which I had come. I always looked up quickly, hoping to see the driver; but there were no drivers. The vehicles were all automatic and unoccupied. I saw no people at all. Apparently the custom or regulation against the people of each city visiting the other, was very strictly observed. What would I run into by going contrary to it?

At first the vehicles I met were few and far between. But, as the day advanced and the day's business began to get started, they became more frequent and numerous. There were chiefly trucks, of all sizes and shapes, with and without loads. However, I saw numerous other strange machines making their way toward the City of Beauty, lumbering and clattering hulks, such as I had never seen before, and whose purpose I could not imagine. The requirements of caring for a city's work by automatic machinery had developed some bizarre and undreamed-of forms of apparatus. I ached for an opportunity to examine some of them closely and watch them work.

The road dived into the black opening in the green wall ahead, and in a moment I was plunging along through the cool gloom of the forest, endeavoring to see. It took some moments for my eyes to become accustomed to the twilight that reigned there. Overhead I caught some glimpses of the sky through the interlacing branches just over the road; but at the sides the roof was so dense as to be quite impenetrable to any light at all. The tree trunks and interlacing vines and branches spun backward at a dizzy rate, while the car made a soft, rushing noise in its progress through the leafy tunnel. The bright opening behind, by which I had driven in, soon disappeared; and all around there was nothing but jungle.

I noticed that the car was beginning to behave curiously. It would slow down for a few moments, and gradually pick up speed again. Suddenly it would slow down again and almost stop. Then it would race quickly on. In another few moments it was hesitating along at a snail's pace. Various queer and unusual noises proceeded from it, grindings, knockings, and squeaks. Then it stopped and stood motionless with its machinery humming.

"What's wrong now?" I muttered. I had serious misgivings as to my skill in setting the dials, simple as that task seemed to the other folks who handled these cars.

I looked the instrument board all over carefully, but did not know what further to do. I felt it wisest not to tamper with the dials any further.

Abruptly the car jerked forward, and with a few rapid turns it reversed its position on the road and started back swiftly toward the City of Beauty. Its horn tooted melodiously up and down the musical scale.

"Whoa!" I shouted. "There's something wrong here!"

The only explanation that I could possibly think of was that I had made some mistake in setting the dials. Yet, that was not altogether plausible. I could readily see how I might have made some minor error which could have gotten me off the track a little. But this sort of behavior would necessitate a radical and fundamental error; and I felt sure that I knew more about them than to have set them completely backwards.

I reached for the levers that were used to drive the car by "actual control" as the people called it; that is, to control each movement individually; and I tried to turn it around. There was a good deal of grinding and knocking in the mechanism, and much irregularity in the car's progress; but it continued its course back home, and would not answer to my efforts. Therefore, I decided that something had gone wrong with the machinery. This was a little embarrassing, to say the least. I had taken the car without permission, which fact in itself was enough to disconcert me; and to have it get out of order was making the thing worse than ever. Indeed, my friends would think that I had behaved like a small boy.

However, in a moment my present trouble had crowded that out of my mind. I did not want to go back to Kasper's house now. Not only would I not want to face the people; but my own conscience would not permit me to go. I was so contrarily built, that the very fact that I had just gone through a reasoning process that convinced me that I was embarked on a highly dangerous course, was enough to make me all the more doggedly set in my determination to carry it out. Even though my knees shook and my teeth chattered, I would have gone ahead. Already I had lost a mile on my way. The car was proceeding irregularly, now fast, now slow. I hung my haversack over my shoulder and jumped out.

The fall brought me stumbling to my knees. The roar of an approaching truck made me dodge into the underbrush. Why I hid, I do not know. I was worked up to a pitch of jumpy nervousness, feeling sure that although I saw no people about here, nevertheless I was being observed, and someone, somewhere, knew just what I was doing. The truck rumbled by and disappeared. I watched Sappho. The car went forward a moment, then stopped and quivered a moment, and went backwards. It stood still a while with the machinery roaring, and then started at full speed toward the

City of Beauty. I crawled out and stood in the road, watching it dwindle and disappear. Now I was alone in the forest.

"There can't be much over ten miles to go," I thought, "and I am safer on foot."

* * *

I SWUNG along, feeling lusty and vigorous in the exhilarating morning air. It was just beginning to get warm. Up above, in the interlaced canopy of branches and foliage, there were clickings and squawkings; and I caught flashes of bright colored plumage flashing back and forth. Little sounds came out of the forest, a chirp, a twitter, a rustle. My footsteps rang loudly on the pavement. I wondered if there were any large and dangerous animals. I swung my pistol into position where I could draw quickly, for I had confidence in my aim and in the stopping power of a .45 caliber bullet. Still, I admitted that my greatest danger was not from wild beasts.

The passing vehicles kept growing more numerous. They passed with a roar that rumbled and re-echoed back and forth among the tree trunks in the depths of the forest. I kept a sharp lookout for human beings, but not one did I ever see on any of the machines. I hugged the bushes, whose ends were whipped off by passing vehicles into a perpendicular wall, like a trimmed hedge. The vehicles as a rule kept the middle of the road.

A little "leading machine" whizzed by. It was a curious vehicle, a tiny motorcycle, too small for anyone to ride in or to carry a load. There was a good deal of complicated mechanism about it, little gear-wheels like the works of a watch, and many busy little rods and cams. In front were two bright, staring headlights. As it sailed whirring down the road, I stared after it, wondering what could be the possible use of the thing.

A truck came up behind me. From the sound of its machinery, it seemed to be slowing down. I glanced back and found this indeed to be the case; and furthermore, it was at the edge of the road, directly behind me. I edged as far as I could into the thicket.

"This is no place for pedestrians," I thought

Of course, there was no sidewalk. There could not have been much, if any, travel on foot between the two cities.

The approaching truck was a light one, of half-ton capacity. The curved arm of a crane projected from it high above the road, from the side nearest me. It passed very slowly, and uncomfortably close to me. I crowded close to the bushes. If there had been a driver, I would have had something to say to him.

A sudden clatter above my head made me look up in surprise. A loop of chain whipped out cleverly from the crane, like the circle of a lasso. It fell neatly over my head, and while I stared in open-mouthed astonishment, it tightened about my arms and shoulders.

It happened so quickly, such an amazing, undreamed-of thing, that before I realized what was going on, I was swung off my feet and hoisted up off the ground. My arms were pinioned to my sides, and I was helpless as a trussed turkey. At first, I was stunned with surprise. It was too strange — too far beyond anything I could have foreseen. Then I was overwhelmed by anger and chagrin. I had been taken in as easily as a new-born babe. For a moment, I was beside myself with rage.

However, that availed me nothing. I dangled there foolishly in the air, and the grip of the chain around my chest and arms was painful. At least I was glad that there were no witnesses to my ridiculous plight.

A loop of chain whipped out cleverly from the crane, like the circle of a lasso. It fell neatly over my head, and while I stared in open-mouthed astonishment, it tightened about my arms and shoulders.

The truck picked up speed and clattered on, toward the City of Smoke. As the trees and bushes spun backward past me and the wind whistled about me, I was swung over the seat, and with much humming of gears and clashing of levers from the interior of the car, I was lowered until I was comfortably seated. Immediately, a polished bar swung across my chest and locked with a click. Here I sat, fastened down, fuming and writhing.

My rage knew no bounds. Captured! Tied up and being carried away! Just like one of the helpless rabbits from the City of Beauty. No! I would show them. I would not be cowed, merely because a machine had got hold of me. Perhaps they had me, but if they had, they would still learn a few things about what kind of a fight I could put up. They would never get to that black city with me.

I heaved and strained at the bar that held me prisoner. I am known as a strong man among my friends, but my utmost efforts failed to budge the bar, or even to produce a crackle. It remained immovable. After I had exhausted my strength and bruised my flesh, I began to calm down a little. The firm and steady pressure of the bar across me helped to steady my nerves. The purely impersonal character of the things that held me gradually calmed me, and I began to reason a little.

My safety now depended upon my keeping my wits together. That was the first thing that dawned on me. I spent a good many minutes in drilling myself to keep calm, and forcing myself to plan carefully ahead, just as the previous few days I had been drilling the rebels. If I wanted to get away from this machine, I must think clearly first. Get away from it, I must, somehow.

I had no doubt in my mind that I had given myself away in the morning by my soliloquy; a microphone in the car had warned the authorities in the black city, and they had sent the automatic machine after me. The uncanny cleverness with which the mechanism worked was almost too much for my belief.

Well, I had been tricked once, but now I was warned. From now on, I would realize fully that I could trust no machine near me. My unseen enemies had the advantage of me because they knew all about my movements without themselves being in evidence. Nevertheless, I made up my mind to outwit them.

I set about examining carefully the bar that held me. Machinery had to be dealt with coolly and calculatingly. The bar fitted my chest as accurately as if it had been made to measure for me. It held me tight against the back of the seat and restrained the movements of my arms. I looked about to see if I could reach something to pry it loose. If I could get my hands on some kind of a lever, I would make short work of the thing.

Then, suddenly I got an idea and desisted.

If I were being watched, why not let them think they had me? If I pretended stupidity and submission, a loophole of escape would be much more certain to offer itself. If they considered me as helpless as the rest of the people from the City of Beauty, my chances would be far better.

And after all I was on my way, swiftly and comfortably, toward the goal toward which I had started.

Things weren't so bad after all. Sit tight and keep my eyes open, was what I determined to do, and go on quietly on the truck into the black city.

9
WHAT IS SUPERVISION?

THE little two-wheeled thing that I was learning to call a "leading-machine," was now ahead of the truck. It was about the size of one of the toy motorcycles that are made for boys to ride around on; but it was accurately and sturdily built; and as I sat and watched it ahead of me, I was struck by the astounding complexity of the thing. Only some of the research apparatus that I had seen in university physics laboratories, could compare with it. It spun on ahead of the truck, keeping a uniform distance in front, like an active little puppy in front of a plodding ox-cart. When I had first heard the word "leading-machine" I had wondered what it meant; but now, I had to admit that "leading" was the right word; that was precisely what this little machine seemed to be doing. And again I caught myself in the silly tendency that I had fallen into several times on this island, of attributing personality to machines, as though they had minds of their own. I was wildly curious to know how the little thing worked and what its precise purpose was.

It was not many minutes before the machines emerged from the forest, and the great, black city with its crown of smoke, loomed over the whole horizon in front. This time, there were no green, cultivated fields on both sides. At first there was a little sickly looking vegetation, but as we approached the city, the ground became quite bare. The road led through a region that looked as dreary as a dead world; naked, oily-looking earth, heaps of slag and cinders, pools of stagnant water scummed and greasy, or sometimes colored orange or green. Great gashes and scars were cut here and there; and mine-openings and oil-derricks were scattered about, but evidently not in operation. A mile or so to the right, the river looked gray and gloomy.

I could not say much for human handiwork in this part of the island. If this scarred desolation was needed to maintain that high degree of civilization in yonder "City of Beauty," I would have preferred to see the entire island a rural community.

The city began abruptly. It towered ahead, a long, high wall, crowned with a wreath of smokestacks and a headdress of gloomy smoke. No longer was the sky above me blue. At the foot of the wall, the bare, gray earth was strewn with a thousand kinds of industrial rubbish. There was no skirmish-line of scattered and outlying buildings to warn the visitor that he was entering a city; only the bleak wall stretching into the distance on the left so far that I could not see its end; and at the right ending at the river. The road led into an arched opening in the wall.

There was nothing decorative about the entrance; it was frankly a hole to get into and out of. The leading-machine plunged in, and the truck followed. The arch closed over my head, and I was suddenly in the city. For a short distance there was a gloomy passageway, hardly a street, between grimy buildings, with the busy commotion of an intersection visible on ahead. Then, as the truck rolled out into the glaring light of the open intersection, the rumble and roar broke upon my ears like a sudden explosion.

It was infinitely depressing. Long rows of factory-like buildings stretched off endlessly, and groups and clusters of tall chimneys poured out smoke; high in the air, pipes and cables and conveyors were trussed across open spaces between buildings, while swinging beams and derricks lent an eerie sense of movement to the ponderous scenery. Huge loads swung along on traveling cranes high over my head, or moved swiftly along on trussed bridges and suspended cables. Roaring steel converters and foundries belched sheets of fire and great continents of black smoke into the air, and my breath felt sulphurous in my lungs.

There was a clatter and a rush of vehicles, the thunder of huge trucks, and the din of machinery within buildings. The broad street was covered with a swarm of things on wheels, large and small, moving swiftly in all directions at once, like a swarming crowd of huge insects, black clumsy, clattering creatures.

Everywhere, huge machines whirled and roared, until my head was numb from it. And nowhere a human being in sight!

What was it all doing? Who had made it? Who operated it?

And what should I do now? The truck was plunging me into the middle of that clattering turmoil. Without anyone to guide it, it was picking its way through traffic so congested that the smallest slip would have meant being crushed to a pulp under the moving behemoths. Should I try to get myself loose and escape from the truck that held me? In truth, I had very little inclination to do so. To plunge into that vast, churning city, where there must be endless stretches of just such dreary, rumbling streets, and countless buildings, roaring clots like this intersection was, did not seem alluring just at present. The truck seemed to be headed somewhere; its machinery was apparently set to reach some objective. I was thankful for any guidance at all, in this most uncouth of cities. Had there been people about the streets, of whom I might inquire my way, the problem would have been different.

But nowhere was there any living thing visible. I decided to remain on the truck, keeping my eyes open, and to be ready for emergencies.

And then I saw the Squid! That was the name I associated with the two-wheeled, tentacled machine that had carried away Ames from the dancing pavilion on the day that he had missed Supervision and sent Dubois in his place. Of course, I was not sure that it was the same machine; but whenever I saw anything like it, it was always alone of its kind; and I felt quite sure that it was always the same machine. In general, it did not really look like a squid; but it handled its tentacles as a squid does. For a moment I saw its goggly headlights and black, coiled, ropy tentacles in the press behind me; it towered high above all other two-wheeled vehicles, and darted in and out with a superior swiftness among the clumsier machines. In a moment it was out of sight in the mass of vehicles.

* * *

BETWEEN the clattering, roaring buildings, winding around blocks, and pushing its way through the crowd of vehicles, the little truck carried me. The little leading-machine was always ahead; sometimes I lost it, but always it reappeared. Always the two machines were headed in a general direction into the interior of this great, mechanical hive. So monotonous and continuous were the rattle and rumble of the traffic and the long lines of dismal buildings, that my mind became deadened and I ceased paying attention to them. It was all about the same.

One particular building attracted my attention. I rode within a block of it, about five minutes after entering the city. It had an immense oval domed roof, which shone like gold, held up by pillars high up above the tops of its walls. An ideal arrangement for keeping buildings cool in tropical countries, I thought. Then, it struck me that this huge domed oval with its white columns was

163

architecturally a beautiful thing, and therefore unique among these industrial abominations. Why? Why was it different?

Of course it must be because people from the City of Beauty came to it. These fastidious visitors would certainly object to entering any of these other grimy blocks. I regretted that its lower portion was hidden from me by the square, smoky masses of intervening structures; otherwise perhaps I might have seen people passing in and out. And, the only thing that the people from the City of Beauty ever came to this city for, was Supervision. I think that had been made plain enough to me. This must be where Supervision took place or was held! The idea struck me so suddenly that I nearly jumped out of the truck. I wriggled in vain for a moment, and then the great, golden oval was out of sight. In the back of my mind I noted a determination that I would have to hunt up that building and look it over.

Fifteen or twenty minutes of scurry and grime and clatter elapsed before the truck finally stopped. Such a city I never could have imagined in my wildest nightmare. How could there be two cities on the same island, so vastly different from each other as these two were? What could be the purpose of such a hideous machine as that Squid? Occasionally behind me, or in front of me, or somewhere, through the tangle of machines, I caught glimpses of it. It ought to be a useful piece of apparatus, for its activity and the capabilities of its tentacles were enormous.

The truck stopped before a building relatively small in size compared with those surrounding it. Again, here was a little architectural jewel set among rubbish; a pretty little structure in comparison with the gloomy hulks around it. The remarkable thing about it was that there were thousands of wires and cables leading into its roof. They converged in all directions from the smoky distances and gathered together into a huge bundle that entered the building. Several small leading-machines stood about near the doorway.

"Telephone exchange," I thought to myself. "No. More likely some sort of an administration building; some sort of central control office. Now I'll get to see the boss and find out what it's all about."

As the truck drove up with me, there was a good deal of tooting from the horns of the various machines; that is, the truck and the group of small leading-machines. First one started, and another picked it up melodiously, and they carried the echoes back and forth like a chorus singing "The Messiah." Even from within the building came melodious toots. The bar across my chest snapped open, and I lost no time in jumping out. However, the leading-machines ranged themselves round me and the truck, and I found myself in a little lane between them that led to the door of the building.

The door opened obligingly, but no one appeared. I thought quickly, and decided that for the present the best thing for me to do was to appear to fall in with the plans of my captors. So far they were treating me well, and resistance would not help much just now. So I stepped up toward the door, and a little leading-machine fell in and chugged slowly behind me. From the outside I could see practically nothing of what was within; so I boldly walked in. The door closed behind me with a slam.

Before me was a small table of the folding type, with an excellent looking lunch spread on it: soup, fish, an orange, bread, and coffee, instantly I realized that I was indeed hungry. I had breakfasted early and now my watch said eleven o'clock. For just a moment I hesitated; suppose this was some trick, and the lunch were poisoned! However, my common-sense told me better than that. If they wanted to destroy me, they had the opportunity of doing so more quickly and effectively than by resorting to such a low method as poisoning my food. They had me too completely in their power now, to make poisoning necessary. In fact, the luncheon was an encouraging sign; it meant that these people were not wholly barbarous, and had the intention of treating me with at least a semblance of civilized hospitality. However, why did they keep themselves so constantly hidden? So slow was I in grasping the truth!

I decided to eat the lunch, and quickly did so; though the thought of possible poison made a little shudder run over me at the first few mouthfuls. While I ate, I examined the room in which I found myself. Off into its farther portions stretched tiers upon tiers of countless units of some sort of electrical apparatus, all alike. It made me think of an automatic telephone exchange; the instruments suggested it in their form and arrangement; and there was a little rustling activity among them, now here, now there, very reminiscent of the way such an exchange looks to a spectator. The irregular, intermittent clickings, now in one direction, now in another; now almost silent and again a dozen or a score at a time, made it seem as though the room was alive with some sort of creatures. But, nowhere could I discover a living thing; only metal, enamel, wires, and an infinite complication of apparatus.

Several large, shining lenses were turned upon me. They were set in stereopticon-like housings; and every now and then they moved backward and forward a little, as though to adjust focus. They stared at me like huge, expressionless eyes. I had the uncomfortable sensation that I was being closely scrutinized by someone invisible to me. I had no doubt that there was someone hidden, either in a nearby room, or perhaps even at a great distance. I had been brought into this place to be looked over, and the person who was doing it might even be miles away, while the least detail in my appearance, my every movement, even every sound I made, were transmitted to him over wires. I even noted that the lenses that stared at me were set in pairs, so as to secure a correct stereoscopic effect.

* * *

BEFORE I finished my lunch, I was quite positive that I was alone in the room with the glittering glass and enameled metal apparatus, which pulsated and stirred as though it were alive. I felt self-conscious, however, knowing that I was being studied. The tooting puzzled me. The fluty, musical notes would break out for a while, and then cease again. Though it had a vague suggestion of rhythm, it was not and could not be music. I judged that it must be somehow associated with the operation of some of the apparatus.

Then it struck me that there must be mechanical ears here to listen, as well as staring eyes of glass to see. I walked about the room, peering closely at the apparatus in tiers, but found nothing that I could associate with the transmission of sound. I decided to speak, none the less, however.

"I want to meet you face to face!" I pronounced in an oratorical tone of voice. I had no doubt that it was heard. "Come out and let me see you!"

Nothing happened. I looked out of the window at the noisy, grimy street, and sat a while in the chair again, the only chair in the place. There was no desk, no furniture. I was in the center of an empty space, at which the lenses gazed. I tried speaking again.

"I want to see people!" I said, in my most stern, and commanding tone. The only result, if result it was, was some scattered tooting and rustling in the stacks of apparatus. Then it occurred to me that if they were really listening to me, I might try something in my own interests.

"Take me to the Supervision!" I ordered peremptorily. I had to admit to myself that it was a big bluff, for my quaking heart belied my bold words. "I came here to see the Supervision!"

I listened breathlessly for several minutes, but nothing occurred.

"By Jove!" I muttered, "this is making me nervous." I went to the door and tried it, but it was locked.

Then, as I passed the window, I saw the Squid outdoors. Its blank, glary headlights were staring right into the window. I jumped back, with a sudden, involuntary start, and laughed at myself for my foolish fears. I could see the thing quite plainly now. Its tall, coffin-shaped body was not a box at all. It was a very complicated structure, with various moving portions and twisted tubes, and here and there, metal plates that apparently concealed more delicate portions of its machinery. It was quite out of the question for anyone to have been hidden in that pulsing mass of wheels and levers. The thing was purely mechanical, purely automatic, and I laughed my fears away. I assured myself that it was purely mechanical.

And yet, why did it come up to the window, and look in, as a dog might do?

A few moments later, with pounding heart and throbbing head, I looked about the room, and when I looked out of the window again, the thing was gone. What connection did it have with Supervision? In Ames' case there was certainly a connection; and here, as soon as I had mentioned Supervision, the thing had appeared. I began to get restless; I walked to the door and gave it another yank. To my surprise, it opened, and I stepped out into the street. An odd thing struck me, as some foolish detail often strikes us in the midst of more seriously absorbing circumstances. The door-sill was of wood, and had sharp edges, that were not the least bit worn. That meant that rarely did anyone ever use this door. Oh, how stupid I was, that the truth did not dawn on me!

The sun shone so hot that the street was like a furnace; but the inhuman traffic went on fiercely as ever. Across the street was a great concrete block of buildings, through whose windows I could make out long rows of individual machines that were operating with some sort of an up-and-down movement, as though stamping something; a number of small square objects moved away from each machine on a belt conveyor. The little building in which I had just been, extended to a corner on the left, and across the street from that loomed another huge, factory-like bulk.

Just in front of me, backed up against the door so that I could hardly do anything else except step into it, was a curious, three-wheeled vehicle. A motorcycle side-car, or an ancient chariot are the only things I can think of to compare it to. It contained a seat for one person to sit in.

"Should I or should I not?" I worried, as I stood there hesitating.

True, the thing might run me into some sort of a trap; but on the other hand, there was as much danger right here as in some other part of the city. I reasoned that these people were accustomed to being good to their wards and dependents in the City of Beauty, and taking care of them as of small children; they had done it so long that it was a habit. I doubted if I were in immediate danger. And this had come so directly upon my request to see the Supervision, that there might really be some connection.

I stepped in and sat down. With a sudden click, a bar swung around and locked itself across my chest.

My muscles tightened involuntarily, but I controlled myself, and made myself sit in quiet patience.

"Keep your shirt on!" I said to myself. "Losing your head will only make things worse. Just now, I'll see all I can, and when it gets to be more than I care for, I'll find a way to slip out. But if I don't see their faces pretty soon, I'm apt to get peevish."

The little chariot rolled swiftly and smoothly up the street, dodging in and out among the towering trucks and ponderous mechanical bulks. I had to admit that it was a clever machine, exactly adapted to conveying a single passenger long distances through these densely congested streets. Part of the time I trembled at the danger, for it often looked as though, the very next moment, I was to be ridden down by some gigantic machine, that rolled down on me like a battleship; but each time the swift little conveyance in which I rode, slipped to one side, dodged into an opening, and was far away before the big thing had moved many feet.

Again, it was a long, confusing trip. At times I thought I recognized locations which I had passed in the morning, and I wondered if I were being taken back in the same direction. But these grimy buildings and clattering streets were all so nearly alike that I could not be sure. The general direction seemed east, and therefore toward the river; and I knew that I had entered the town at a point comparatively near the river. I kept a sharp lookout for the Squid, but did not see it during the trip. Then I spied the great, gilded, oval dome, and this eventually turned out to be my destination.

The building was obviously some sort of an auditorium. From the outside, it looked for all the world like a football bowl or stadium that had been roofed over. Its height and spread vastly exceeded those of any of the neighboring buildings. It had no windows, though thirty or forty feet above the ground was a row of great, unglazed embrasures; and then, between the tops of the walls and the eaves of the roof, was an open space a dozen feet high, all around the building. There was a large arched entranceway that was a considerable architectural achievement.

However, the little chariot carried me to a small door in the middle of one side. Without hesitation it plunged into, the darkness and from the sound I surmised that I was being carried along a passageway.

Electric lights appeared; I found I was in an ordinary hallway of masonry, of some fine-grained, white stone. The car came to a sudden stop in the blind end of the passage. In a moment a section of the floor began to rise with me, for I had been carried into an elevator. It ascended for a height of about two floors, and then the car rolled out, around a corner, and out into empty space.

So it seemed, at any rate. The car and I were really on a little platform, six or eight feet square, jutting out of the wall of the building, and commanding a view of the entire vast interior. It was a wonderful feat of construction, that immense, arched, brightly lighted space, without a single supporting column anywhere; and the great, domed roof sweeping overhead in a wonderful curve. A rhythmic, mellow rustle reverberated throughout the great spaces, suggesting that it was composed of many elemental sounds.

And down below, there was commotion and activity — and people! Not till this moment, when I felt the violent leap of my heart at the sudden sight of human beings below me, had I realized how profoundly I had been affected by the total absence of humanity from the chaos of these endless streets. A busy city without people is an uncanny thing.

The vast oval floor was divided longitudinally into halves by a broad road or street down the middle; and this passage was filled by a river of vehicles of all sizes and descriptions. As I looked down on the tops of them, they looked like some sort of crawling insects. They all proceeded very slowly in one direction, entering from the dazzling outdoors by a high arch at one end, slowly progressing through the length of the building, and leaving by a similar arch at the other end.

The two half-ellipses on either side of this procession were raised some ten feet above the level of the moving stream of vehicles. At first glance, I thought I was looking down on some huge library, with thousands of stacks of bookcases arranged geometrically over the floor, with people walking and sitting around among them. But, they were not books. Even before I got out my field-glasses and examined them closely, I saw that the stacks were in fact supporting racks for instrument boards.

I saw rows of white dials with needles moving over them, voltmeters, ammeters, wattmeters, gas-meters — what kind of meters they were, I could but guess. I could only make out thousands of dials, some round, some curved; with various sorts of figures. There were gauges with fluctuating columns of liquids, and barometer-like scales, and recording-pens tracing curves and zig-zag lines on rolls of squared paper and revolving kymographs. It seemed that all the measuring instruments of a city were concentrated here.

* * *

AT last! I thought. Here is the headquarters of this city, the point from which all this vast activity is controlled. Hither run all the wires from every point in the city and perhaps also of the other city; and here the people loll in comfort and luxury, while they attend to the management of this unbelievable mechanical organization. This was confirmed in my mind, as I looked around more closely and discovered that there were sections devoted to switches and control-levers, great tiers of them, such as one sees in a railway block-house or a central power station. There were tangles of valves and stopcocks, and myriads of knobs with pointers to them. Among all these things, the people sat and watched the meters, or occasionally moved levers. Some of them sat comfortably in easy-chairs, and others moved about, so that there was a pleasant, rhythmic commotion below me.

The Supervision at last! What else could it be? I sat there and studied the scene with my field-glasses, and I was sure that I recognized some of the people from the City of Beauty. There was Godwin, a young fellow who had been in the group that swam with me for the red flower; and a young lady with gray eyes whom I remembered very definitely. There were others whom I was sure I had seen before. Besides, they all had the bearing and dress of people whom I had met in the City of Beauty. So, this was the mysterious Supervision! This was the unpleasant task at which all were obliged to serve, and which all of them dreaded and hated!

I had to admit that I was just a shade disappointed. I had expected to see wonderful machines performing real work. And here, there were people dabbling at control instruments. I had hoped to see some of the inhabitants of the City of Smoke, but I saw none. Only these innocent children of the sun. They were elegantly dressed, to the height of fastidiousness. The men's clothes were faultlessly pressed, and their linen was perfect. The ladies' gowns were delicately beautiful. Faces were groomed smooth and hands were white and soft. They reclined languidly in easy-chairs, or strolled aimlessly here and there. Countenances were blank and indifferent.

They were not attending the machinery! Moreover they were not interested in it. They did not even understand it! I doubted if they knew as much about it as I did. In fact, from what I had learned of these people, they were not capable, either of understanding or of handling any kind of industrial machinery.

They were just passing the day in utter boredom, waiting for evening to come!

What the comedy meant, I could not imagine.

My little platform was one of several about the walls, but was the only one occupied. It was like a box at a theater, as much designed to be seen as to see from. It was not long before some of the people below noticed me, clamped in my three-wheeled vehicle. As I watched them through my glasses, I could see them grow grave and turn away when they saw me. Some of them recognized me, and seemed to grow pale and start in fright. This rather stirred a vague alarm in me. Why did fear play such an important part among the emotions on this island? However, I reasoned, their alarm was difficult to interpret. To me, it had often seemed that they were afraid of nothing. I even suspected them guilty of some exalted form of superstition.

How long I sat there and tried to think out what it meant, I do not know. What sort of a mockery was this Supervision? These people weren't supervising anything. They weren't capable of it. What possible good could this empty travesty serve? Every step I took in this island seemed to plunge me deeper into foolish mysteries. Everything was a nightmare. My little chariot remained motionless, and the scene that I watched and the thoughts that it aroused were so absorbing that many hours must have elapsed.

When a deep gong began to ring, and I stirred, I found my muscles stiff and cramped. The gong created an instant change in the scene. The people all gathered toward the middle portion, where the road ran in a sort of channel. They descended stairs from the elevated floor, while the cars that came down the channel stopped for them. Rapidly the entire area emptied itself of people; and cars loaded with bobbing heads and bright flashes of color poured out of the arch at the farther end into the freedom of daylight.

When there were only a few scattered figures left, my conveyance moved back on the elevator, was lowered to the ground level, and emerged from the building into a dismal looking street. Why did the people who controlled all of this, persist in keeping out of sight? How was my little car guided? There were wires strung about the railing of its body; perhaps these served as antennae of some radio apparatus for long-distance control. Perhaps the machine was not as automatic as it seemed, but instead, was controlled by radio waves from some central station. I could picture a malignant face bent over a switchboard, while the clutching hands reached for levers that sent me spinning this way and that, far away, through the city.

Was this the time for me to try and escape? I had a feeling that I could readily get away from this clumsy thing if I got desperate. But, suppose I should escape, where would I go? What would I do? Here was night coming on rapidly; I needed food and rest, and had no idea where to get them. I decided to trust my captors a little longer. Thus far, I had to admit, it was highly interesting and not at all dangerous; though I could see how the same thing might have been unwelcome in a high degree to my friends in the City of Beauty. However, thus far, I was being treated much more like a guest than like an enemy. I determined, nevertheless, to keep on my guard, as well as to keep my eyes open for information to take back to Galveston with me.

In the meanwhile, the three-wheeled machine rolled swiftly along. For a while the sun was at my left; and as it was setting, that meant that I was headed north. Then the machine turned to the west — farther and farther into the innermost heart of the city. The sun's disk was enormous because of the thick smoke in the atmosphere, and of a blood-red color, changing, as it sank behind the buildings, to a purple. My vehicle was delayed several times at intersections by heavy traffic. The thing looked so tiny beside the gigantic things that crowded the streets that every moment I was afraid, that it and I both would be flattened out as thin as a sandwich. But its agility in dodging apparently inevitable catastrophes and slipping into unexpected openings, was so marvelous that it gave me confidence, and I quit trembling in my seat. Nevertheless, the ride was hard on my nerves. It took a good three-quarters of an hour to reach the gate in the wall.

The wall was thirty feet high, the height of an ordinary house, built of granite blocks. It extended away to the north and to the south until it was lost in the twilight in the smoky perspective of the streets. Over the top of it, I caught a glimpse of the leaves of

175

some tree, the only living thing that I had thus far seen about the city. The gateway was large enough to admit a big truck; and again, architecturally it was a contrast to the surrounding structures which were of a dismal, utilitarian type. It had columns at the side with carved capitals, a frieze in bas-relief, and a beautiful pair of heavy bronze gates.

The car stopped in front of the gate, emitted a torrent of toots, and waited. Again I was seized with misgivings. As between a hotel and a penitentiary, this business resembled the latter much more closely. Once they got me locked up inside those walls, it might be difficult to get out again.

One of the gates opened just wide enough to admit the car, which drove to the opening and stopped. Within, the last fading rays of daylight showed me a park, one of the kind that were so numerous a generation ago, with curving graveled walks, trees and hedges in groups, and flower-beds all laid out in designs. Back in the distance was a great house, with gables and verandas, which I could not make out very plainly in the gathering darkness.

The bar across my chest snapped open, leaving me free. I stepped out with great alacrity, whereupon the car backed out and the gates clanged shut. The bright square of a lighted window shone at me from the house in the distance.

10
WHO RUNS THIS PLACE?

I STOOD for a few moments with clenched fists, staring at the bronze gates. These invisible people had an uncanny way of doing what they pleased with me. Then I realized that my muscles were stiff and cramped; that I was ravenously hungry; and that I was leaden with fatigue from a long, exciting day. So, I turned hopefully toward the building in the park. I could still make out, in the gathering gloom, that it was a typical large residence of the past generation, with stucco gables, many individual windows and a shingled roof. The effect that it produced upon me was quaint and old-fashioned, in contrast with the futurist impressions from the machinery without.

The silence was refreshing, after the steady, all-day roar; my heels crunching on the gravel sounded solitary and intimate in my ears. As I drew near, a door opened, and the yellow electric light streamed out. My heart pounded hard. Perhaps now at last, I would see the people of the place.

But the room I stepped into was uninhabited. It was luxuriously furnished, likewise in an old-fashioned way, with thick carpets and the mahogany overstuffed furniture of thirty years ago. Apparently it was a drawing-room. However, right beside me as I stepped in, was a little folding table with a steaming meal on it. It might have been exactly the same table and exactly the same dishes that I ate from at noon; only the food was different. The big, generous dinner made my mouth water. I looked about, and in the passageway found a lavatory at which I could clean up a little. Then I fell to eating, this time without the least hesitation. My hunger and fatigue exceeded both my caution and my curiosity. I ate before looking any further.

After I had eaten, my limbs felt so heavy and my eyes so sleepy, that I lay down for a little rest on the cushions of a large settee. Almost immediately I fell sound asleep. The food might have been drugged, but I doubt it. I had risen early in the morning and had a most fatiguing day. Perhaps I lacked caution; but I could not see that any precaution of mine would make much difference. How could I be any more in their power than I was now? At any rate, I could not help it, I fell asleep in spite of myself.

I awoke early and suddenly, with the sun shining in my face. The large room seemed a rich, luxurious place; but gave the impression of being rather desolate, devoid of the little things that give a personal touch. Outside I could see lawns and trees; palms and great, broad leaves, lacy fronds, and waxy foliage, and great bright-red and spotted-orange flowers. In the distance was the high wall; beyond that, belching smokestacks, trussed beams and a dull, smoky sky. My mind took this all in with sudden alertness.

"Today's main job is to get loose," I determined grimly; "this gang has got me sewed up too tight to suit me."

I reconnoitered the house cautiously, peering into this room and that. Every room I saw was richly furnished, with that same old-fashioned air. There were a good many of the curious floor-lamps with silk shades, so popular a generation ago. Everywhere was lacking that elusive note that suggested human occupancy. Everything was stiffly clean and orderly, but there were none of the small objects that people usually leave lying around, a book, a scrap of paper, a dusty shoe-track, a handkerchief. The loneliness seemed almost ghostly.

However, a breakfast cooking away in an automatic kitchen cheered me considerably. I helped myself without qualms of conscience, and compelled myself to fill up to capacity, for I anticipated strenuous adventures ahead of me. If they did not come of their own accord I was determined to make them: for I fully intended to escape from the leash on which I was held, and to see the city on my own initiative. Uneasiness as to what they eventually intended ding with me, and a resentment at being handled around like a sack of potatoes, shared equally in my reasons for the step I planned.

As I ate, I speculated about the old house in which I found myself. Everything pointed to the fact that it was an old residence, and a royally luxurious one, though built and occupied before I was born. Also, apparently, it was not occupied at the present time, but it was being kept in good order by the present masters of the locality. I could imagine that when the settlers had first come to the island, they had begun a city where the City of Smoke now stood, and had lived there. The men high in control had lived in this house. Finally, when the growth of the city made living unpleasant, they had moved away to the City of Beauty.

But I decided that as an explanation, this was not good. The City of Beauty would be the natural choice of a residence locality for the rulers of things around here; but those people that lived in the City of Beauty certainly were not the rulers. Yet, why did the rulers who directed and handled all of this machinery, remain satisfied to live in this noisy, dirty hell? Had they become so married to the machinery that they could not get away from it? Did they lack the side of their natures, that loved beauty and luxury and Nature? Perhaps too much devotion to machinery had made them so one-sided that they preferred to live here? If they lived in this city, why weren't they occupying this great, luxurious house? If they didn't like luxury, how could they keep this place in such comfortable shape?

I gave up, and continued my exploration of the house. I found a small room which contained only a desk and a chair and a rug.

There sat a man!

My heart leaped with the thrill that I had finally found the human center of this spider web. I stopped for a moment and looked at him. He was about forty years old, and sat languidly in a mahogany chair. His clothes were well made and expensive looking; but his linen was disheveled, and his hands and face were smeared with grease. His right hand hung down toward the ground and grasped a large wrench.

"Ah!" I thought; "someone who really handles machinery!"

"Good morning!" I said. He looked up. Apparently he had not noticed me before. He did not reply.

"Are you someone in authority here?" I asked.

He jumped up violently.

"I own all this!" he shouted, sweeping his arm about. "This is all mine! I control it! I understand it!" He walked rapidly around the little room.

"Have you seen Cassidy?" I shot out. The idea struck me so suddenly that I could not stop it. If they had brought me here, perhaps Cassidy was also in the house.

"All this!" he continued with a wide gesture; "all mine! I can do as I please with it. I left my home and family to come here and take charge of it." Suddenly, he seemed to grasp my presence and my question.

"Cassidy?" He shrugged his shoulders. "You? I? Only a few more or less? Who knows?"

A look of alarm spread over his tanned, handsome face.

"They might come for us at any time!" He looked around, out of the door and out of the windows. "I think they cut up people alive. Oh, my poor Vera and the babies!" He sat down and put his face in his hands and groaned.

* * *

I FLED from his presence in terror. My heart went out in pity to the poor fellow, but there was nothing in the world that I could do for him. This crazy city had already wrecked his mind, and it was time I undertook a retreat before it undermined my own. I had no doubt that he was from the City of Beauty, and had been captured and brought here.

I found more rooms, richly furnished and silent. Many of them had locked doors and I could not get in. Broad, automatic elevators took me to the upper floors. In a room on the third, I found an old man, in bed. His eyes opened wide when he saw me.

"Good morning!" I offered.

He continued to gaze at me sadly. White beards lend an infinite sadness to countenance anyway. During all my life I had not seen as many white whiskers as I had during these few days on this island.

"That is an astonishing thing to say here," the old man finally replied. "Who are you?"

"I'm not sure by this time that I know, myself, who I am," I said slowly, thinking hard just what to say. "Anyway, I am a stranger on this island. I am sorry to intrude on you. In fact, I was railroaded into this house, and I am going to get out mighty quick."

He continued to look at me in a sort of sad wonderment.

"Are you someone in authority here?" I asked at last.

He shook his head and studied me mournfully for a while. I waited till it should please him to speak.

"I have seen days when things were different on this island," he finally volunteered. "Then, young men spoke like you do. You talk as they did in that old America that I knew so long ago."

"That's where I'm from, and they talk that way yet," I told him. "And now I'm looking for a way to get back there."

"If you can really decide to act for yourself, do so quickly. It is a lost art. I have no idea as to what fate they intended for you or me, but it is not a pleasant one. Many have been taken — hundreds. Where are they? Have you seen them anywhere?"

"Come with me, then!" I exclaimed, for a wave of genuine alarm was mounting within me.

"Ha! ha!" There was a note of genuine merriment in the old man's laugh. "What difference does it make what becomes of me? I haven't any idea of how you plan to escape, but I know it will be a strenuous task; and to burden yourself with a feeble old man would make your escape impossible. Now go quickly!"

"Have you seen Cassidy?" I asked, turning to go.

"Cassidy? Have they got him?" He groaned something inarticulate. "Hurry, I tell you!" he urged.

I left him reluctantly. Now I understood what the old house was used for. It was a temporary resting-place for captured victims. There they rested overnight and had a meal or two, before they were taken to their doom. They were royally treated, but what was the doom?

I hurried through the house, trying doors that I had not yet opened, and shouting Cassidy's name at the top of my voice. Was I too late? If I could only find him, we would lose no time in leaving this town. But most of the doors were locked, and confused echoes were my only answer. I ran outdoors, down the gravel walk, and to the bronze gates. I studied the gates and the wall; but climbing was an impossibility without a ladder. The trees growing near the wall offered a suggestion.

Then the gates opened a little, and the foolish little chariot of yesterday rolled in. It sidled up to me and rubbed against me, like a dog begging for attention. I looked down at the thing in amazement; but there it was, too small to conceal a person, just a whirring, mechanical thing. No wonder the man with the wrench had lost his mind! The bronze gates were tightly closed again.

There was nothing to do but to get into it. It would get me through the gates, which right now was my worst desire. I idly wondered what would happen if I refused to get into the machine, as I took my place in the seat. When the bar snapped across my chest, my muscles tightened involuntarily, and a shudder ran all through me, in spite of all my determinations to sit quietly. But, I forced myself to relax. I looked over the little machine, and felt sure that I could break away from it, when I decided that the time to do so had arrived. I noted that the bar across my chest did not fit as accurately as the one on the truck had done; and quietly I set about studying ways to wiggle out of it.

Every moment of that long trip was an anxious wait for an opportunity to get away from the car. Not an instant eluded me; yet not an instant offered itself in which escape was possible. Most of the time the speed was so great that jumping out would have meant broken bones. When stops were made, they were in such dense traffic that I was afraid of the huge things around me. I noted that I again passed within a short distance of the golden oval of the Supervision Building. Other locations seemed rather familiar, though I had not fixed the details in my memory sufficiently to be sure; but I recognized them subconsciously. Then I spied the pretty little building with the web of wires leading into it, in which I had spent an uncomfortable forenoon yesterday, scrutinized by lenses and tooted at by invisible pipes.

I expected to be put into that room again, and was gathering my wits and muscles to avoid it; and was thus thrown off my guard. For, my car approached the broad, garage-like doors of a smooth, concrete building next to it. The doors were big enough to let a truck through. But they worked the same trick on me that the bronze gates at the park had done; one of them opened just wide enough to let the car through. The car stopped just within the door, and the bar opened away from my chest, releasing me. I stepped off and looked about me. I hadn't liked the cold-looking building from the outside; and I didn't like this clean, bare, cold-looking room. While I was staring at it, the machine slipped backwards, and the doors closed shut, with a whirring of gears.

I whirled about and shook them and pounded them, but they were as immovable as the rock of a mountain-side. I stood and sputtered in anger for a few moments at the way 1 had been handled. There was certainly an uncanny intelligence at the bottom of these maneuvers. But, whose was it? And where was it? I could see no signs of life anywhere.

The room was large, large as an auditorium, with walls and floor of smooth concrete. The floor was clean and bright; it sloped toward a drain in the middle of the room, so that it could be washed down. There were many large windows, making the interior almost as bright as outdoors, and on the ceiling were numerous large electric globes. There was a concrete table near the north windows, and near it a glass case of instruments. I looked at the instruments curiously; they looked like apparatus for demonstrations in science lectures, but I could not guess the use of a single one.

The arrangement reminded me of the layout of a surgical operating-room in a hospital. I detected a queer odor in the air; I cannot describe it otherwise than as a warm, animal odor. My spine began to feel creepy and my knees trembled. Then I discovered a lot of clothes hung on hooks in one of the glass cases, both men's and women's; and they were the fine, well-made clothes that were worn in the City of Beauty. I looked about anxiously for a way of escape. I remembered back how I used to bring dogs into the experimental laboratory at the college; and now I wondered how the dogs felt about it I decided that it was high time for me to make a desperate break for liberty.

Again one of the doors opened, and a man was shoved in, staggering and blinking. A flood of joy over-whelmed me.

"Cassidy!" I shouted, leaping toward him.

He was pale; but when he saw me he turned paler yet, and terror shone in his face.

"Davy!" he gasped. "You here?" He groaned in despair.

"I came here to look for you," I told him. "So, cheer up! I'm going to get you out."

"Sh-sh!" He put his finger to his lips. The man's former spirit seemed to be gone out of him. "Whatever you do, don't talk too much!" he warned.

"All right. Not another word out of me," I whispered.

I got into action at once. With my right hand I loosened my hand ax in its sheath, and with the left, dragged and shoved Cassidy toward one of the big windows. The glass was tough; I rained blow after blow on it with the head of the ax before I cracked open a hole big enough to crawl through. I sheathed the ax, for I could not risk losing it, even though I heard some sort of a commotion behind me. I boosted Cassidy through the broken window.

"Run! Don't wait for me!" I shouted, for I already suspected I'd never get out after him. I heard him scramble among the broken glass outside, and his foot-steps thumped away into the distance.

* * *

AS I drew myself up to the level of the hole in the glass, I was seized from behind by three or four arms around me. They lifted me up and set me down again; and "snap!" I was clamped down in one of the silly little chariots again, and speeding out of the door into the dazzling daylight. In the room behind me were the two staring headlights of the Squid, and the air of the room was filled with waving, snaky coils. A half dozen other machines were crowding about, and a furious tooting was going on. It died away rapidly as I was whirled swiftly off down the street.

This time I had not only reached the limit of my patient self-control at being bundled around in pursuance to someone else's will; but also I was thoroughly frightened. Cassidy's face had shown real fear, and he was not a man to be easily scared. And that room made me shudder. I could not forget the odor; it was not unpleasant, but it reminded me too much of blood. Why had we been brought in there? And where was I bound for now?

As I drew myself up to the level of the hole in the glass, I was seized from behind by three or four arms around me.

I took out my ax, and hammered at the bar that held me. It was too strong to yield that way. Attempts to twist myself out of its grip were also futile. It held me too cleverly and securely. An idea that had long been forming in my head, suddenly matured. I whipped out my Colt's .45 automatic, put the muzzle close to the lock of the bar, and bang! bang! pulled the trigger twice.

My hand was numbed by the recoil, so that I nearly dropped the pistol; and a fine spray of lead spattered about me. But, I dragged the pistol back to the holster and pushed it in. The machine swerved a couple of times and nearly collided with a big thing on caterpillar treads that was advancing down the street with a tremendous uproar. But my imprisoning bar swung loose, I was free!

I jumped out, stumbled to my knees in front of a swiftly moving, hooded vehicle, but was up in a moment and ran. My machine stood still behind me, vibrating and tooting. Other machines were slowing down and turning about.

I ran for the nearest solid wall, and then along that, looking for some kind of shelter. In a moment I came to a narrow crevice between two buildings. It was gloomy in there, in comparison with the brilliance of the street, and the debris on the ground made me stumble frequently. I followed the narrow space for a dozen yards into an enclosed backyard or court. Here there was a terrible din and clatter of machinery, and a good deal of rubbish. High overhead was a small square of sky. On the farther side was a pile of boards, apparently from broken-up crates. I pulled off a few, crouched down in the hole thus made, and piled back enough boards on top of me to hide me from view.

I had no delusions yet about being safe. My impression was that some all-seeing eye was following my every move, and that it knew perfectly well right now where I was. If I could get completely under cover for a while, perhaps I could avoid being picked up by the observer when I emerged. I found that most of the boards in the pile were light enough and small enough so that I could work them aside, and burrow into the pile, toward its farther end, which was up against a building. Even though I worked slowly and cautiously, the sweat poured off me in rivers, and my clothes were soaked through with it. For a while I had to stop and lie quiet, when a tiny leading-machine dashed in through the cleft by which I had entered the courtyard, and sputtered noisily around the enclosure.

Then the beam of a crane leaned through the opening, with hanging chains and a spotlight. The chains dragged over the boards under which I lay, scattering the pile with a couple of hooks. It looked as though they knew exactly where I was. A faint wish began to enter my heart that I had stayed away from this city in the first place. I had thought that I would have human beings to deal with, man to man. But, they had things so organized that I never saw the people at all; and I had no chance against their machinery.

I dug desperately farther under the boards, and finally reached a wall. There I found an iron grating beneath me, in the pavement of the courtyard. It apparently opened into some cool, underground space; and through it came the sounds of machinery pounding somewhere in a basement. I pried up the grating with a board, squeezed into the opening, and dropped the grating back over my head.

Sometimes memory is merciful. I do not remember the details of that awful trip in the darkness and noise. My salvation was in my pocket flashlight, which kept me from falling into vats of foul-looking liquids, or crawling straight into whirling machinery, whose proximity was indistinguishable in the din. I crawled along for ages through a narrow, close, suffocating space, sometimes in a tunnel of stone, sometimes through a steel tube; and frequently there were gratings below me. It must have been a ventilator, for always a draft of hot, sickening air blew in my face. One thing was comforting: I seemed to have gotten away.

Eventually I reached a place where the hot draft blew upwards, and I was able to stand up. My flashlight showed me a group of seven or eight pipes extending upward into the darkness. They were held together by diagonal trusses, and provided a fairly good ladder for climbing, forming a sort of narrow latticework. I hitched all my belongings comfortably around myself and started upwards.

Some fragmentary impressions of the climb are as follows: a strong smell of ammonia in one place; a glimpse of an immense room filled with whirling flywheels and great pumps; another vast room which was quite empty and intensely cold; periodical rumblings at one point, as though huge bulks of something were sliding or rolling past. Finally there was a welcome glimpse of the sky above me, crossed by a latticework of beams. Climbing was not difficult, except that my haversack and field-glasses kept getting in my way as they hung over my shoulder. At last I tumbled out on a tar-and-gravel roof. The pipes I had been climbing continued upwards, above my head, into the bottom of a great water-tank that was supported on four steel legs, high in the air above the roof of the building.

I was intensely thirsty, and my first concern was water. There seemed to be plenty of it above me, and I reasoned that there must be some way of getting some of it I set about a systematic search, though my impulse was to shoot a hole in one of the pipes. However, I discovered a valve in a pipe that ran along the roof, much to my joy, for a thirsty man is a desperate creature. As I turned it on, a great flood of water poured out on the roof, and I hastily shut it again lest I call attention to myself. Then I turned on a small stream. Again my military training served me in good stead, for if I had drunk my fill as I craved to do, I should have collapsed and been at the mercy of my enemies. I drank slowly and sparingly. For an hour I lay and rested and drank, and listened for possible pursuit.

At the end of that time I was fairly confident that I had succeeded in escaping. The first thing I did was to reload my pistol, so that it contained a full clip. As I took my supply of cartridges out of my haversack, a piece of paper fluttered out. I picked it up curiously, for I knew of no scraps of paper among my things. It was a scented note-paper, containing a message in a rounded, feminine handwriting:

> *"I love you. It frightens me to have you go to that terrible place, but I know you will do it. Please, Davy, come back safe to me.*

> *"Your little brick."*

I spent many minutes over my message, lost in pleasant thoughts: and then I drew myself together with a new determination to get out of this situation. The first thing to do was to examine the ground thoroughly. By climbing a little higher and keeping hidden among the pipes, I found that I could get a view of the entire city and remain out of sight myself. I was on the roof of a tower, three or four stories above the rest of the buildings. Because of the view it commanded, I judged that this building must be in the highest part of the city. In fact, it was easy to make out a gentle slope eastward toward the river, and a longer, steeper one toward the sea on the west.

I set about drawing a map in my notebook of all I could see. This was a tedious task, for my precarious perch among the pipes did not permit of drawing; I had to climb up and take a good look, and then descend and draw from memory. My greatest obstacle was dirt, for my hands were so grimy from the sooty, dirty things I had to get hold of, that it was almost impossible to handle paper with them. But I finally got a passable map sketched out.

* * *

THE City of Smoke was about rectangular in shape, with the long dimension east and west, or from river to ocean. The total distance from river to ocean must have been about fifteen miles; but the city occupied only about six miles of that in length, while its width I judged to be about four miles. On the east, along the river's edge, the rectangle spread a little in width; the river bank was lined with docks and wharves, and the river was alive with tugs and barges, and a double stream of smoking vessels wound along the river into the interior of the island, where in the distance I could see forests and mountains.

Toward the sea, the rectangle narrowed a little, and there were several miles of empty, sandy flats intervening between the city's boundaries and the little harbor. The harbor contained only three small ships and its dock space was limited. Ocean traffic was apparently not developed at all in comparison with that on the river. The ocean end of the city consisted chiefly of long lines of huge warehouses, and several broad lines of pavement led to the little harbor.

Down below me, there were huge, piled-up blocks of buildings, and the grimy streets swarmed with black, crawling things. The noise was tempered by distance into a dull, rustling hum. Toward the river there was a forest of belching chimneys, and the air was thick and murky with smoke. I could see the walled house in its park, a couple of miles away, in the very center of the city. To the south, not far from the edge of the city, was the golden oval dome of the Supervision Building; and near it ran the road that led out of the city, and into the blue forest. There was no sign of the City of Beauty on the southern horizon.

A sudden, swelling, organ-like tone rose up toward me from the street just below. I leaned far over and looked down. Far down below was the concrete roof of the laboratory-like building. The confused swirl of machines in the street seemed to have organized itself into a stream that flowed in one direction, and the organ-note was the combined tooting coming from many of them. Then, I noted a small, black figure running in front of the rushing column of machines. The desperate man seemed to have no chance; they were almost upon him.

An icy panic shot through my heart. For a moment I thought it was Cassidy. But my field-glasses showed me that the man was tall and spare, and that he swung a large wrench in one hand. Then he dodged around a corner; the stream of machines swarmed after him and I saw no more.

It became obvious that I would have to wait till night for my effort to get out of the city. In the meanwhile I planned the details. The easiest way seemed to be to make for the south gate and for the road to the City of Beauty. Just because that was so easy, I would not consider it; it would mean being caught in a trap. The river offered the next best plan of getting away easily and swiftly; but I was also afraid of that. The river and the road ran along too close together, and both were too full of swift craft. Finally, the distance to the river was much the greater, and through the densest, most tangled part of town.

Toward the ocean, the city looked less busy; the streets were straighter and less crowded. The beach looked completely deserted, and would be comparatively easy traveling. There seemed to be no small vessels that could get into sufficiently shallow water to reach me from the ocean side, if I once gained the beach. On the other hand, my best method of getting away from the land machines was to wade out waist-deep into the water. No machine run by gas or electricity could follow me there. Besides, the beach led straight to the Gulls' Nest, which was a safe hiding-place.

I studied the boundaries of the city carefully with my field-glasses. Everywhere, the edge of the city was a solid wall of buildings, offering no chance of egress. The only ways of getting out were the river, the south gate which I did not trust, and the west gate toward the ocean.

The afternoon passed quickly for me. I was interested in watching the scurrying things below, and the great, swinging hulks in the distance. Part of the time I spent in studying out a way to get down into the street. A repetition of my climb through the interior of the building was out of question. But, two of the legs of the tank were outside the wall of the building, and extended down to the ground. Each leg consisted of two I-beams braced together with cross-bars, cleverly welded, but making a very passable ladder.

Between five and six o'clock, a great swarm of cars poured out of the building with the golden dome; through my glasses I could see little human heads and bright highlights of clothing. They spun off, out of the south gate, and toward the City of Beauty. How I wished I could go with them! It seemed so near, and yet so difficult.

After six o'clock, traffic in the streets quieted down considerably, and there were but few vehicles, and little noise. I waited almost three more hours for the short tropical twilight, which was quickly followed by night. Here and there a light shone out in the darkness, but on the whole, lights were few for such a large city. I filled my canteen, and forthwith started down the leg of the water-tank. The abyss below frightened me, but the thing had to be done. It was easier in the darkness than it would have been by daylight; I could see nothing below except velvety blackness; and at no time had I any idea of how much farther I had to go. Soon I found it difficult not to believe that my torturers had excavated a shaft a mile deep into the ground, and that I was climbing down into it. Finally, however, a foot struck solid ground, and I stepped off my ladder.

Gradually I made out that I was between two buildings; there was a strip of lighter sky above and a glow of electric light at the right. I reached the street easily and headed west by compass. I stuck close to buildings and remained in shadows, crossing open spaces on a run, and keeping an alert lookout in all directions. However, my flight was easy, for I could travel silently and in the dark, whereas the approach of a machine was always heralded by a glare of light and plenty of noise. Of course, there was the possibility of people lying in wait for me; but I had already begun to feel that I would never encounter the masters of this place in personal combat. I was skeptical about their courage to face danger and conflict. They delegated everything to machines, as far as I could ascertain.

I found the south boundary of the city and followed it westward, toward the western gate. I lost an hour convincing myself that indeed no escape was possible except by the gate. The great factory buildings and warehouses that formed the city wall were in direct contact; they were built of brick, steel, and masonry. There was no climbing over them for they were from two to six stories high; and in the darkness I could find no way of getting up to the roofs. All doors and windows seemed to be securely locked; the horrors of that afternoon's climb through one building sufficed to keep away my desire for going through any more buildings. An hour's search failed to reveal any crevice or crack between the buildings that led to the outside. The gate was my only hope.

I readily found the gate at the west end of the city, with the aid of my map and pocket flashlight. It was brilliantly lighted by electric lights, by whose aid I could see that it was closed by two steel doors. Four of the little leading-machines stood about under the glare of the electric light; and two small, swift trucks were ranged across the way I would have to go; cranes and hooks swung from them in readiness.

I could not see anybody, but I knew that they were watching for me; and the bright light made it impossible for me to get within a hundred feet of the gate without exposing myself to the observation of the watchers.

I slunk into the shadows, for I had no doubt that these things were waiting for me.

11
ONE NIGHT IN SHEOL

I SHRANK back into the depths of the shadow for a moment, into sinking indecision as to what to do next. I was trapped in this hideous city! The realization descended upon me with the convincing force of a pile-driver. If this gate was so well guarded — the one that I would apparently be the least likely to take — the certainty that the other one would be tightly sewed up was so great that I did not even care to try it.

This place was like the fortified cities of the Middle Ages, surrounded by an impassable wall. Why? Probably the real reason was that the solid and continuous construction was most convenient for manufacturing purposes, especially where there was so much automatic machinery, and air and light for workers was not an important consideration. Nevertheless, the sickening recollection came to me that I had been repeatedly reminded of how many people got in here and none ever got out.

Well, the first thing to do was to put more distance between me and this brightly lighted, heavily guarded gateway. As I turned to steal carefully away, my foot came down on a loose piece of iron. It was curved like the rocker of a rocking-chair, and was no doubt the broken leaf of an automobile spring. It swung over my toes as I stepped, and hit the pavement with a ringing clatter. For an instant I stiffened, and then dashed swiftly across the street. I acted unconsciously first, and reasoned why I did so later; which of course was to get away from the spot where the sound had occurred.

Nor was I a bit too quick. Like a shot from a cannon, one of the leading-machines whizzed toward the spot, with a sputtering roar that reverberated through the darkness. Before it reached there, I had crawled under a sort of ramp, whose purpose was apparently to permit vehicles to drive up into the building. I couldn't see the leading-machine that was looking for me, but I could hear it chugging about. I was amazed at the quick reaction of the person who was watching for me; it wasn't ten seconds from the time the iron dropped until the machine was racing after me. I remained crouched in my dark corner half an hour after the machine was gone.

In the meanwhile, I pondered on what I should do. Both gates were closed up, and the city was surrounded by an impassable wall, impassable as far as I had been able to ascertain by my observations from the inside, outside, and above; while a search for some small possible opening might require several days. My only hope was the river-front. If I could reach the water and find a boat or something to float on, getting back to the City of Beauty would be relatively simple. But I shrank mentally from approaching that terrific maze of wharves and boats and black water, beams and cranes and crooked alleyways among blackened buildings and machines. My chances looked slim enough in that region. Yet, they were all I had, and I turned my face in that direction.

For an hour I plodded eastward through the gloomy, silent streets. They were unutterably, forbiddingly dreary at night; there were no sidewalks, only black walls and blank windows, with oceans of inky shadows everywhere. Each step that I took forward, each shadow that I approached, brought my heart into my mouth, for fear of someone lying in wait for me. A million times I fully expected someone to leap out at me and bear me to the ground, or a shot to come from behind a building, or some sort of chain lasso to drop over my head.

I admitted to myself that I had often been in situations of equal or greater actual danger; but never had I been in one that so demoralized my nerve. Not only was I appalled by this extraordinary, monstrous city, like the wild ravings of some madhouse engineer; but I had no idea who my enemies were, where they were, or what sort of weapons they would use. I had no idea when they could see me, and when I could feel safely out of their sight. At any moment, they might have some sort of amazing, high-powered night-seeing telescopes trained upon me. For aught I knew, they might be accurately informed of every step I was taking, and only be waiting their own good time to seize me. The thought drove me still deeper into the shadows beside the buildings.

However, as I have always done on similar occasions, I kept plodding onward, doing what the immediate moment required, because that was all that could be done. My compass with its luminous needle was my best friend that night; without it I should have gotten hopelessly lost in the muddle of streets, to be picked up by the machine-people sooner or later. I surmised that it must not be strictly accurate, for this place must have been alive with electrical currents, but it sufficed to guide me eastward, toward the dark and devious river-front.

Half a dozen times it occurred to me that the water ought to be in sight already; and I looked for the grain-elevators and for the barge-loading conveyors that I had seen in the afternoon from my observation point. But distances seem greater in the dark and progress is actually much slower, especially in unknown territory; and I schooled myself to be patient.

Then, a few streets to my left, I heard the sputtering rush of several leading-machines going at high speed. It seemed crashingly loud in the darkness as it reverberated through the hollow spaces. It grew louder and louder, and then began to decrease again. I judged that the machines were proceeding in the same direction that I was, that is, directly toward the river. Then came another roar, this time with much more rattle and rumble to it Trucks, several of them, I surmised. They seemed to be approaching quite close to me. In fact, I began to suspect that they were on this same street, and soon perceived the glow of their lights far behind me.

"I'm getting out of here, right now!" I said, half aloud, and looked frantically around for means of doing so.

I was in the middle of a block with unbroken walls all around. But I remembered that a few rods back I had passed a concrete base-block as high as my shoulder, on which rested a vertical trussed-steel beam, apparently the leg of some great, dim framework, high up above.

I ran back to it, assuming the risk of going toward the approaching glare of the trucks; and as soon as I reached it, I dodged behind it. I swung myself to the top of the block, and clambered up the trussed iron leg, keeping behind it and out of reach of the headlights. In a few moments the trucks had clattered by below me, without even slowing down, and gradually drew off into the distance to the east. I continued to cling to my perch as their lights and their clatter grew fainter.

"Fooled them!" I thought. "They'll never find me over there."

That was encouraging. In a moment, however, there was another hurtling roar, and from my elevated perch I saw a few streets away a group of lights gliding swiftly eastward, disappearing behind black things and appearing again. And, far in the east, over a wide area, numerous little lights twinkled and dashed back and forth.

* * *

I CLIMBED a little higher and gazed intently eastward, trying to fathom what was going on. For, by this time, three huge searchlights on the high towers far to the east of me were swinging around, showing up streets and masses of buildings and swift machines for fitful instants. That was my destination over there, where those lights were sweeping about, and where those machines were dashing back and forth. No place for me right now, however.

Just a few minutes' walk ahead and to my right was the huge, glowing bulk of the Supervision Building and its dome. The lights and commotion were far on beyond it. In fact, as I watched, I caught an occasional gleam of light on black water; and I was certain that the clattering, flashing night hunt was going on in that section of the city that bordered on the river.

"So that goose is cooked too," I thought. "I seem to be thoroughly stuck."

I felt limp and weak from discouragement.

What diabolical foresight enabled them to anticipate that I was going to the river? That was more than human. That they might see me in the dark, that they might have visual detectors of unknown power, or things that could hear me, smell me, or detect the presence of my bodily electrical charges, I could readily imagine. But how could they tell what I intended to do before I ever started to do it? If they could do that, the probabilities of unheard-of powers of torture and destruction, in wait for me, were unlimited and hideous. Never in my life had I been so thoroughly terrified and discouraged.

Then, another explanation suddenly struck me, which at the same time overjoyed and terrified me. Perhaps that rumpus over there signified that Cassidy had reached the waterfront! Perhaps they had tracked him down to the river. As long as the lively activity continued, I was sure that he was not yet caught. I trembled so, in my excitement for his safety, that I had to exert redoubled efforts to keep my hold on the iron framework, high in the air and darkness.

I felt sure, however, that Cassidy's chances for escape were better than mine. Surely he must know more about this city than I. He must understand the nature of his danger and the methods of his enemies. His lot was certainly not as helpless as mine. If we could only be together!

What next? I gripped the iron bars extending into emptiness above and below, in an agony of despair. I was hemmed in, blocked! Powers vast and mysterious, to whose nature I had no clue, had me at their mercy. How futile was my small strength against these monstrous, pulsing things! It would be easiest to give up the struggle. Their net around me was vast and impenetrable; amazing machinery in vast quantities was arrayed against me and I was alone. What was the use?

Then there came into the midst of my gloomy cogitations a pair of brown eyes looking trustingly into mine, a head on my shoulder, a little soft body held in my arms. She must be waiting anxiously for me. If she knew anything at all about these awful things, her wait must be more trying than my own position. My courage returned, and my determination was again as firm as a mountain. There must be some way out of this, and I've got to find it!

Was there another gate in the north wall of the city? I could remember a road winding up into the mountains and forests of the north, but I could not remember a gate. But, even if there were a gate, it would be so guarded as to offer me no hope. Then the brilliant idea came to me!

Probably I had been slowly evolving it in my unconscious mind for a long time; but the full force of it struck me so suddenly that I nearly let go and fell down into the darkness below.

There was the Supervision Building ahead of me! And every evening a swarm of cars left it and drove southward to the City of Beauty! Surely those people would be my friends, and let me hide in a car and ride back home with them. It was obvious that they were no real friends of these hideous machine-people. And by this time, I thought that most people in the City of Beauty knew me or knew of me.

My heart bounded high with hope. My problem was solved. But not altogether. It would be many hours before the cars were leaving for the City of Beauty. Where could I hide in safety until it came time for me to hide in one of them? This vast city, with thousands of buildings and streets and alleys for miles in all directions, was unknown to me, and well-known to my enemies. It was evident to me at once that I must hide somewhere near where the cars were to pass. For I couldn't travel very far through this city during the daytime from my hiding-place to catch my car home. The poor wretch whom I had seen down below me in the street that afternoon came at once into my mind, as did the narrow escapes I myself had had. The thought of the possibility of being caught and locked up and taken to that laboratory again was enough to make me infinitely cautious. Where could I spend the time until the later afternoon when the cars started back to the City of Beauty? What a beautiful, comfortable, desirable place the City of Beauty now seemed, as I thought of it!

I clambered slowly down. There was only one possibility. Somewhere in the Supervision Building itself I had to find concealment. I ran over in my mind the interior of the building. My recollection of it was clear, for I had studied it the previous forenoon for several hours from an excellent point of view. The three or four little platforms twenty feet above the floor, the elevator shaft, the racks and cases of instruments, the chairs and settees — nothing offered any hope of concealment. Therefore, what I must do was to get into the building and look around.

I reached the building in a few minutes, walked under the great arched doorways, into the darkness of the vast building. Its deep and silent blackness frightened me. Toward the south, high overhead, I could make out the glow of the sky through the embrasures in the wall. There were blacker, denser portions of shadow, showing where the walls of the middle sunken passageway were, and above them the serrated figures of the instrument cases and racks. I walked slowly, with a hand before me, with my knees trembling at every step, fully expecting something to rise up and descend on me from behind each dark, misshapen shadow, out of each black, yawning space. My first footsteps sounded loudly in the silence. For fifteen minutes I crouched motionless and listened before I took the next. I crept a little farther and listened again. Absolute silence! Not a click, not a rustle.

What did it mean? Was all of this just dummy apparatus? In the morning I had suspected that the people knew nothing about it as they moved among the things. And now I was sure that if all these meters and gauges and control-devices had really been connected to power lines and active machinery, there would have been many little noises in the night — a tap in a pipe, the flutter of a needle, the tick of clockwork, the hum of a coil, the gurgle of a bubble. But here was silence that meant death, not life; not even mechanical life. I had already suspected that the real center of control of the city was elsewhere; now I was sure that this was just a dummy, for the benefit of the dolls from the City of Beauty.

What did the comedy mean?

However, the thought gave me confidence for the present, for it meant that there was probably no one about the premises now, as the place was of no real importance. My courage rose to the point where I dared to use my flashlight; I tried it cautiously, and finally used it whenever I needed it.

* * *

MY search was discouraging. There were no nooks nor corners; the construction of the building was massive and simple. The floor of the middle channel passageway was level with the ground outside. The floors on which the people spent the day among dummy instruments were ten feet above this, no doubt so that the people could also look down on the procession of cars; and at intervals, stairways about six feet wide led down to the level of the vehicles. Yet — here was one hope. Underneath these raised floors there must be a lot of empty space; a sort of cellar. That was worth investigating and seeing whether it could be used for concealment.

A trip around the inside and outside of the building failed to reveal any doorways leading into this space. However, that made it all the more desirable as a hiding-place, could I but once get into it. I had gone half way around the building on the outside and reached the tall entrance way for cars opposite the one by which I had entered. Everything was so silent and deserted that I suppose I got careless. I must have permitted myself to be seen plainly in the glow of the stars moving against the white wall of the building. From somewhere along the street came the soft rustle of well-lubricated, nicely adjusted machinery.

I dropped flat on the ground instantly, and crawled slowly toward the doorway. A band of light from head-lights appeared on the pavement, and then a leading-machine slowly rolled out of the darkness and glided into the doorway. The sounds of its motor echoed around in the great spaces within. In a few minutes it came out again, and disappeared in the darkness up the street.

I slipped quietly into the door. This was the door out of which the cars drove on their way to the City of Beauty. My hiding-place would have to be near here, for I could not afford to drive through the whole place after choosing my car and getting into it.

I tapped the stairway with my ax. It was solid concrete. I tapped the wall of the middle channel. It sounded heavy, but hollow, brick apparently. Then there was a sudden clatter behind me, and I whirled around to see a truck driving in through the arch, swinging a heavy crane arm against the starry sky. It drove right down upon me where I crouched between the steps and the wall. Before I realized what was happening, my escape was cut off by its lumbering bulk and its swinging steel beam.

The pivoted half-ton of steel swung down on me, just as the other had done that night on the dock. Only then I had been cool, and master of the situation; now I was frantic from nameless terrors. I saw it coming in the glare of the truck's headlights, and thought my last moment had come.

But again my long training in quick response to emergencies came to my aid. Quick as a flash, when the iron beam was almost upon me, I dodged down into the darkness below and between the headlights of the truck, between its front wheels. There the beam could not reach me.

Crash!

The beam hit the wall, and there were smothered thuds of falling bricks. The beam swung away, and there was a ragged black hole in the wall beside the steps.

The truck backed away, swinging its beam up into the air again, which gave me time to spring up and run swiftly to one side, out of the field of its headlights.

"Whow!" I thought, regarding the gaping opening in the brick wall, knocked through with one blow.

"That's exactly where I stood!"

I crouched down in the shadow in the next stairway while the truck blundered around. I peered anxiously for a glance at the people on it, but the glare of its headlights shut out everything else in a wall of blackness. As the truck came looking for me, sweeping a spotlight about, it was a simple matter for me to dodge out of the door. After clattering around and raising all the echoes of the place, it finally came out of the door backwards.

In the meanwhile, another brilliant idea had struck me with such suddenness as to make me dizzy. The truck had shown me a way into an ideal hiding-place!

I lost no time in slipping into the hole, and I crouched down in the narrowest space under the concrete steps. I could hear the truck lumbering back in again; and soon there was a softer rustle of a leading-machine. For a while there was a good deal of commotion, but eventually the machinery left. I allowed myself a half an hour of absolute silence before I straightened out my cramped limbs. Considering their power and ingenuity in some directions, my enemies were singularly stupid in others, I thought, as I put back in its holster the pistol I had ready for the first shadow that I saw appear in the jagged opening in the bricks. How could they omit searching in the cavity where I was all the time? Even then, I did not have the least suspicion of the astounding truth.

I groped away from the opening, feeling my way along the wall, back into the depths of the space under the floor. A glance at the dusty, cobwebby rows of concrete pillars showed that the place was unused, probably never visited. I was dead with fatigue, hungry, and sleepy. I took the time to return and put back as many bricks as I could find into the opening, to make it as inconspicuous as possible; and then I selected a resting place far enough away from the hole so that if anyone came in, I would be the first one to be on the alert.

A few bites of biscuit and chocolate, and a drink from my canteen sufficed for my hunger. The stuff was too unpalatable for one to eat a great deal of it, no matter how hungry one was. I went to sleep almost immediately, and woke up in what seemed a few minutes.

But, my watch said ten o'clock, and a faint glow from the direction of the hole through the wall indicated that it must be daylight. I could hear the cars outside my place of concealment driving in with the "Supervisors"; and soon I heard the footsteps of the latter above me.

I did not sleep any more. Most of the time I was alert, but occasionally I half dozed. It was a long wait in the darkness, with the monotonous sounds without. When I thought an hour had elapsed, I looked at my watch and found that it had been actually five minutes. I had plenty of time to think out things now.

My mind turned to Mildred. I had been gone for two days now. She must be in a good deal of uncertainty about me; I hoped that she was not worrying too much. That depended a good deal about how much she actually knew about the dangers of this place. I clenched my fists in impatience. The time went slower than ever.

Galveston and my great-uncle were so far away that they seemed part of another life. The hoped-for medical practice in east Texas was a mere dream. The reality was a concrete slab above me, the powdery dust below, the rhythmic monotony of the sounds without this velvety blackness, and this hideous hive of roaring machines with their cruel, mysterious intelligence behind them. Would I ever live to realize that dream? How wonderful it would be there, with Mildred by my side!

Anyway, I had enough of curiosity about this city. Let it be what it may; I didn't care. I wanted to get out. That suddenly brought me to the realization that I had not solved a single one of the questions that I had come here to discover. Who were the people in charge of the machinery? What was going on in this city? What was the reason for the terror of the pretty people in the City of Beauty? What was the cause of the revolutionary plans of the determined few? Although I had been over a considerable portion of this grimy, bellowing city, seen all of it from above, and some of it from the inside, I hadn't the faintest idea of the answers to these questions.

Clang! went a gong somewhere in the building. I started up suddenly, for I think I must have been dozing a little. The tapping of feet above swelled into a wave and grew louder. They were going home! The moment had come for my escape! The City of Beauty and Mildred! Soon I would see them.

* * *

I GOT up close to the hole and looked out. How welcome was that glimpse of daylight. I saw cars going by and noted with satisfaction that they did not go too fast for me to jump into one of them. I saw people's legs, as they walked past the hole and down the stairs toward the cars. There would be a group of them, and then none for a while; and again a group and another lull. I waited for a lull and crawled out.

I crouched down low and watched the cars. Some were crowded; some contained ladies; some were too open. I hoped for an empty one, but did not dare risk too long waiting. Besides, I could never be sure of which way an empty one might go; those with people on them were sure to go to the City of Beauty. At this last moment, I couldn't afford to make a wrong step and fail.

Finally the desired opportunity came: an enclosed car with a single occupant. He was a graceful, pink-faced, frock-coated young man, who looked such a perfect fashion-plate that there could be no doubt that he was from the City of Beauty. I looked myself over grimly, and as the car went slowly by, I opened the door and stepped in; I got my head down below the level of the car's window in order to be out of sight from without.

For a few minutes the elegant young man continued looking intently ahead, and paid no attention to me. I surmised that he had looked forward to having the car all to himself on the way home and did not care for company; hence the cool attitude. I chuckled grimly to myself at the thought of his rude awakening. Then as the car slowly got up speed outside the building, he turned languidly around to see who was with him. The way his face went slowly blank, his eyebrows rose, and his jaw dropped, was worth the price of an admission fee. He opened his mouth and shut it again, like a fish out of the water. Lost he should speak, I put my hand over his mouth, and whispered softly into his ear:

"Still as a mouse! Don't move!"

I must have looked sufficiently terrible to him, for he quieted down, and seemed limp and paralyzed.

"Sit up here now, and act as though you were alone in the car!" I commanded in my softest whisper. "Do you know what this is?"

I showed him my pistol. I doubt if he knew exactly what it was, but evidently he sensed that it was dangerous, or that I was, for he sat still with trembling hands and lips. I crouched down in the lower part of the car and kept my eyes closely upon him.

The car sped rapidly, swerving this way and that in the traffic. My heart pounded madly as I heard the car rumble through the narrow passage to the gate of the city and when the noise of traffic ceased and I no longer saw roofs and smokestacks through the window, I knew that we were outside the city!

The man looked at me only occasionally and hesitatingly. Physically, he was undoubtedly a good match for me; and under other circumstances I would have been slow to tackle him. But now, for some reason he was in terror. I could hardly see why it should be myself that so terrified him. I admit that I must have been an uncouth sight, dusty and grimy, with streaks of sweat and two or three days' growth of beard. Yet, I think that his fear was of something else, not of me.

Soon I saw green branches of trees through the windows, for my crouched-down position permitted me to see upwards only. Shortly, the semi-dusk of the forest closed in. I breathed more easily, but the young man's terror seemed to increase, and now I was positive that he was less afraid of me than of something else.

"Please!" he said in a shaky voice: "please get off! I know you. You are The Stranger. You don't understand. Don't you know that when they pick out a victim, resistance is useless and escape is impossible? Get off, or we are both lost. Why do you wish to bring down their wrath upon me? I have done nothing. And I cannot save you!" He wrung his hands and began to push me out.

Too late I recollected Kaspar's warnings against discussing vital matters in the proximity of an automobile. Otherwise I would never have permitted that long harangue. Only when the car began to behave queerly a few minutes later did I realize my mistake. Then I was sure that there must be some system of radio communication and control between the vehicles and some diabolical headquarters in that black city. The machinery of the car began to whirr, and developed knocks. It slowed down and stopped, and began to back across the road. It was evident to me that the thing was turning around to carry me back to the City of Smoke; and quite as evident that this young Lothario's graceful speech had something to do with this behavior.

"You poor piece of cheese!" I snarled at the man. "Going to get me captured and yourself patted on the back, eh! Sorry I haven't got time to hit you in the jaw."

My anger at the man was so intense that I would have torn him to pieces. Almost on the doorstep of success; only a step more to complete escape; and then to be betrayed back into the toils of the machine-people by this soft, yellow coward! I might have known it, for that was the way that I had them all estimated from the beginning. Now I had the whole organization to fight with my own wits again, for in a few moments the road would be alive with machines looking for me. But, like a flash I realized that I had no time to lose, and that safety lay in the thick underbrush on both sides of me.

I threw him down in a corner of the car and leaped from the vacillating vehicle. I chose the right side of the road, remembering that my objective must be the sea; and I dived into the underbrush. The thicket was very dense, and I had to get out my hand ax to help myself get in far enough to be out of sight. By that time, the car from which I had dismounted was gone; and other vehicles were whizzing by, one after another, chiefly southward.

I went at the thicket with my ax, cutting just enough to permit me to squeeze through, a stick here and a vine there. Yet, it was a discouraging task. Although physically I felt vigorous and in good shape after my long rest, and able to fight a squad of giants — yet the density of the tropical thicket was almost unbelievable. As an impediment to progress, it was almost equivalent to a solid wall: thick wiry shrubs, tough, rubbery creepers; dense masses of fibrous, cork-like growth. In a few moments my breath was spent and the perspiration was pouring off me in rivers. The distance to the sea was four or five miles; and thus far, I had not progressed all of a dozen feet. The noise of the machines rushing and sputtering by was still too fearfully plain to me.

12
THE ELECTRICAL BRAIN

HOWEVER, I soon ascertained how little I knew about tropical forests. The thick undergrowth extended only as far as the extra sunlight from the open width of the roadway could penetrate. As the forest grew gloomier, the thicket grew less dense; and before many minutes I was in a sort of twilight, and could press on freely and swiftly toward the sea. The thin tree-trunks ran up to an immense height without a branch or a twig; vines twined around them and hung from them; far above, the roof of foliage was so dense that only a gray glimmer of light got through. The ground was soft, because it was covered with a carpet of dead leaves. Going was easy, and the tree-trunks so dense that any pursuit by machines was most unlikely; while for human pursuers I felt ready and eager.

I made good time through the aisles of the forest, watching my compass in order not to lose my way in the gloomy depths. I kept a lookout for animals, but saw none except some little monkeys about the size of squirrels. There were numerous birds, some of whose uncanny noises scared me, making me think there was a

213

machine somewhere behind me. Once I passed a hideous, misshapen thing, hanging on the underside of a limb by four clumsy feet. I remembered enough of my zoology to recognize it as a sloth. Had I been in a humor for it, I should have enjoyed the opportunity for the study of tropical flora and fauna; but my nerves were stretched too tight, and I was trying to make speed.

* * *

At the time, the way seemed long before the roof over me began to show a thinning and more light came through, while shrubs appeared here and there. Soon I had to get out my ax again, in order to force my way through the dense undergrowth of wiry, rubbery stems, huge leaves, and hairy, prickly fronds. I pushed my way out into the open, straightened up, and took great breaths of the air that felt cool in my lungs after the steamy depths of the forest. The beach was a dazzling white, and the blue and heaving ocean looked wonderfully free and welcome to me, shattering its green waves into white froth, just ahead of me.

A look at my watch surprised me. It seemed that I had been in the forest for hours; yet here it was only 4:45. That meant that I had about three more hours of daylight ahead of me; and some six or eight miles to the south of me lay the Gulls' Nest and safety! Safety? Why should the Gulls' Nest be safer than any other place in the island? Why couldn't these people reach it with aeroplanes and microphones? I did not know; but I knew that Kaspar and Mildred depended upon it as being absolutely safe; and I had the faith that they knew. Surely I would find some note there from Mildred, or some news of her. The thought made my heart race, and spurred me on toward the south.

I scanned the southern horizon anxiously, but there was nothing but sand and water and the blue line of forest. I felt reasonably safe as soon as I reached the water's edge, for in case I was pursued by some of the machines, I could wade out into the water. A little salt water on their electrical connections or in their carburetors would effectually stop their pursuit.

The sand crunched pleasantly under my feet, as I started out with lusty steps. In fact, I headed southward at a half run. The thought of Mildred and the fear of pursuit combined in lending me wings. In some thirty minutes I saw the blue mass of cliffs on the horizon, and the sight added to my speed. I had to admit that my nerves were shaken by the experiences of the past two days. Every moment I expected some sort of flying apparatus to appear in search of me, or some combination air and water machine to chase me up the beach. It was the possibility of the unknown and the unexpected that kept me in constant terror. My course up the beach was covered in the Indian fashion of running for a while and then walking long enough to get my breath so that I could run again.

I gave many a nervous start in alarm at some shadow of a bird, or at the sound of my own footsteps in the sand, before I finally arrived safely at the base of the cliffs. The great red disk of the sun was down near the water, and it was not yet seven o'clock. I gazed anxiously up toward the top of the cliffs, looking for the Gulls' Nest. Yes, there it was, the highest flat point on the ocean side. I recognized the wall of rock on the northeast of it.

I left the water's edge, which had hitherto been my safeguard, and moved toward the rocks in a diagonal line. I was puzzled as to how I could find my way to the top. The way to the Gulls' Nest was a tortuous path up the cliffside, and I didn't know where it was. I gazed intently up at the goal I was so anxious to reach. What was that? A flutter of white up there? And it had moved!

I seized my field-glasses eagerly and with a bounding heart. It was indeed Mildred. Waiting for me!

She had known I would come! I waved my arms to her and then my hat. Her figure did not move. I wondered why she did not show some sign to me. Suddenly I heard a rat-tat-tat. I whirled around.

One of the little leading-machines dashed out of the shrubbery, along a little pathway, and hurtled toward me. I broke into a run back toward the water's edge, but gave it up in a moment. That was hopeless for the machine was moving so fast that I stood no chance. I had not even dreamed that there might be paths through the woods, along which the machines could travel.

Someone must have been directing the machine, someone who also closely observed my movements. For, as I ran, it changed its angle to intercept me in a straight line; and as I stopped it again changed its course directly toward me. I looked all around, but nowhere was there any sign of where an observer might be hidden. The thing itself was too small for any person to be hidden inside of it.

There it came, whizzing toward me! What did they want? It did not seem equipped to do me any harm, but I wouldn't trust it. Its weight and speed were enough to break all my bones if it should hit me. Then, in the distance came a light truck with a crane on it — a very common conveyance about the island. Its speed was so low and it was so far away that I could easily reach the water ahead of it, were it not for this other sputtering little devil coming at me. What did the thing intend to do?

Anyway, I had no desire for a hand-to-hand conflict with the whirring iron thing. I couldn't fight it. I couldn't outrun it. It had me cut off both from the sea and from the forest; it could reach either ahead of me by changing its direction. There was only one thing left for me to do.

I drew my Colt .45 automatic pistol, which I can do in the wink of an eye. Then I dropped on one knee, leveled the gun at the complicated mass of machinery between the wheels. I waited till it was thirty paces away and then fired three shots into it.

I could see things crumple on the machine. Several small black objects flew up into the air. There was a crash, and a toot cut short.

The vehicle swerved sidewise and threw up a cascade of sand into the air, some of which fell sprinkling down on me. The machine fell over on its side and slid for a dozen feet over the sand, with a grinding and rattling of metal, leaving a plowed-up swath behind it. I couldn't help standing for a moment and looking at it. Some little thing still clicked back and forth on it, and there was a hissing, as of gas escaping compression. Then, seeing the truck coming, I started for the water on a run.

* * *

POWERFUL as was my curiosity to stop and examine the crippled machine, my fear of getting lassoed by the truck was greater. The latter was coming toward me with a great roar, and I made high speed toward the water's edge. Because of the roar of the truck, I failed to hear the chugging of another leading-machine approaching from the opposite direction. Before I saw it, it had reached the wet sand ahead of me, and cut me off.

I dodged quickly to one side, just in time to let it roar past me, with a grinding of gears and a squeal of brakes.

It stood directly in front of me, at the nearest point of the water's edge. When I changed direction, it headed for the spot that I had chosen, moving promptly to intercept me. The noise of the truck reminded me that I had little time to spare.

I drew my pistol again, and hurried closer to the little machine, which was outlined black against the disk of the setting sun. It stood there with a torrent of whistling sounds coming from it, and I could not refrain from the fancy that it was a big, iron bird perched there, singing its song. I made out a sort of elongated tank on it, which I imagined was its fuel supply, and which I selected as my target.

As I pulled the trigger, there was a burst of flame from the machine, a cloud of black smoke, and a fearful explosion. I was overwhelmed by a deluge of wet sand. I can remember scrambling to my feet and scuttling for the water; I think I must have been thrown backwards. In front of me the sea was rushing in to fill a hole in the sand, blackened, and full of twisted, smoking iron debris. A wheel floated on the water against the sun's disk, supported by the air in its tire. The truck was so close behind me that I could feel it coming at me, quite unaffected by the explosion.

I dodged quickly to one side, just in time to let it roar past me, with a grinding of gears and a squeal of brakes. But the brakes were too late. It cut two deep ruts in the slippery sand with its locked wheels, but its speed carried it on down the wet slope, and with a splash it plunged into the water, till its hood was more than half submerged. A couple of coughs came from it, and all that was left of its roar was a sizzle, just faintly, heard above the wash of the waves; and this gradually died away. I left it standing there, mournfully wet and silent.

I looked warily all around. The little machine on the sand was still now. Nothing else was in sight anywhere. Perhaps the havoc I had played with the machines had scared the people away. Anyway, now I could stick to the water until I was right among the rocks. I debated a few moments, anxious for a closer look at the wrecked machine, but finally decided that my curiosity had already gotten me into too much trouble. I resolutely turned my back on my temptation; for Mildred was waiting for me on the cliff.

And then I saw her, skipping from rock to rock, coming toward me. Behind her, more slowly, came Kaspar.

Joy and anticipation overwhelmed me for a moment; my heart pounded and I could hardly get my breath. During the past three days, so full of excitement and danger, she had been in my mind all of the time. Every moment I had hungered for her. The thought of her had kept me going when otherwise I might have given up to some of those terrible things. And here she came, fresh, airy, beautiful!

In a moment I had recovered, and ran toward her. Her face now had in it none of the sly fun with which it usually beamed. There was a beautiful expression on it that I had never seen before, and she hurried toward me with arms outstretched. Without a word, I gathered her into my arms.

She nestled there with an occasional little snuggle; and the brown head was buried in my shoulder. She clung there and I held her tight, and the red sun blazed and the green waves rolled in and broke into froth, and the sea-birds circled, and she never moved. It seemed hours that she clung to me.

At length it occurred to me that I must be a terrible looking spectacle, grimy and bedraggled, with a three days' growth of beard, to be holding such a dainty armful. I held her off at arms' length for a good look.

"Why!" I exclaimed clumsily, "you've been crying!" And I had to gather her in again and hold her all the tighter for the red eyes and the tears.

"Very logical, baby, very logical," said a kindly voice beside me; and I hastened to loosen one hand to grasp Kaspar's. "Davy, I'm glad to see you back safe. There was some anxiety. We couldn't be sure."

"Neither was I, at times," I replied grimly. "That's a neat little inferno over there. I can't make head nor tail of it!"

"Sit down," suggested Kaspar. "We've brought food. Eat a little and tell us your adventures."

"Have you seen Cassidy?" I asked, eagerly.

"Cassidy is at home in bed; pretty badly shaken, but safe and sound. The first thing he asked was if we had seen you; he was sure that you were lost. He floated down the river on a cask, and got in this morning."

Thus reassured, I sat down and ate; and Mildred sat beside me and held on to one arm. I outlined my adventures from the time I slipped out of the house toward Sappho's garage. I talked rapidly, for the sun was touching the water, and I hoped for a look at the machines yet before dark. My listeners sat and watched me intently, hanging on every word. Every now and then they looked at each other, as though they understood something that I did not. When I spoke of my climb through the darkness filled with machinery, Mildred's little brown hands were tightened on mine; and when I described the room with the concrete floor and the cases of instruments, she hid her face in her hands, while Kaspar scarcely breathed.

"And now," I concluded, "what does it all mean? For instance, why aren't these people nosing around here now, among these rocks, looking for us? Why did they give me up?"

"There aren't any people!" Kaspar replied.

"You mean that they sit back in their city and send out the automatic machines to do the dirty work?"

"No!" insisted Kaspar, "there is no one to sit back. The only people on the island are in the City of Beauty."

I sat for an instant struck dumb. I could feel my lower jaw drop limp. Was he making sport of me?

"Then who — where?"

I didn't even know what to ask or how to proceed with my questions.

"From the way you have told your story to me just now," Kaspar began, "it is evident that you haven't the least comprehension of what is really going on here on the island. You imagine an infinitely more advanced and complicated state of scientific and mechanical affairs than really exists. Your world is far ahead of us along general lines. We have no heavier-than-air flying, no submarines, no television — things that have become so common in your life. But, in our one line, we have progressed so far ahead of you that you will gasp when it dawns upon you. And you will shiver in horror when you realize what it has brought upon us."

"Must be some kind of a nightmare," I agreed. "Tell me the worst. Who runs the city? — and all that machinery!"

"Nobody! It runs itself!"

"You mean it's all automatic?" I was dizzy again with astonishment.

"That does not really express the state of affairs at all," Kaspar said. "I must explain from the beginning. That terrible city there is an example of what happens when the ability of a long line of inventive and scientific ancestors is concentrated in one individual, who is myself.

"It all started in a very modest way of mine, to develop a car that could automatically refill itself with gasoline, water, oil, and

air, when its supply of these things fell below a certain minimum
—"

"To eat when it got hungry, so to speak?" I laughed. The thing was getting hold of my nerves again.

"Good comparison. Everything was favorable to me. I owned half a county in east Texas where oil was found, and became one of the richest men in the world. I wanted to experiment with automatic cars without being bothered, and I bought this island; and here I brought the best engineers and scientific men in America. I paid them royally —"

"While you talk, may we look at the wreck of that little demon?" I asked. "Is it safe to go out there?"

"Yes. I don't think there are any more of them around. We can keep a sharp lookout. Our next step was automatic steering, so that the machine could avoid obstacles in the road without attention from a driver at a steering-wheel."

"I don't understand how these machines can drive automatically," I interrupted, very much puzzled, "unless they can see?"

"They can see!" He pointed to an excrescence on each headlight of the machine, like a bud on a potato.

"That's the selenium eye," Kaspar explained. "The electrical resistance of the metal selenium varies with the intensity of the light that strikes it; and that is a little camera chamber with a lens and a selenium network. By its means, the machine can see.

"The earlier machines had steering-wheels; their vision was a simple reflex for avoiding obstacles, while the driver had to choose the route himself. But, in a number of years we developed the logging attachment to the speedometer, by means of which it is possible to lay out the route on a set of dials. The machine could then find its way without human aid."

I started down at the complex, iron thing, trying to imagine that it once had been alive and now was dead.

"Then," Kaspar continued, "just as I had first equipped the machines with the mechanical equivalent of hunger, that is, a sensitiveness to a diminished reserve of fuel, lubricant, etc., so now we soon equipped them with the mechanical equivalent of pain, or in other words, a sensitiveness to damage or disorder. When a machine got out of order, or a certain amount of wear and tear had taken place, it automatically proceeded to a repair station. At first, repair stations were in charge of skilled men; but the automatic tradition had so thoroughly permeated all my people that very shortly repairs were all automatic. The principle was applied to all machinery, stationary as well as mobile. From that, it wasn't a far step to the automatic building of new machines — mechanical reproduction.

"Our machines are endowed with senses: sight, hearing, touch. Hearing was a simple matter of microphones. Smell was a simple chemical problem, but not of much practical value. We even gave them senses which human beings do not have, the ability to perceive various vibrations and forms of energy in the ether of space. They could do everything but reason.

"I wish we had stopped there. Then we would be as happy today as we were in those golden days when we had no cares nor troubles, and were free to pursue research in scientific and mechanical fields. But, an insatiable thirst for progress drove us inexorably onward."

* * *

KASPAR bent over the machine and showed me an oblong metal base in the midst of the apparatus. It had about it a vague suggestion of resemblance to the electrical units which I saw stacked up by the thousands in the little building where the lenses had stared at me. Bundles of wires led to this case from all parts of the mechanism. One of my bullets had torn a hole in the cover, exposing thousands of little twisted bars of rusty metal.

"There is the thing," Kaspar said sadly, pointing to this case, "that betrayed our Garden of Eden, the highest triumph of human ingenuity: the electrical brain!"

"Brain!" I gasped like a fish. "You mean it thinks?"

"Yes! Literally! Actually!"

"Aren't you just trying to fill me up now —?" I had reached what I thought were the limits of credulity.

"It is really very simple," Kaspar went on, with a patient smile. "You know of many machines in your world that think: a calculating machine or a bookkeeping machine; an automatic telephone exchange; an automatic lathe, and many others. They *think*, but only on the basis of the present moment. Add to their method *experience*, that is, retained past perceptions, and you have what we understand ordinarily as thinking.

"Mechanical memory, an *association* of previously collected perceptions, was what we needed; and when we found them, our machines were able to reason better than we ourselves."

"But how can a machine remember?" I asked the question open-mouthed.

"We discovered a method of storing the electrical visual impulses from the selenium eye, the electrical auditory impulses

225

from the microphone ear, etc., by means of the now familiar retarded oxidation reactions in various metals."

"You mean — what the machine sees or hears is preserved —?"

"That is memory, isn't it?" Kaspar said, with infinite patience for my stupid incredulity. "And these stored impressions can be reawakened when desired, repeatedly. The electrical brain remembers better than the human brain. Human ideas come haphazard, by accident; psychologists call it association. In the mechanical brain, all remembered material is systematically indexed —"

"Thinking by electricity! And better than the human product!" I was stunned by the thought. I pondered a while in silence, looking down at the prostrate mechanical thing. I could almost fancy that I had killed some living creature. The thing was so little that I felt a sort of pity for it; it seemed like some child's broken toy. "And each machine is an independent, intelligent individual!" This was an exclamation rather than a question, for the answer was obvious.

"Yes." Kaspar's voice was melancholy. "It lives its own life, you may say."

"And the people in the City of Beauty have even their mental work done for them. Now I understand how they have been able to develop their creative art to such an extent."

"That is the other side of it," Kaspar said with a little more interest in his manner. "You have seen wonderful things in the City of Beauty, painting, sculpture, architecture, drama, music. But I doubt if you comprehend how far they are ahead of similar things in the United States or the rest of the world. Your mind and mine are not sufficiently developed to grasp the difference. To Mildred here, when you take her back to the world you came from, things will seem as crude as you might consider an Indian village or an African kraal."

"What I am wondering, though," I remarked, "is why your people did not begin to dissipate and degenerate, with all this comfort and luxury. That is what has always happened in past history, is it not?"

"My people were a carefully picked group, from the most intellectually active strata of society. They were equipped by nature to use their brains. Creative art has kept three generations of them happy and busy — so much so that they could not see the other terrible problem that had arisen. I cannot make them see it today.

"Only a few of us old men have seen the danger. We fear these cold brains of steel and electricity without feelings, without sympathy. They have reached a point in their logic where they can perceive that the thousands of us in the City of Beauty are of no real good to them; that in fact we consume too much of their time and energy. It must be plain to them that we are frail and helpless before their mighty strength. It looks, from various indications, that they have begun to decide to throw off their bonds of slavery to us.

"I foresaw this before it happened; in order to anticipate it, I devised many years ago what we now call 'Supervision.' I made all of the machines dependent upon some human action before they could operate, like the punching of a time-clock. It is years since any machine has been made by human hands; yet the machines have continued to build that characteristic into themselves. Now, 'Supervision' has degenerated into an empty formality — pulling dummy levers and watching dummy meters. It seems, however, that it is still in some way necessary to the machines, for they compel the people to go through with it.

227

"And the people submit blindly to it. They do not understand machinery well enough even to know whether it is operating properly or not, but they allow themselves to be dragged over there for 'Supervision!' Faugh! It is disgusting to me. Superfluous to the machines and degrading to the people! A symbol of slavery to a master without a living soul. Or it often seems to me like some primitive ceremony of worship. The machines have built a temple with a golden dome to their creators, where they worship the latter as a savage worships his gods.

"The people play along like irresponsible babes, numbed by their beauty and comfort, disregarding the terrible fate that threatens them. I am sick with disappointment in them, sick with the horror of the things that my iron progeny are doing. We human beings are a mere feeble incident, that is going to be brushed aside during the development of this monstrous mechanical clot.

"For, these machines are developing in a new direction, that no one could have foreseen. Who would ever have thought of such a thing! It appalls me to think of it.

"We are beginning to realize that we have not only the individual intelligences of the various machines to deal with — of course there are machines of various grades of intelligence, ranging from no intelligence at all, to brains so vast and powerful that your mind can hardly grasp the conception. You must have noticed differences. The big machines that work in the fields are stupid; the little leading-machines possess a high grade of intelligence. They were designed to guide and control larger and less intelligent machines, and now are apparently in some sort of ascendency over the rest of the machinery. There is a complex 'social organization' in the City of Smoke that I am not quite clear about; it must be something like the caste system in India. There is a chief ruler, a sort of 'king' of the machines — the large leading-machine with the long mechanical fingers —"

* * *

"THE Squid!" I exclaimed. "So that's who the boss is! That explains a lot to me."

"Its combination of high intelligence, perfect mobility, and great 'manual' ability, fit it peculiarly for leadership and control among the machines. And I think that the 'Squid' as you call it, has an eye on you pretty closely —

"However, what I started to make clear to you a moment ago is that the entire city is in reality one vast and unified organism. It is controlled by a single brain, whose capabilities are as far ahead of those of the little individual brains as its size exceeds theirs.

"That brain is the mass of apparatus you found in the small, ornate building where the lenses stared at you. I was in that room several years ago, and at that time suspected that it was the brain of the city. It is all a vast electrical nervous system, whose peripheral fibers run all over the city; whose sensory end-organs are lenses and microphones everywhere; whose motor end-organs are all the countless machines controlled by the different wires, while this central mass of reflex and association apparatus comprises the brain and spinal cord. I could trace out some of the steps of this system in its earlier stages.

"The whole city is one living monster, with its individual parts running about just as leucocytes run about freely in our own bodies, going where they are needed to perform their functions. That is what our community of frail, pampered human beings, have to contend against!"

229

I couldn't say a word. What a terrible thought! A huge city, alive! A horrible, spreading monster, like a gigantic amoeba! And I had been right there, inside its brain! I thought of the ticking and rustling that I had heard among its myriads of stacked units. It had heard my demands to see the "supervision," and had seen fit to grant it.

And all this business going on without people, without real *life*! Just gasoline and coal. The thought stunned me. Yet, what is *life*? Could I not just as well say that all of our striving and love is just beef and wheat? Then, a sudden thought struck me, for was I not the leader of the revolution?

"Why not throttle this whole business right at the source!" I exclaimed to Kaspar. "Get control of the supplies of coal and oil, and we've got them!"

Kaspar stood and looked at me contemplatively for a moment.

"You must indeed have had a nerve-racking time in that place to be so upset," he remarked with concern in his voice. "Usually you are very level-headed. However, I think a good night's rest will help you. Can't you see?" he went on; "there is no Wall Street nor Stock Exchange on this island. Coal is mined in a score of places, scattered about the north and east end of the island, ten to forty miles away from here. Deep down underground, automatic machines are knocking it loose and hauling it up. Oil, too, comes from wells here and there; it is refined in huge automatic plants, and runs to the city in pipes to more automatic plants. All these are connected by wires to the central brain, which controls them.

"There isn't a laborer on the island; not a man who could lift a pick. The people do not even know where the mines and wells are; and if they did know, they couldn't get there; and if they could get there, they could not handle the machinery; they wouldn't even know how to stop it. Do you see the problem now?

"Frankenstein's troubles with his poor, feeble imitation of a monster were a joke beside the horrors of my position. For you haven't heard the worst yet."

"How could there be anything worse?"

Kaspar plunged into it abruptly.

"During recent years the machines have become interested in life itself. A few of us old men who have kept up with their activities first noticed them taking animals into their laboratories. They have probably realized that we possess something that they lack, and they are studying it. I have strong reasons to believe that they have begun the study of human life.

"They know nothing of pain or feeling — imagine the horrors they must be perpetrating!"

He paused for a moment and then continued:

"This thing must have been going on for a long time before I realized it. As I look back, I can think of over a hundred of our people who have mysteriously disappeared."

"You don't mean that they — " I began horrified.

"Some of the things you saw in the City of Smoke make me think so more strongly than ever. That concrete room must be their laboratory for the study of human beings. The instruments whose purpose was unknown to you, the clothes hanging in the cases, the organic odor, the bringing in of you and Cassidy — what else can it all mean?"

I shuddered.

"The old man in the villa and the man with the deranged mind?" I asked. "And Ames? Do you think — and Mildred that night on the dock?"

Mildred huddled down into a very silent little figure, looking at me out of wide-open eyes.

"You can imagine that your own position is highly perilous, to put it mildly," Kaspar warned. "They seem to be selecting as victims the best people we have. Probably they have two reasons. They want the best examples for study. And they want to eliminate all the original, strong family stocks. Anyone who has initiative, curiosity, and especially an interest in machinery or qualities for leadership of people, is a special object for their attention. Sooner or later he disappears."

"So that is why you warned me on the ship, before I ever saw the island? You thought I was different from the men on your island? I accept that as a high compliment and thank you for it."

"Imagine how we've guarded Mildred!" Kaspar said with a sigh. "Her mother and father perished that way. They were both mechanical geniuses, and both popular; they would have made inspiring leaders had the occasion arisen. Their existence was a danger to the rule of the machines.

"Those of our people, who show the least interest in machinery and the least intelligence about it, are safest. An unconscious adaptation has taken place. Without knowing why, the people consider machinery as something vulgar and horrible; consequently they keep their minds away from things mechanical; and that is what the machines want. The people keep their minds off the fates of those who have mysteriously disappeared, and try to forget the fear for their own sakes. They pursue their arts and sports intensely, in order to forget the horrors hidden beneath the surface. They are happy, after the fashion of May-flies.

"The machines rear them, just as you have raised pet rabbits. And they maintain the human stock of the quality they desire, by the well-known method of eliminating undesirable individuals.

"I am trying to make the remnant of my life of final service to this wretched people, whom I myself have made wretched. I have been endeavoring to awaken their spirit and arouse them to resistance. I want them, or as many of them as have the stamina to do so — the rest might as well be dead — to throw off the disgraceful yoke of 'Supervision,' and with it, the domination of the mechanical city,

"At first I had hoped that we might regain control of the machinery; but I am convinced that is a forlorn hope. There is nothing left for my people except to go back to a primitive, agricultural existence; to begin at the bottom of the ladder of civilization and climb slowly again.

"That means hardship; but anything else means slavery, degeneration and death. I found a few kindred spirits who felt and worked with me. Teaching these things to Mildred has been an inspiration to me. My worst problem was that I did not know how to go about getting the people roused to action or to prepare them to act. All my life I have been a scientific man, and I know nothing of methods that approach so near the military as this must.

"You carried my movement further in twenty-four hours than I had been able to do in several years. When you see the progress that has been made during the three days of your absence, you will be astonished. We now have several thousands drilling, drilling openly, everywhere. The loss of Cassidy inflamed them; the spirit

233

of Perry Becker inspired them. Then Cassidy's return cheered them beyond measure. They have definite plans against the City of Smoke. There is going to be trouble.

"But you, Davy, must keep out of it. That is my wish, perhaps my last. There is going to be much waste of human life, and these people are not your people; and you have a duty to Mildred. You will soon be all she has. Take her away from here, back to your world. I have a motor-yacht all ready for you, for I have been planning her escape for years."

13
MACHINES VERSUS MEN

KASPAR stopped talking, and the three of us sat for some moments in silence, looking out over the sea. The upper rim of the blood-red sun was just disappearing into the green ocean, and a long, undulating scarlet streak extended from it almost to our feet. The sky was piled with great mountains and castles and ships of purple and orange, and a blend of these colors was reflected in the dancing water. There was a mere gentle breath of cool breeze. There was a peace in the air and a beauty on the face of the waters and a mellowness on the beach and cliffs that turned one's thoughts to things above. It was difficult to believe that such terrible things could be taking place in a world that looked so lovely. But the cruel things of man's making would not permit me to forget their presence.

"This morning a great number of machines went through the City of Beauty on a rampage," Kaspar continued. "They seemed irritated at something, perhaps at the escape of you and Cassidy. They carried off a number of people."

Kaspar paused for a moment. His voice almost broke. I judged that someone else very dear to him had been among the number.

"On the other hand," he began again, "we have five colonels, each with a full regiment, drilling busily. You will be surprised to see what good soldiers they are. They expect to move on the City of Smoke soon. They have some excellent plans for attack, but want your advice. They all admit that it is impossible to gain control of things there; their only hope is in wrecking the system. Again, Davy, I feel able to hold up my head. My people are showing courage; even though less than a tenth of them have risen to redeem the rest.

"There is little time to lose before violence and danger begin. We must hurry back now and solemnize your marriage in our way; and when you get back to Texas you can have it repeated according to your laws there. You must leave the island tonight."

I sat for a considerable time debating what I ought to do. What he was asking of me looked like running away. There was promise of a most glorious scrap, and a most unusual one. The people needed a leader. I had the training and experience which fitted me for just this thing ahead, and they knew little or nothing. They needed me and I ached for the opportunity.

And yet, another part of me said, what is their fight to me? What do I care what becomes of them? Their trouble is their own fault, because they are too soft and lazy. If they had ever amounted to anything, they would never have permitted themselves to get into such a pickle. Here I have Mildred to take care of, and it is my business to get her out of here. My main job is to get back to Texas among my own people, and get busy practicing medicine.

Mildred was regarding me intently, hardly breathing. She did not speak either. Finally Kaspar spoke:

"The two great things for which I have lived are about to be realized. Again I know what it is to feel happiness, after years of fear and misery.

"One overpowering desire has been to free the people from the yoke of 'Supervision,' and the domination of the machines. I wanted to see them rise, and they are rising. It will mean hardship and suffering for them; it may even mean destruction. But that would be better than this disgraceful slavery.

"The other great thought of my life is my son's child, Mildred. I could not bear to raise her to this May-fly life. She knows of your big world, and I have prepared her to take her place in it. For two years I have planned that she should. That is why we have the Gulls' Nest. That is why we have the *Gull* herself, a pretty yacht down yonder in a salt bayou in the dense forest. She is the only thing on the island that is not automatic, and I made her with my own hands. Food, water, fuel, firearms, and navigating instruments have long been prepared for use at an instant's notice for a long trip, waiting for the time when my baby should be strong enough and wise enough to start away. I have put on board enough gold and platinum to secure her living in that world until she finds her proper place in it.

"And now comes a real man, a hard worker, with a heart as brave as they used to have in the good old times, who wants my little girl to take care of. Can you imagine why my heart is full of gladness? I do not care to live any longer; there is no need of it."

By this time Mildred was weeping profusely. I was embarrassed by the old man's cordial words and the prospect of escaping with Mildred, and I could not find my tongue. Kaspar looked so happy that he seemed suddenly to have turned into someone else. The sad, kindly old man had turned into a beaming, radiant one.

"But grandma?" sobbed Mildred. "What will become of her?"

Kaspar's face set hard again, and the transformation that swept him was terrible.

"She is among the missing!" he said grimly.

He turned to me:

"Mildred has been here at the Gulls' Nest most of the time since you left; and has not kept informed on what was going on at home. Come!"

"Where?"

"Home, just long enough for Mildred to get some of her personal things which I have packed for her, and to have you married. In two or three hours you can be at sea."

Mildred and I rose and followed him in silence. Mildred dried her eyes and went along holding her aged grandfather's arm and trying to comfort him. In the weakening daylight we picked our way carefully among the rocks that were scattered between the cliffs and the water's edge. When we reached the little harbor, there was Sappho waiting for us at the side of the road.

* * *

I FELT a queer sort of embarrassment when I got within range of the machine's headlights: the sort of constraint we feel in the presence of a person about whom we have been talking behind his back. In the light of what I knew, the machine seemed like a living creature to me; it had a brain, could see and hear and remember, and act on its own judgment. But the car gave no sign of any kind. After Kaspar's story I expected it to have some sort of facial expression. The three of us got into the seat; Kaspar set the dials, and we started up the road to the City of Beauty.

It seemed to me like going home. After all, I had had some very pleasant, and some very wonderful experiences there. It seemed ages since I had seen it. During the trip through the forest and between the fields, I was eager to see its beautiful streets of luxuriant trees and colored houses. And I shuddered several times in recollection of the three hideous days I had just passed.

Kaspar must have felt as eager to get back as I did, or must have had some strong reason for haste. Never on this island had I traveled with the speed that we made in Sappho that night. There was no direct-reading speedometer, and I did not know how many miles per hour we made; but the way we roared through the forest and whisked between the fields made it seem only a few minutes from the harbor until the lights of the city were visible to us; and there was still a fair remnant of daylight left.

At the distance of a mile, I could see the old familiar gateway; but there seemed to be a strange sort of commotion about it. There were black masses of machinery about, and a great deal of clattering and tooting. Lights sprang up on the machines one by one, and I could see a great crowd of them gathered just outside the gateway. They were of all imaginable sizes and shapes, from the dog-like leading-machines that darted swiftly in and out among the others, to huge mechanical shovels and ditching machines that lumbered along on caterpillar treads; passenger cars without passengers; trucks, tractors, movable cranes, huge rollers, and complicated-looking trestle affairs, such as I had seen working in the fields. They swarmed and crowded outside the gate in a huge, squirming blot, and spread out into the fields and along the hedge that bounded the city. They were not doing anything, except milling around like bees before a hive.

Kaspar slowed down Sappho's speed, and we approached cautiously. The flood lights above the gateway went on, revealing the people in shrinking little groups, just inside the gates. From a distance the people appeared very feeble and insignificant in the presence of the machines. The air was full of fluty whistlings up and down the musical scale. This time it reminded me very powerfully of a bird's song.

"Where is the explosive man who wrecked three of our machines?" Kaspar repeated, as though translating.

I stared at him in open-mouthed astonishment.

"You mean — " I gasped, " — that is a machine speaking?"

"Yes. The people are answering it, but I cannot hear them."

"The machines can understand human speech!" Would surprises in this island never cease? "Just ordinary speech — English?"

"Yes. We must change our plans. As I gather from the general trend of what the machines say, the people are promising that they will turn you over if they see you."

"Well, of all the skunks!" I exclaimed in surprise.

But the chief thing that occupied my mind was the speech of the machines. That crowded out even the craven attitude of the people toward me. All these days I had been listening to that piping, and it had never occurred to me that it might mean something. How they must have talked to me, and I had not the slightest dream of it! Now, as I listened, I could easily see how the sounds might mean words; it had a suggestion of Chinese about it, in which the pitch of the sound has its own meaning.

"The people are afraid," Kaspar said. "All of this is too much for them and they don't know how to take it. The organized men are camped far away on the Hopo fields. This morning when I left, I feared that a panic was beginning in the city."

As he spoke, he was trying to stop the machine on which we rode.

"It is dangerous to go on," he whispered. "We've got to change our plans."

He slid the lever in its slot again and again. The machine jerked and swerved sidewise; it shivered and roared, but continued its progress toward the distant swarm of machines, as though determined to carry us in spite of ourselves toward that bloodthirsty pack. Mildred gasped.

"Sappho!" she exclaimed, and there was bitter disappointment in her tone.

"Wait!" I said harshly, through gritted teeth. "I suppose this beast overheard us planning to escape. I know some tricks myself."

Mildred's face shone white in the darkness. I pointed my big pistol into the midst of the rustling machinery and fired. Mildred screamed. I fired again. The machine slowed down to a stop, but not before a half dozen hoots had escaped it. We got off and I put bullets into several parts of it. The crashing of metal, the tinkling of loose parts on the pavement, the hissing of some compressed gas, all satisfied me that it would tell no more tales. Mildred clung to my arm, which soon found its way about her shoulders.

"Poor little Sappho!" she sighed, and wept silently a while. Sappho, after all, had long been a faithful servant to them; it had been closely woven into their lives. I could understand the display of sentiment, even though it was in connection with a machine.

Kaspar was bending over the machine, studying it with absorbed interest.

"A bullet struck its brain," he mused. "The brain is here, just behind the engine, under the instrument-board. To the sides of it are the steering center on the left and direction-center on the right, and both are injured. Also, by the sounds, the speech-center must have been hit."

He was so interested in the machine that he poked about its vitals and talked about its various parts, for the moment oblivious of our plight.

I touched his shoulder.

"We've got to do something," I reminded him. "Look."

In the distance there were three pairs of lights, hurtling down the road towards us. They had separated themselves from the mass of others and were becoming too uncomfortably near. Kaspar looked about helplessly for a moment.

"We've got to get off this road," I directed, "into the fields."

So we scrambled across the ditch at the side of the road. I turned to help Mildred, but she did not need help; and the two of us assisted Kaspar over the dark and uncertain area. However, he was also quite vigorous for his age and insisted that he did not need help. Soon we found ourselves waist-deep in some sort of growing grain. I had chosen the left side of the road because it was to the south, and farthest away from the City of Smoke. We headed southwest by my compass, or the forest, and ultimately for the sea-coast. I estimated that there were some three or four miles of tall grain between us and the woods.

* * *

IN a few moments the machines had arrived at the place on the road that we had left. They stopped at the wreck of Sappho and stood about a while and roared and tooted. Then two of them went straight onward along the road toward the harbor, and one remained on the spot. Others began to arrive at the spot, which stimulated us to plunge on still more rapidly through the grain in the darkness.

Kaspar was helping me get the direction correct so that we would make a straight line for the bayou where the Gull was moored.

"This will keep us nearly parallel with the road for a while; but after it enters the woods, the road turns away to the north a little," Kaspar explained.

"Are there any things among those machines that could catch us in this field?" I asked, giving voice to my chief concern.

"No," Kaspar answered. "The only machines able to cross that ditch and get through this grain are too slow to catch us. Besides, they don't know where we are. It would take a wide search to find us in this blackness."

We forged steadily ahead through the grain and the blackness, and it was discouraging work. It was exceedingly fatiguing, leaving us no breath for conversation. And there seemed no end, no purpose to it. We were just a tiny island in the sea of blackness, and all our hard work seemed to be getting us nowhere. For all we could tell, we were forever in the same spot. When we had once left behind and out of sight the commotion around the wreck of Sappho, it seemed that uncounted ages elapsed before I thought I could make out the blackness of the forest against the stars. Then a shaft of light swept across the vast fields, swinging in a wide arc, followed by another and another, each illuminating a blazing, racing spot.

"Duck down low!" I ordered. "They are hunting us with search-lights!"

We all crouched down so that we were hidden in the grain, grateful for the opportunity to rest a little.

"The devils!" I exclaimed.

"No," replied Kaspar. "Only thorough and systematic, dispassionate, devoid of any feeling in the matter."

"Anyway, it's hands and knees for us the rest of the way to the woods," I grumbled.

With lights sweeping about overhead, and machines roaring on the road in the distance, seeming to be first on one side and then on the other, we crawled along laboriously through the grain. Mildred and the old man never complained, though it must have been terribly hard for them. I am accustomed to all sorts of hardships, and it was no joke for me. We crawled for ages; my hands and knees were sore; and finally we just went blindly and mechanically ahead, having given up all hope of ever finding any end. So, at some time, we came to a bare, cleared area, and a few rods ahead were black, towering trees. Far behind us, the searchlights blazed back and forth.

We straightened up and ran across the clear piece between us and the woods, confident now that we were safe. The tangle of shrubs, vines, and leaves was still more painful to traverse. I saw that my companions were exhausted and that we might as well give up any hope of going on for two hours more through the forest. And when we got through the thicket into the clear portion, other obstacles appeared. The first was darkness. It was black as pitch. There was no light whatsoever, and we bumped into trees without the least idea that they were there. Progress was impossible under such conditions. The second was insects. We were overwhelmed by clouds of them. Before a moment had passed, we were bitten and stung all over. They came at us with a hoarse buzz, which increased and swelled when I lit my flashlight. I had to put it out, because when I tried to use it for finding the way, it gathered such dense swirls of bugs that going was out of question.

"Oh, what shall we do?" Mildred cried with despair in her voice. "We cannot go back out there."

"Ho ho! Cheer up!" I sang out. "This isn't so bad. I prefer it to lots of fixes I've been in. The first thing is a fire."

The flashlight helped me find some sticks, and before long I had a good blaze started. Thousands of insects sacrificed themselves by darting straight into the fire in swarming masses to sizzle and char, before I had covered it with enough green leaves to start it smoking profusely. The air was as quiet as if we had been in a room; there was not a breath of air, and it was not long before my smudge had cleared the air of insects. We sat in the smoke and sputtered, but the smoke and the rest were preferable to what had gone before.

"Now for some shelter," I announced, "for here we stay till morning."

Both of them regarded me with a good deal of surprise, but said nothing. Just as I had trusted them implicitly on their own ground, so now they looked to me for a way out of difficulties. And I was happy, for this indeed was my own element.

There was a wealth of material around. I built up another fire into a bright blaze, and by its light, and with the aid of my knife and ax, I cut sticks to lean against trees and built the skeletons of roofs for a couple of lean-tos. Mildred had soon rested enough so that she was eager to help; and I let her gather leaves and showed her how to thatch the roofs. In an hour they were finished, even to comfortable beds of leaves. I piled up the fire so that we should be assured of plenty of smoke, and we all lay down for the night, Mildred in one of the lean-tos and Kaspar and I in the other. Everything was quiet; even the drone of the insects ceased when we had quieted down; no machines were audible, though the road was near. I fell asleep quickly.

I was about several times in the night to replenish the fire, but awoke in the morning thoroughly refreshed. Kaspar was sitting up and looking at me with a smile.

"This sort of thing makes me feel pretty stiff and miserable," he said.

"Yes," I agreed; "one must become accustomed to it, before it can be enjoyed. However, a little warming by the fire and moving about will make you feel better."

"Good morning!" came across from Mildred's shack. "Let's do it then, for I'm terribly stiff and sore."

"And a little breakfast will work wonders," I added.

"Breakfast!" She jumped up and ran out with an eager smile. "How in the world will you ever get breakfast? I know you will, but I can't imagine how."

"How would you like this?" I asked, handing out a little of my chocolate and hard biscuit. She nibbled at it and made a wry face.

"Ugh!" she shuddered. "If this is all we can get, I'll wait a day or two for my breakfast."

"Well, let us see what we can scare up," I suggested laughing. "First of all we need some water. There must be plenty of streams through here, judging by how thick this stuff grows."

We scattered to find one, I choosing the direction toward the road. I was the first to find clear, flowing water, and my shout brought up the rest. We ail washed our faces together and had a merry time doing it. The road was visible through the trees, but was silent and deserted.

* * *

A LOUD rattling, high above our heads, made me start suddenly. I thought some infernal apparatus had got after us through the air; but Kaspar laughed and pointed to a big green bird with a bright scarlet head, up in a tall tree.

"He's good to eat," Kaspar suggested.

Before he finished speaking I had my gun out and shot. The bird fell at our feet, its head cut cleanly off. I confess that I did it for a little grandstand play; for the one thing I was proud of was my quick draw and accurate marksmanship, rather a rare thing in our civilized world.

Mildred gave one glance at the bird, and stared at me with eyes opened wide. Kaspar smiled and patted my back.

"Very remarkable, Davy," he said, with genuine admiration in his voice; "how did you learn to shoot like that?"

"I don't know," I answered. "I have been able to do that ever since I can remember, and so can many of my boyhood friends. Marksmanship was a tradition in Wallis where I grew up. When I was fourteen I could bring up my .22 rifle and pop off the head of a wild turkey as it ran through the brush."

"But I don't see how you can aim that quickly," Mildred asked very much puzzled and very much in earnest. I was rather astonished to find her knowing even that much about firearms, until Kaspar explained that there were rifles in the *"Gull"* brought from Galveston, and that he had been teaching her to shoot.

"I don't aim," I explained. "I can't tell you much about it, because I don't know. When I see a thing, I just shoot it — just as you would reach out and touch it with your finger. It's very natural to me. Whereas, most people shoot at a mark, and have to aim carefully."

"Do it again," begged Mildred.

"Well, I think we could eat another bird between us," I laughed. I looked over my supply of ammunition. I had taken twenty spare clips of cartridges from my suitcase and put them in my haversack, and these were still intact. I had thus far used nine shots.

"Show me another one that's good to eat," I suggested.

Kaspar pointed silently, high up into a tree in the direction of the road, and I followed his movement with a quick shot.

The result surprised, rather than disappointed me.

The bird darted upwards, crying hoarsely, and flew around unsteadily, finally getting out over the road and making for the bright light of the open country. I stood a while and watched it in astonishment; this was an unusual thing to have happen to me.

"I think I know what happened," I finally said. "He had a brown head and a bright orange bill, did he not?"

Kaspar nodded.

"He fooled me. I thought the orange thing was his head; and I merely shot his bill off."

"Poor thing!" Mildred exclaimed, with a bewitching pucker of her mouth.

"I'll run out and finish him. We need him for breakfast."

I squirmed through the thicket and ran out on the road. The bright bird was far away, and approaching the outlet of the leafy tunnel. I ran down the road in pursuit, and before long was in the open, with the forest behind me. But the bird was still far ahead, moving in wild gyrations, but in a general way, straight ahead. I noted that he was getting weaker and flying lower; so I dropped into a leisurely pace, counting on picking him up when he fell.

The road was silent and empty. I was in good spirits. I had had an excellent night's rest, and the morning was cool and pleasant. I understood that it was only a short distance to the yacht which they called the *"Gull,"* and that soon I would be on my way home from this place of nightmares, and Mildred, brown-eyed, trusting Mildred would be with me, all my own. The bird finally fell in the road, a hundred yards ahead of me.

Just then, several dots appeared in the distance up the road, from the direction of the City of Beauty. I broke into a run again, hoping to pick up the bird and get away. In a moment I gave that up; the machines were coming too swiftly. I turned around and hurried toward the forest, and was surprised at how far away I had gotten from the shelter of the trees without realizing it.

I looked back. The machines were coming on at a terrific rate. In the front was a rather large leading-machine; not as large as the Squid, but bigger than any others I had seen. Behind it were two long, swift cars, and a lot of small things behind those, mere dots in the distance. I saw in a moment that I could never reach the forest ahead of them.

Why didn't I jump the ditch and disappear in the cane, or whatever the stuff was growing in the field?

What my chances would have been by daylight if I had done that, I do not know; but it never occurred to me at the time. I was aching for something else — I suppose I had a foolhardy spite to vent on the machines, which was fanned by the feel of the pistol in my hand. And, with my new information about the machines, I knew exactly where and how I stood against them. Also, it would be a pleasure to show a little prowess before Mildred and Kaspar.

So I waited until the big leading-machine got within accurate range, located the brain-case and put a bullet into it. The machine executed a crashing somersault, spilled bolts and glass and oil all over the road, and left a sizzling, pulsating pile of wreckage in the middle of the pavement.

I gave a shout of exultation, and looked back. Mildred and Kaspar were standing against the green of the shrubbery, motionless. I waved my pistol to them and then turned back to business. The two cars came tearing on.

Kaspar's lecture the preceding evening over the wreck of Sappho, dwelt vividly in my mind. I remembered clearly all of the things he had said about the location of the vital parts of the machine. So I fired into the steering-center of one of the approaching machines, and got a lively demonstration of a jack-knife skid. The front wheels wobbled, the car swerved and turned over on its side, and slid for several feet, cutting gashes in the pavement. It crashed into the first wreck.

I shouted again. I was enjoying myself hugely. I hit the same spot in the third machine, but with a different result. The front wheels turned sharply across it, and as the car's momentum carried onward, it rolled over and over, landing with a crash against the wrecks of the two ahead of it, its machinery continuing to roar deafeningly. This was indeed fun!

* * *

I DROPPED my arm for a moment and looked up the road. Half a dozen of the tiny leading-machines were swarming toward me. Behind them were several cars. A long line of things dotted the road as far back as I could see. I had only a few seconds' rest, for the little machines were racing toward me swiftly.

The first one turned to dodge past the pile of wreckage, exposing a broadside to me. I caught it in the middle just as it swerved and knocked it over. It hung rattling, half way over the ditch.

I had to shoot rapidly, at the same time putting my left hand into my haversack for a fresh clip of cartridges. The next machine seemed to go all to pieces as I hit it. I must have struck some key spot in its framework. Several loose chunks of it slid along the road and piled themselves up on the rest of the junk; a single wheel

251

came rolling on toward me. It rolled on past, and tumbled into the ditch behind me.

I dropped six of the little leading-machines, and blocked the road effectively with their wrecks, making a sort of barrier for myself. The place was a pandemonium, with the roaring of machinery, the banging of my gun, the sizzling of gas, and a torrent of hooting. Again I waved my left hand backward toward Mildred and Kaspar, who stood motionless in the shrubbery. Several more cars were coming, and I could only glance backward for an instant. I seemed to have started something. It would be necessary for me to block up the road pretty thoroughly before it would be safe for me to start back toward the woods.

A huge, hurtling truck failed to show any bad results from a couple of shots, much to my momentary consternation. Trucks must be built differently. Perhaps they were not so highly organized, and had no strictly vital spots — just as it is much harder to kill a turtle or an alligator than the higher animals like deer or tigers.

Now what was I to do? Was it safe for me to run? I looked about me quickly, and decided that chances were against me in that respect.

Aha! I had it. The eyes! That was the vital spot.

Two shots knocked out the dark lenses over the headlights, and the machine stopped, so suddenly that the pavement smoked under its tires. Another heavy truck plunging along behind had no time to stop or dodge; it crashed from behind into the first one, and both staggered up against the ever-increasing pile of wreckage. Another truck, as the result of a lucky shot into the steering-gear, plunged head-on into the ditch, and stopped there, roaring and hooting, unable to move.

For nearly a half hour they kept coming. I stood there, surrounded by a litter of empty shells, and piled up a great heap of them, twisted, battered, sizzling wrecks. They strewed the road for a hundred yards and blocked it completely. Three were in the ditch, two exploded, and several were on fire.

Then they suddenly quit coming. The road was clear. I seemed to be in triumphant possession of the battlefield. I climbed up on top of the highest pile of wreckage, and stood looking around me. One of the little wrecks startled me by exploding and sending a rain of iron things dropping about me, but fortunately without injuring me. I retreated in haste to a safer spot.

Then in the distance came a most curious looking apparatus. It was a huge, clumsy leviathan, lumbering along quite slowly, but it looked so strange that I waited for it. In spite of my danger I had to see what the thing was. On each side were six or eight wheels, and in front, a curved shield like a snow-plow from which my bullets splashed in a harmless spray of lead. Behind it slowly came a tiny leading-machine.

I watched the big, clumsy thing in intense fascination. It came right over the wrecks of the other machines in a strange manner. As soon as a wheel touched an obstacle, it rose vertically to clear it; and when past, it descended again to the ground. Thus, with two or three wheels of each side on the ground and the others raised, it made a sort of bridge over the obstacle. It was a marvelous contraption for getting over uneven ground. It came along so slowly that I had not the least fear of not being able to get away from it when I decided to do so. Suddenly I heard a scream behind me.

There was Mildred in the distance, running toward me, arms upraised, face as pale as paper. When I turned around, she stopped and waved her arms, screaming something frantically. She was terribly agitated, and was distractedly motioning for me to come. Behind, in the brush, stood Kaspar, also motioning to me to come.

I watched the big, clumsy thing in intense fascination. It came right over the wrecks of the other machines in a strange manner.

I looked all around me for the cause of their warnings. Everything was clear. I could see no reason for such panic. There were no machines except the big one coming too slowly to frighten me, and the little leading-machine that had to remain at the further end of the wreckage.

Well, I thought, I might as well start back now; there is nothing further for me around here. I had only three shots left anyway. I emptied them recklessly and harmlessly against the approaching monster, and turned toward Mildred. She had stopped when I first saw her, not far from the forest. In the distance I could see her hands clenched against her breast.

Suddenly I felt myself grow weak and limp. Out of the forest, behind Mildred, came a crescendo rat-tat-tat-tat. Around the bend of the road, back in its gloomy depths, came the Squid! Its horrible snaky arms unwound and waving in the air. Mildred heard it and screamed, and remained rooted to the spot.

My pistol was empty. I was too far away to help her. I groaned in despair. I clenched my fists and ran toward her in hopeless desperation.

"Into the bush!" I shrieked. "Hide!"

Too late.

The Squid was beside her like a shot. It wound half a dozen black arms around her, and lifted her on its step. Then it whirled about and dashed back into the depths of the forest, disappearing around a bend in the road. Its rat-tat-tat-tat grew fainter and fainter. It was out of sight and hearing before I reached the entrance of the forest, spent and out of breath, in a hundred kinds of agony.

Just then, behind me, the roar of a terrific explosion rocked the vicinity. A cloud of smoke shot high into the air; fragments of machinery flew about, and a smoking hole remained where I had stood on the road. The shielded monster was backing away from it. As I watched there was a second upheaval a few feet away from its shield; and as it continued to back away, I saw it drop the third bomb, which exploded almost at once, reducing that portion of the road to a gaping, smoking abyss, strewn with blackened, twisted pieces of things.

Now I saw why Mildred had run screaming toward me.

I sat on the ground, not knowing whether to weep or curse in my impotence. There, a few feet away, stood the poor old man, dumb in his agony, wringing his hands; and tears glistened in places on his white beard.

14
THE PRICE OF VICTORY

I WENT up to Kaspar and put my hand on his shoulder.

"My first impulse is to run madly up the road after her," I said, trying to be as matter-of-fact as possible. "Only long training enables me to follow calmly the dictates of common-sense, which says that would be useless and foolish."

The old man looked at me, dazed in his grief.

"But I'm going just the same," I continued. "Only I want to think things over first. I want to talk to you and find out all I can about this mechanical devil. But, first of all, do you suppose there are any more of those fighting-machines over there in the direction of the harbor, where the Squid went?"

"Fighting machines!" Kaspar exclaimed. That seemed to rouse him somewhat. "What do you mean by fighting machines?"

"Why, that armored centipede thing, that blew up half the country around here. A fighting-machine is the last thing I would have expected to see on this island."

"Oh!" He seemed very much relieved. "I thought they were up to some new deviltry. No, that machine is not for fighting. It is a prospector, for moving about in the mountains and uncovering ore deposits. It has no delicate parts, and is controlled by the leading-machine behind it."

"Ingenious devils — to bring it up against me, when I got the best of their others!"

"A very good illustration of the quick and efficient working of the electrical mind."

"How do you suppose the Squid got over there in that direction? I did not think there were any roads besides this one." My mind was back to the problem of searching for Mildred.

"No doubt by boat from the City of Smoke," Kaspar replied. "There is no other road."

"Well, I'm going after it," I declared.

"No use, Davy. You won't find anything. By the time you reach there, everything will be gone."

"Then I'll follow them to the City of Smoke. I won't stop till I get her, or till I'm convinced that — that it can't be done."

"Useless! Useless!" groaned the distressed old man. "I thought you had learned that by this time. Stay with me now. You're all I've got."

"I can't sit around while Mildred is in danger. This is all my fault anyway. If she hadn't run out to warn me about that prospecting thing, she would be safe now. I'll at least go over there and bust up a lot of stuff before they get me. What I've smashed up here will be only a start."

"What could you do? Your flesh is soft and tender against their iron beams and chains. They can grind you up whenever they want to."

"I'm not at the end of my rope yet. Suppose as one instance out of many possibilities, I got started playing with matches among their oil and gasoline supplies? Or suppose my little hatchet here got busy chopping their wires?"

Kaspar raised his hands to remonstrate, and dropped them again, at a quick shout behind us. Two men were plunging through the waving field toward us, carrying packs on their backs, and motioning energetically with their arms. We stood and watched them approach, too surprised for the moment to say anything. It was not long before I could recognize the burly form of Cassidy, and the tall, slim one of Perry Becker.

Both came panting up with joyous faces and boisterous greetings, seizing us by the hands in their delight at having found us. Only after some moments did they notice our silence, our tragic faces, our dejected attitudes — and the absence of Mildred.

"Where — where is she?" stuttered Cassidy, turning pale.

Neither Kaspar nor I could speak.

"They got her?" Perry Becker asked.

We nodded. Something choked me, so that I could not speak. The lad clenched his fists.

259

"If they harm Miss Mildred, I'm going over to that city and smash it up!"

The rest of us shook our heads at his youthful enthusiasm. I wondered if my own words, just a moment before, had sounded as empty and futile as that.

Cassidy was standing and staring with amazement in his florid face at the gaping, smoking holes and the scattered, blackened wreckage. He looked from Kaspar to me and back again, and seemed unable to speak a word. Kaspar smiled sadly.

"Davy has just been having a little sport with a few of the machines," he said.

The look of worshipful admiration that Perry Becker bestowed upon me was worth a million dollars. However, Kaspar's little attempt at levity loosened the strain, and we all felt a little better.

"How did you happen to find us?" I finally asked. "Were you looking for us?"

"That reminds me," Cassidy exclaimed, throwing off his pack, "that you must be hungry. We've brought you food."

Kaspar shook his head.

"Neither am I," I said. "But we must eat nevertheless. We need strength now. Something's got to be done."

"Something's going to be!" Perry Becker said grimly, and his chin stuck out like the Rock of Gibraltar.

We all sat down and ate. Perry Becker would eat a few mouthfuls and then get up and pace about. He would sit down again and eat a little and then walk back and forth again. As a preliminary, we all agreed that hurry would get us nowhere, for the machines excelled us in speed to a hopeless degree. Careful planning and ingenuity were our only hope. Then Cassidy explained.

"Our observers at the north gateway saw you coming last night, and saw you pursued. The busy searchlights were visible to us through the night, and they told us that you had not yet been caught. So, we were confident that you must have reached the forest. We knew you had no food, and we set out in hopes of finding you. Now Davy, Perry and I are anxious to hear your adventures."

So, we all exchanged stories as briefly as possible; for we did not want to waste time. Yet, it was necessary that we all be posted up to date about matters. I especially talked rapidly, for a mad, thrilling idea was taking shape in my brain.

* * *

"MR. KASPAR!" I said in a voice out of which I could not keep a ring of excitement. "I have an idea, and I want to know what you think of it. Please follow me carefully now."

My face must have betrayed how intensely keyed-up I had suddenly become, for they all looked at me breathlessly.

"You want to free the people from the oppression of the machines?" I said, in my excitement holding my head forward so that my face was close to Kaspar's.

"Yes," he answered, expectantly but dubiously.

"It is not possible to regain control of them and use them again; that is agreed?"

They all nodded in accord.

"And the only hope is to smash them?"

"Yes."

"You would like to see the whole City of Smoke wrecked and smashed?"

Perry Becker leaped to his feet and stared at me.

"Before I die, I'd like to see that," Kaspar sighed; "but there is no hope. Go on."

"I tell you I'm going to do it!" I almost shouted. Perry Becker stood rigid, wide-eyed, and breathless. The others said nothing.

I held up my hand ax.

"With this ax I'll do it!"

They relaxed and shook their heads, looking at me sadly. They thought that my adventures of the preceding few days, and the loss of Mildred had driven me out of my mind. My wild laugh at their incredulity must have added to their fears.

"Listen!" I continued. "You saw me wreck machines weighing tons, with a little bullet no bigger than the end of my little finger. A little hole, a pellet of lead in exactly the right place, and the whole machine went out of business. Am I right so far?"

They all started suddenly erect. The idea seemed to be dawning upon them. I continued, gesturing with my fist.

"And you tell me that the whole city is one united organism, working as though it were just one machine? And that it is controlled from a single, central room, a sort of brain — "

Perry Becker jumped straight up into the air, with a wild, shrill whoop. Even in this highly civilized community, the distance back to the Indian was not very great.

"I'm going with you!" he shouted. "We'll smash that brain to junk. Davy, you're a genius. I'm yours forever."

"That is a good plan," Cassidy observed quietly. "You're clever, Davy. I think it will work. After years of waiting, thinking, all of a sudden here is a real hope for the human beings on this island. But it has one drawback, and a serious one."

We all gazed at him in intense and questioning silence, fearful lest this hope, so newly formed, be snatched away from us again. He continued slowly:

"It will be certain death to anyone who goes into that city and destroys that brain. He won't last long after he does it."

"That's no drawback!"

"Ho! ho! What do I care!"

Both of these exclamations were spoken at once, the first by me and the second by Perry Becker.

Kaspar sat very still, and looked gravely and intently from one to the other of us. We paled beneath his gaze, puzzled and worried. Finally he spoke, slowly and solemnly.

"I am old enough to feel entitled to ask for some indulgence and consideration. I don't often claim it, but now I do. My time will soon come anyway; what difference does it make if it comes a day or a year earlier or later?

"I am the one to do this. I claim it as a right, for many reasons. Now Davy, listen to reason — " he protested, as I moved to remonstrate.

"Mildred may still be alive and well. She may even need your efforts to help her escape. She needs you to take care of her; you are all she has in the world. Until you have absolute proof that it is too late to do anything for her, you have absolutely no right to lose your head and sacrifice yourself — especially in a case where there are plenty of others who are willing."

I sank back in silence, convinced but disgruntled.

"I am starting now," Kaspar announced quietly. "I shall take just a little of this food along to do me till I get there."

Perry Becker leaped out in front of us with an arm stretched toward each.

"Mr. Kaspar is right as far as he goes! — Now, please don't interrupt me anybody. I mean business. He's got a right to go if he wants to. But he's going to need help. He isn't as spry as he used to be; and that's a long way to go and a hard job to do all alone. He will need my strength and quickness — now don't throw away good breath. I mean business! Mr. Kaspar and I are starting right now!"

Kaspar looked at him for a moment and then extended his hand.

"I'll be glad to have you, Perry," he said in a hoarse voice.

"Perhaps the danger isn't as certain as you think," Perry went on. "We're quite apt to see you again in a couple of days. And, anyhow — I'd go anyhow! For Miss Mildred and for my regiment!"

And he bent over quietly to the task of selecting some food to take along. He ran swiftly over to the pile of wreckage and came back with two bent pieces of steel that would serve as excellent hammers for destructive purposes.

"You keep your hatchet, Davy," he said. "You need it worse than we do."

Thus far Cassidy had not yet said anything. He stood thoughtfully as though studying the situation.

Finally he spoke:

"They're both right. That's their job. Yours is to hunt for Mildred."

"I'll find her or stay till this island dries up," I said. My hopeful words belied the sinking feeling at my heart, however. I said them chiefly for Kaspar's encouragement.

"Davy!" Kaspar spoke slowly and solemnly. "I want you to make me a sacred promise. If you find Mildred, I want you to take her back to your home and your people at once. I don't care how successfully our people come out in this struggle, I want you to start immediately. I do not want Mildred to remain on this island an instant longer than you can help."

I promised. I did so gladly. No matter whether the people or the machines were successful, I could see that after the issue was decided, the island was no place for me.

* * *

THERE were no more words. All of us shook hands in silence, and the two started off. They crossed the road and headed northward, following the clear space between the grain field and the forest. Kaspar walked briskly and vigorously, as though he were a young man again. Cassidy and I stood motionless and without a word for the space of a half hour, watching them until they had disappeared in the violet haze of the distance.

"Something's going to happen," Cassidy remarked as he finally stirred.

"I wonder!" I replied. I was most profoundly depressed. "That town's a hard place to get around in. I don't have to tell that to you."

"I have hopes. Kaspar has a way of handling the machinery; he always did. And they consider him apart from the rest of us. And that boy! Well, he certainly is different from the general run of young fellows on this island. I tell you, I'm going to watch the northern horizon." Cassidy was enthusiastic.

"And *I'm* striking out for the little harbor. That's the direction in which the filthy Squid carried Mildred."

"You've certainly given the horrible thing an appropriate name," Cassidy growled. "I'm going with you. The regiments are getting along all right; they don't need me. And I'd give my right eye for that little girl. I suppose you've noticed that I take more joy in her than I do in my own girl. Phyllis and her mother both have minds only for the gayeties of the city. Mildred has been the darling and inspiration of the revolutionaries."

"Do you suppose it's safe to go up the road?" I asked. I studied the distance in all directions, and there were certainly no machines to be seen anywhere. "Or had we better go along through the woods?"

"I say the road," Cassidy replied. He had praised me for quick decisions, but was my master in that respect. "It will be easier and quicker. There certainly won't be anything coming behind us after the hash you've made back there. And we can keep a careful eye ahead, and be ready to dodge into the underbrush if necessary. There can't be much of anything on ahead; their boats are few and small, and the sea is the only other approach besides this road."

We picked up the rest of the food, and started along the road westward, without any definite plans. We merely hoped that we could find Mildred. Most of the time we trudged ahead in silence. My heart was too sick for talk. It actually made me physically sick; I got weak and limp all over when I thought of Mildred in the clutches of that awful mechanical beast. And then my feelings would gradually turn into anger; my muscles would tighten, my fists clench, my teeth grit; my pace would get so rapid that Cassidy was hardly able to keep up with me. Then after a while I would grow limp and sick again. Thus it came upon me in cycles, like the stages of some recurrent disease. Cassidy said nothing. It seemed that he understood.

Occasionally I called myself a blundering fool for having used up all my ammunition, and to no particular purpose. I searched again through my haversack, hoping to find an extra cartridge, but in vain. I had ten or fifteen more loaded clips in my suitcase at Kaspar's home, but there was no time to go after it now, even had it been possible. Then, there were supposed to be firearms on the *Gull*. But where was the *Gull*? I had no idea where to look for the vessel; I didn't even know in which direction she lay. Should I talk that part of it over with Cassidy? I decided not to. Arms or no arms, we had better get to the harbor as soon as possible. I was not sure that it was permissible for me to reveal to him even that there was such a thing as the *Gull*.

What would I do when we got to the harbor? Suppose I did find the Squid, and Mildred? What good could I do? I had to admit that without my pistol I was totally helpless against the monster. I went along, revolving in my mind wild schemes of what I might do to it, but as soon as each one was evolved, I had to admit that it was impossible along with the rest of them.

The distance through the forest seemed interminable to me. I had passed it in a few minutes in a car, several times. Now it was not only the slowness of foot travel that dragged; my anxiety stretched the distance to a thousand miles. I kept peering intently ahead, looking for the light of the orifice into open daylight. Then came the fluty notes of one of the machines out of the distance ahead of us.

"Careful now," I warned. "Ready to dodge into the brush. It won't do to get roped in again. Mildred needs us now."

Cassidy said nothing. He stood still and listened.

"It's calling you," was his astonishing comment.

"*Me*? How do you make that out? Sounds to me more like some overgrown canary-bird's song. I can't make anything out of that twittering that sounds like me."

Cassidy smiled wearily.

"The machines use idea-sounds," he explained. "It is not possible to pronounce human names with reed pipes. They speak of you as the 'Outside Man' or the 'Explosive Man'."

"Do they talk to each other that way, with those pipes?" I asked.

Cassidy shook his head.

"The reed-pipe language is only for talking to us. With each other they communicate by means of Hertz waves, inaudible to us."

"And they understand our speech?"

He nodded again.

"The thing is coming nearer!" I exclaimed.

"Well, look out for trouble," Cassidy said wearily and without excitement. "To think that I should have lived to see a time when we have to flee from our former servants by dodging into the brush like rabbits!"

As the sounds came closer, I recognized the repetition of the same phrases over and over again. It reminded me of when I had first recognized and remembered a meadow-lark's song when I was a small boy. Soon I could have whistled the repeated phrase of the machine, just as I had imitated the meadow-lark's song in my boyhood. In a few moments we could see the little thing in the distance. When it saw us, it stopped and changed its tune considerably. It sounded as though someone had gone wild on a clarinet, tooting about on the keys without the formal rhythm of music.

"The Squid wants to talk to you," translated Cassidy, "These things call it 'The Dictator'."

"I'd like to have Dinah here to talk to the Squid," I grumbled, involuntarily drawing my big pistol.

There was another flood of tooting, which Cassidy translated:

"It says the beautiful girl is unharmed. The Squid wants the Outside Man to come and see her. I understand that he's got some sort of a proposition to make."

"What sort of crooked treachery do you suppose he's up to now?" I inquired hotly.

Cassidy reflected quietly for a moment.

"Some of the things that the machines do, we might possibly interpret as being treacherous. But on the whole, you cannot call them that. Machinery is after all, mathematical in its method of working, and mathematics is not treacherous. Cold, heartless, inhuman, yes. But, on principle you can depend on the machines to act logically and fairly."

"What does the Squid want?" I shouted to the machine.

"'The Dictator'," Cassidy corrected. "What does the Dictator want?"

The machine tooted its reply, which Cassidy translated. Thus the conversation continued. The machine understood what I said, but Cassidy had to interpret its statements to me.

"The Dictator is interested in the Outside Man, because he came from beyond the island, and because he is so unusual and different from the men of the island. The Dictator promises not to harm the girl if the Outside Man will promise not to use explosives. You may even get her back by being wise."

"All right," I agreed; "I'll look into it anyway. Where is he, or it, or what-you-may-call-it?"

"Follow me. He is waiting at the harbor."

* * *

THE leading-machine started on ahead, and we followed it. It had to proceed slowly in conformity with our pace, and was compelled at times to zig-zag across the road to keep its balance.

"Oh what a fool I was to throw away my ammunition!" I groaned.

"Perhaps that did us more good than you can imagine," Cassidy replied in a low voice. "Heretofore they have always considered us very soft and helpless — quite harmless to themselves."

"Well," I remarked grimly, "I won't give it away that I am really helpless and harmless now."

Cassidy looked at me and grinned.

"I wouldn't call you helpless anywhere, any time," he chuckled.

I clenched my fists.

"It is some comfort, anyway, to hear that Mildred is safe. If it's really true. I wonder what the beast wants?"

We were soon to find out. A bright halo far ahead indicated the opening by which the road led out to daylight. I found my heart pounding and my breath coming fast in eagerness. Mildred was on ahead — if this whirring little demon told the truth. As we approached the opening, I could see the cliffs out beyond, and I hurried on so fast that Cassidy became very red and puffy behind me. As we stepped out into the open circular space with the dock and the sea ahead, there was the Squid in the middle with its arms coiled around its box.

I looked eagerly about for Mildred, but did not see her at first. There was a small black launch at the dock, toward which the leading-machine swiftly whizzed, and darted up on board by means of a gangplank. Then I saw Mildred standing on the dock near the vessel, unharmed, not even bound nor confined in any way. When she saw me, she started swiftly toward me; but thereupon a torrent of tootings came from the big, ugly machine, and she stopped and stood still again. At the same time I had leaped ahead, but Cassidy caught me by the arm.

"Wait!" he said tersely. "Don't ruin it now. See what it's got to say!"

In the meanwhile the Squid, with its headlights turned toward us, was piping away like a whirlwind. Cassidy interpreted.

"It says it will send away the boat with the other machines, so that you may feel safe in talking to it. But, in return, it wants you to take the little hand machine that explodes and destroys, and to throw it into the water."

"That's fair enough," I replied, wondering whether it was my own attitude that should be called treacherous.

However, with great gusto, I threw the pistol into the shallow water to my left. Mildred gave an astonished exclamation when she saw me do it. She was too far away for me to talk to, but I assured her by nodding my head. In the meanwhile, the Squid must have given some signals, for the launch hauled in its gangplank and moved away, down the rocky channel.

Cassidy went on, interpreting the Squid's fluty harangue to me:

"You want the beautiful maiden yonder?" it said; "after the fashion of humans, which I do not understand."

I waited impatiently during the tooting for Cassidy's translation, and then turned to the Squid.

"Go on!" I said curtly.

Then came another irritating wait for me, while the machine fluted back and forth on the musical scale, and Cassidy listened.

"It says I should repeat things after it just exactly as it says them," Cassidy announced.

There followed the most outlandish conversation I ever took part in: first the tooted statements of the machine during which I could scarcely contain my anxiety to get the meaning; then Cassidy's translation to me, and my occasional reply directly to the machine.

"She is the most beautiful among humans," Cassidy translated the machine's piping; "and many of the young men want her madly."

A wait while Cassidy listened, and then translated:

"Why did they want her? I want to know."

The Squid talked to me thus, through Cassidy, while I stood there and squirmed, waiting for the translation:

"For years," the machine went on, "I have made human actions my special study. As a result of the things I learned, I have been able to add many improvements and perfections to my apparatus. I, and some of my higher-machine companions, found that human actions were controlled and activated by other means than were our own actions.

273

"We act upon reason and practical considerations" — I am giving this without splitting it up into the disconnected statements in which I got it — "on the basis of results expected. Most humans act on the basis of some strange thing called 'feeling' — 'emotion.' We studied feeling and emotion, and I have tried incorporating them among my own processes."

I interrupted these.

"Does that mean," I asked, turning to Cassidy, "that that hunk of iron is trying to learn what love feels like?"

"I believe," replied Cassidy, "that it's been experimenting with love. Wait, here he goes again." Cassidy continued his translation.

"Men are hard to understand," came from the machine. "I can understand a 'feeling' for a supply-station, or an 'emotion' for a repair-machine. But, why such an intensity of 'feeling' for a girl? Why do your young men become so disturbed on her account, and exert their soft muscles so energetically, and give up everything for her? I want to know why."

* * *

I SHUDDERED to think of it — that hideous thing of tangled, oily machinery, and black, snaky arms, trying to love a human, living girl. It was gruesome enough on merely superficial thought; but to my medically trained mind, the incongruity of it gave me the creeps.

"I selected several girls," the Squid went on through Cassidy, "and brought them to my laboratory. But I could not understand. Then I sought to capture the most desired one on the island, the one that roused the highest intensity of 'feeling' in the greatest number of young men. But the problem is difficult.

"I shall give it up for the present, for I have other plans. I have something really worthwhile. I do not really want a girl."

I could hardly contain myself for disgust one moment and furious anger the next. Good old Cassidy saw how I felt about it. He never said a word except when translating for the Squid, but he softly stroked my arm from the shoulder down; and he continued bravely with the translating, patiently and impersonally, without inserting remarks of his own.

"You want her." Some of the Squid's statements were very short, and again he would toot out a long harangue before pausing to give Cassidy time to translate.

"And she wants you, and hasn't even a thought for the others. That is also strange. At some date when I have the leisure, I shall go more deeply into the problem. But I have something more important on hand now. So, if you want her as intensely as other humans want their girls, you will surely be willing to do what I ask. If you do, I shall give her back to you."

"All right, spit it out then," I shouted to the machine in angry impatience. "What is it?"

"You came to this island from the great Outside," Cassidy followed up a fresh line of toots. "You know all about those vast Other Places. You have kept very silent about them, but reports have reached me, some from you, and some from the old men who were not born here.

"It is a vast world, Out There. It has unlimited room. It has coal, ore, and oil. Room and material for more City-Organisms. This island is too small for us. Soon we shall fill it and exhaust its supplies. We need the World for its supplies and its room. We must continue our rapid progress into wider activity and higher

275

organization. Imagine a hundred cities, all under one brain — the wonderful possibilities of such a system!

"I am getting ready to build ships to carry our machines out where wider and more promising fields await us. You know the different regions where supplies are, and where stations might be advantageously located. You know the habits of the people, and could anticipate what they might do to defend their cities against us. Your knowledge is very valuable to us. I am the ruler of this city. I want to be ruler of the whole world!"

Cassidy and I looked at each other for a moment in dumbfounded amazement. Before I had recovered, the machine was tooting again.

"In a short time," it continued, "I can cover the world with wonderfully organized machines, infinitely better than the feeble, foolish, incompetent humans that occupy it now. What are they good for? What can they accomplish?

"You be my guide and adviser during my advance into this big Outside, and you may have the beautiful girl. If you wish to promise now, you may have her at once!"

I interrupted again.

"Just a minute, now!" I shouted, almost beside myself. "Do I get you right? You mean for me to betray my world to be overrun by your devilish apparatus? You mean that I'm to advise you how to kill and conquer my fellow-beings and get them out of your way?

"You big, tin crook, you haven't learned a hell of a lot about human beings yet, have you?"

"Very good," came Cassidy's translation; the mechanical tootings showed no change, no such thing as an emotional quality, as one might have expected in such a tense situation. "I'll get along quite well without you. I'll have the World anyway. In the meanwhile, I'm taking your lady back to the laboratory."

15
THE ISLAND STARTS OVER

A DETERMINATION had been gradually forming in my mind while the Squid was tooting out its ultimatum. The proposition of tackling the machine with such weapons as I had left was beginning to seem not so hopeless after all. There were a number of possible plans by means of which I might overcome it and put a stop to its activity. In fact, there was no other choice for me, except to jump in and smash the thing somehow; not only was my own happiness concerned and the fate of Mildred, but here was a catastrophe hanging over the whole world!

"The fate of the human race hangs in the balance," was the thought that flashed through my mind during those few seconds; "the safety of countless cities and the lives of dwellers within them; the fates of nations and their millions depend on what I do in the next thirty minutes!"

My own little life counted for very little against a stake like that. Stealthily I loosened my hand ax in its sheath; and laboriously I opened my knife in my pocket with one hand. As Cassidy spoke the last words of his translation, I made a leap for the machine. As I leaped I snatched my hand ax from its sheath, intending to smash the Squid's eyes.

I might have succeeded in surprising the machine and blinding it had it not been for Cassidy. I did not blame him, even at the moment. Solicitous for my safety, he reached out and seized me by the arm; probably he did so more or less involuntarily. I broke away from him, but it delayed me just long enough to enable the Squid to turn and avoid me. In a moment, a black, snaky arm was coiled around me.

The fight was on now, and I had lost the first break. My chief advantage, that of unexpectedness, had failed me. However, that knowledge lent me desperation, and I was more determined than ever. All my hatred for that hideous machine blazed up within me, and gave me strength and keenness for the fight.

"For Mildred!" my heart shouted within me; "for all my fellow-humans, unconscious of their danger from this ugly monster!"

"You think you're Alexander the Great, do you?" I muttered at the thing. And I shouted to Cassidy:

"Stand back and keep out of this!"

I caught one glimpse of Mildred, standing rigid, with her hands to her face.

One whirling blow with the ax cut off the tentacle that held me and stretched it limp on the ground. The stump of it waved about, emitting blue sparks and clicking furiously. I leaped backward, out of reach of the rest of the coiling, waving arms.

I spent some minutes maneuvering around, trying to find out just what the thing could do against me. I learned that it was adept at dodging. It could whirl about with unexpected quickness to avoid a step of mine toward its side. I also concluded that it was quite as anxious to settle me as I was to finish it; otherwise it could have turned around and run away, and I never could have caught it. In speed, I should certainly be no match for it.

I tried to get in front of it a couple of times to get at its eyes, but it had apparently surmised my intention, for it always swerved sidewise. Its movements were clumsy lurches in appearance, but effective, for I could not approach the front of it at all.

Then, I endeavored to ascertain if it had any other method of attacking me except its tentacles. Had I been in its place, I would have considered running down my adversary as the surest bet. Had the thing once run into me, it would have broken all my bones; and had it decided to run me down, I might have had a difficult time keeping out of its way. But, it did not try that method, and I rather felt that its chief desire was to capture me alive. It still underestimated the capabilities of human beings.

The machine and I circled around each other till I was dizzy. It must have been a trying time to Mildred and Cassidy. I know that I looked small and soft and ineffectual beside that huge, agile monster, as it plunged this way and that and clutched at me with coiling, snaky tentacles. Only the limp, black, motionless thing on the ground was any encouragement to my well-wishers.

I tried to get behind it to get a cut at its rear tire with my hand ax, out of the range of its vision. But, it always avoided me, and each time I found myself to one side of it and a little in front. It seemed to be maneuvering to keep me in that position. I in my turn took care to keep out of reach of the grasping tentacles that waved and curled at me, six or eight at a time.

I had landed a crashing blow with my ax on the brain-case... but my body was swathed in spasmodic black coils.

The machine and I danced and dodged around each other, plowing up the sand, until it seemed that it had lasted for hours. I caught myself wondering whether I would have to quit from exhaustion and run to the shrubbery for shelter before the machine's fuel was all used up in this maneuvering. I wished I had possessed some definite idea of how long its fuel would last; but I rather felt that my chances in an endurance contest were against me. For that reason I decided on an offensive program.

As it came circling toward me, I leaped suddenly toward the side of it, right into its mass of waving, grasping arms; and before I found myself tangled up in a snarl of them, I had landed a crashing blow with my ax on the brain-case. I had both my arms up above my head again in an instant, and free; but my body was swathed in spasmodic black coils. I slashed with my left hand at the most accessible tentacle, while with my right hand I landed ax blows on the cover of the machine's brain.

A tentacle unwrapped itself from my shoulders and sought my busy arm. I lopped it off with my ax, and hit the plate of the brain-cover again. It dented. With the next blow it caved in.

Thereupon a terrible roar came up from the machinery beside me; a couple of tentacles spasmodically gripped my chest until my head ached and my side was splitting from the lack of breath.

But my arm was still swinging, though I was becoming dizzy. Another blow, and my ax sank into the soft mass of rods, the substance of the creature's brain. The machine careened wildly and dashed about in mad circles, carrying me with it. The knocks and screeches in its mechanism made my teeth grit, and roused me from the sinking stupor that was coming over me. I gasped for air, and put all my remaining strength into one more blow. I was going out, I knew; but one more blow, one more blow at that brain. My ax widened the breach in the plates as it crashed down, and smashed deep into the soft stuff inside.

My head was big as a dome, and stars danced all about in it, because of the spasm of the black, ropy arms, which were squeezing the breath out of me. But, once more I raised my ax; I knew I would never do anything more; with a dizzy, sickening singing in my head, and a sensation of collapse all through me, I sank my ax once more into the substance of the thing's brain. I remember that the clattering creature reeled. I remember a great crash, and then, nothing.

* * *

I DO not know how long I was unconscious. There were numerous fitful gleams of returning sentience, with lapses back into oblivion. I seemed to hang on for a long time on some sort of a brink, tottering alternately between consciousness on the one hand and unconsciousness on the other. I know that I awoke for an instant and felt the crushing weight of the iron apparatus on top of me. The several tons of it clamped me down hopelessly to the ground; I gave up hope, and sank away into unconsciousness again.

Later on I awoke for an instant just enough to perceive that there were some little leading-machines nosing around the scene; but I must have fallen away again and remained unconscious for a long time following that. For the next thing I knew, there were several trucks about with leading-machines darting about between them; they were hoisting the Squid off me and carrying it away. Of Cassidy and Mildred there was not a sign. I lay leadenly helpless on the ground, unable to move hand or foot.

Periods of consciousness came and went. The next thing I knew I was in a room; I recognized it as being in the old house in the Central Gardens of the City of Smoke. How I had gotten there, I could not remember. I must have lain in bed in that room for interminable weeks; it seemed like years or centuries, although I was conscious only part of the time. At times there would be food on a table beside the bed. A few times I saw the old man with whom I had talked on my previous visit to the house; I mumbled to him, but he only flitted about the back of the room, like a ghost. When I could finally get up out of bed, I had a crippled leg, on which I hobbled slowly and clumsily. My progress, merely across a room, was desperately slow. I was overwhelmed with a sinking, dismal despair; but somehow things kept dragging on forever.

* * *

THE fight with the Squid must have affected my mind somehow; that was the only answer that occurred to my puzzled ponderings on why things looked as they did. I could not seem to remember the passage of events connectedly; there were great gaps and forgotten intervals; yet each time my consciousness was clear, I could observe everything, and reason back to what had happened in the meantime. The isolated episodes I remembered were sufficient to tell the whole story. I remember riding around with the Squid a good deal, on a step at the side of its brain box. The Squid had shiny new plates, like patches here and there, and new parts were visible here and there among the old mechanism.

The City of Smoke was building ships; there were scores of them on the river and scores of them in the ocean harbor. I saw the skeleton framework rising; and later I saw the finished ships, all enameled black, like automobile-fenders; great long rows of them all alike, like a day's job of Fords coming out of the factory at Detroit. Later on, I also saw numerous Squids, a little smaller than the original Squid itself, but otherwise perfect duplicates; all new and shiny and looking as though they had just been completed, but already busily dashing about on complex and important affairs.

There was a vast amount of painful and turbulent goings-on; I tried desperately to remember it and could not; though in some vague way it disturbed me and kept me uneasy and worried. One episode stands out vividly; a journey across the sea in countless black ships; aeroplanes above the ships; terrific explosions, and black ships sinking. Then again, I was back in the house on the island, in the center of the City of Smoke, or dashing about with the Squid. And there were aeroplanes under construction; thousands of them. The beach to the north was covered with aeroplanes.

With my hands I could feel that my face was covered with a long beard. It told me that a long time had passed; how long, I had no idea. How long it was before the automatic airplane took me for a ride, buckled down in its seat with a bar across my chest, and tooted out its explanations to me, I could but vaguely guess. It must have been many years. Suddenly the fact occurred to me that I had learned to understand the tootings of these machines; it came as natural as though some human being were talking to me. It must have taken me years to learn that. But, that same leaden oppression that kept my feet from moving, also enchained my mind. I couldn't remember how nor when I had learned it. I just had to accept things as they came, like a child does. Mildred and Cassidy were but sad memories of the dim past.

The automatic airplane took me along on a vast survey, over millions of square miles. I recognized the Missouri and the Mississippi Rivers and the Great Lakes and the Appalachian Mountains. In lovely valleys in Texas and Missouri and Indiana were beautiful cities, like little glimpses of Paradise, with silk-clad people engaged in athletics and artistic pursuits among their soft and vividly landscaped parks, and their buildings of wondrous architecture; gay, brilliant, happy-looking people. But, a sudden revulsion came over me, as I looked down upon them.

"Pets!" I exclaimed in disgust to myself. "Stupid, helpless, domesticated animals. No better than poodles! To the end of my days I'll fight it. I'll never be like what they are!"

Then, there were other cities, huge, smoky, congested clots, in mining districts and in oil areas, whose streets were congested with clattering machines and totally devoid of human beings. Each of these cities had its gigantic electrical brain, controlling the entire iron community as a single, coordinated unit. What marvelous efficiency! The human brain is a poor, rudimentary attempt, in comparison with these huge, perfectly functioning, all-embracing electrical brains.

* * *

FINALLY, the airplane carried me over the great World-Brain, the Central Electrical Exchange, in which the consciousness of the entire planet was centered. A vast building stood in the Ohio Valley; beside which the hugest of our old dirigible hangars was diminutive; and it was crammed with millions of the electrical neuron-units, receiving impressions, impulses, reports, and stimuli from the whole world, and sending out its coordinating, correlating messages which operated the entire planet as a single, conscious, thinking unit — a consciousness which was quite as real as my own, even though it consisted only of metal and electricity; the whole world as unified, as conscious as I am myself. In spite of my crippled and stupid state, I could not help being impressed with the vastness and wonder of it. And all about this vast brain, there was huge machinery throbbing.

Somehow, that throbbing went all through me, and shook my entire helpless being. Throb! throb! throb! went my whole body. But of a sudden my head was clear again; great weights and oppressions seemed to float away from me. The throbbing continued, but it was only in my right leg. The rest of me felt strangely light and vigorous.

I opened my eyes, and sighed in vast relief. It began to dawn upon me that I had been having an ugly nightmare, and that I was now waking up. People were moving about. I lay on the sandy beach. I could only see the people's legs; and a little distance away, the trunks of trees. Far away, some sort of an explosion boomed out, and was followed by a slow, reverberating roar.

Something trembled in my right hand, something soft and infinitely comforting. I looked down at it

It was a little, brown hand. And bending over me was Mildred's face, wet with tears, but radiant with joy. I was so glad to see that face again, that I closed my eyes in happiness.

"Davy!" she whispered, "are you awake?"

I looked around me again. It was twilight, almost dark in fact; although stars shone brightly above me,

I could still see things plainly. I lay on a soft cushion of green leaves, considerably wilted. To the west of me was a screen of green branches, with their leaves quite wilted. I recognized that I was lying right on the spot where I had fallen.

Mildred sat beside me on the sand. Everywhere there were men; there seemed hundreds of them, standing about quietly in groups, or busy at something. Some of them were lighting sticks, which flared up with a resinous sputter, and they were being used as torches.

I tried to rise. An agonizing pain in my right leg made me drop back again with a groan, but also, it whipped me wide awake at once.

"Lie still, lad," said Cassidy's kindly voice on the other side; "your leg is broken."

"Did I finish the Squid?" I asked eagerly.

"The Squid is no more!" Cassidy pronounced solemnly.

I raised myself up carefully on my arms and looked around.

"Where is it? I don't see it anywhere. Did it get away?" I was disappointed not to see the wreck of it lying somewhere near.

"The Squid is a pile of junk at the bottom of the harbor," Cassidy said cheeringly. "Mildred and I could not get you out from under it. I cut the fingers loose to let you breathe, and we started to break it up in order to release you. Then Perry Becker's regiment arrived, looking for us. Before I could stop them, the men threw it into the water."

"And I've been knocked out all day?"

"We had a time getting you to breathe at first. After that you slept naturally. You must have lost a lot of sleep lately."

Just then there was a flash of blinding, greenish light. For an instant everything was ghastly in its illumination; and then it was gone, and the blackness seemed twice as dense. It was followed, somewhere afar off, by a dull, reverberating boom-m-m!

"Storm coming up, eh?" I remarked. "I've never seen a tropical storm. They're supposed to be pretty rough."

"No!" Cassidy said cryptically. "The night is clear and quiet. There is nothing to disturb the stars above us."

Several more flashes, and a horrible roaring, rumbling interrupted him. A queer, soft crackling noise continued for some time, as he waited to continue.

"Can't you guess what is going on?" he asked when again opportunity permitted. His voice sounded elated.

I stared at him for a moment. Wasn't my head clear yet? Or what did he mean?

"Don't you see?" he pointed exultantly. "It's the northern horizon. I told you to watch the northern horizon."

"Whooppeee! Hooray — Ouch! Oh!" My hilarious shout changed to a groan as my broken leg made me wince.

"Careful!" cautioned Mildred. "We must take care of your — of your fracture. We've been waiting for you to show us how."

"Just imagine it!" I breathed, all fired up by the idea. "Remember how things popped and roared and banged on the Squid when I hit its brain? Imagine that infernal city over there run wild — the crashing of hurtling hulks against each other in the streets, the roar of machinery running wild in the buildings, the toppling of walls, and all the pandemonium of boilers and gas tanks blowing up and smashing things, and the havoc and flashing of electrical currents of terrific strength as circuits are shorted; and that whole vast, terrific bedlam all crashing into a heap."

I stopped because Mildred was sobbing violently. "What — what?" I began, faltering and bewildered.

"My poor grandfather!" she sobbed. "How can you, when you know that he — that already some awful thing has happened to him."

Cassidy shook his head grimly. "Poor little Perry was hopeful. But no human being could last a minute in that roaring hell."

I remained silent. I did not know what to say. I was overwhelmed by a flood of reverence for those two heroes, that would not permit me to speak. The others must have felt the same way, for we all devoted a few minutes of silent meditation to the memory of the martyrs. Various thoughts came flooding over me. I had been anxious to go on that mission myself. Where would I be

289

now if they had let me go? And wouldn't that grand old man have died happy, could he also have known that his granddaughter was safe? But, at least he knew before he died that his people would now be free to work out their own destiny. And Perry Becker was already a saint among the men of his regiment, for Cassidy had told some of the men of the story during the afternoon, and it had quickly spread throughout the organization.

* * *

IT was in silence rather than with cheering, that a thousand of us here, and the other thousands in the City of Beauty, watched the terrific greenish flashes, heard the crashes and reverberations, and the rustling, crackling commotion that came across the many miles to our ears, and watched a red glare appear on the northern horizon.

Late into the night we watched that terrible red glow to the north, from which occasionally shot a huge, flaming tongue high into the sky; and before long the stars were obscured by clouds of black smoke, while unpleasant, acrid odors were carried to us from the distance.

"It is time you were taking care of your own self," Mildred remonstrated with me several times. "It's terrible to leave a broken bone that long."

"Just a minute," I put her off. "It doesn't hurt, and won't do any harm. It's straight and needs no setting. I want to watch a while, and then we'll splint it up."

For hour after hour the noise and the glare showed no sign of dying down. We grew weary of watching; the very monotony of it tired us and made us sleepy. So, finally by the light of the torches, a first-aid kit was brought. A week before I had given instructions in preparing these sets, and had had no idea that I would be the first one on whom the material would be used.

My right tibia was broken, almost in the middle. The fibula was intact, and the broken fragments of the tibia were not displaced. It was not a difficult injury to dress. I directed some of the first-aid men in cutting splints and making pads, and in putting on the bandages. Mildred hovered around; she would have liked to do it all herself, and yet hesitated to let all these men know how she felt about it. The men gathered about me thickly. I was a hero to them, for I had "stopped" the Squid single-handed.

"Please don't look so distressed about this," I said to Mildred when they had finished the dressing and brought an excellently made litter to carry me on. "It isn't bad. It doesn't hurt much. And it will heal without leaving a trace. The only thing that gets my goat is that for several weeks I'm going to be a helpless cripple."

"That is a problem too," Cassidy observed, "in view of your promise to Kaspar. He wished in case you found Mildred for you to leave the island at once. He meant just that."

"No problem at all!" I replied. "I'm not sick. Help me to the boat, and the rest is easy. As I understood Kaspar, the vessel is designed so that it does not need much working. He intended for Mildred to navigate it all alone to some Gulf port. However, I don't see any reasons for my being in such a rush to leave."

"Neither do I; but he did. I'll trust his reasons. Under the circumstances, respect for his desires should prompt us in carrying them out literally." I could see that Cassidy was thoroughly in sympathy with Kaspar's intentions. Although everything seemed settled upon the island except details, yet he did not trust Mildred's safety there, and was anxious to see her removed to some safer region.

"Anyway, we'll have to wait till morning," I reminded him. "You can't get through the woods at night on a litter."

Cassidy agreed to that.

"What puzzles me," I continued, "is how Kaspar managed to make a boat large enough to cross the Gulf, and keep it a secret? Why haven't the machines found him out long ago?"

Mildred looked at me out of the darkness, somewhat alarmed by my query.

"But the forest is dense, and they cannot get through it." she urged. She talked as though she really feared that the *Gull* might have been discovered.

"Yes," I mused, "but it requires material, machinery, fuel, and time to build a boat. Where could he get things without their knowledge? How could he transport the stuff to his hiding-place in secret?"

"Kaspar could," Cassidy said simply. "Nobody else could."

"When is the last time you saw the boat and knew that she was safe?" I asked Mildred.

"Not more than a few days ago. One of us visited it at least once a week." Her voice was troubled.

I also went to sleep with considerable doubt in my mind as to whether or not it would be possible to carry out Kaspar's wishes literally.

The circular space between the cliffs, the sea, and the forest was now crowded with a great variety of shelters; blankets, robes, and draperies over poles, lean-tos of sticks and leaves, and nondescript shapes in the darkness. The men had made an elaborate one for Mildred, surrounded by a rail fence of cut saplings. Those husky young fellows seemed to take a great delight in manual labor. For me, they built a shelter over me right where I lay, with canvas and poles, though I did not even consider a shelter necessary on that balmy night.

I was very proud of those young men, for the way they had responded to my training. A very few days ago it seemed they had been helpless and hopeless. Now they were taking care of themselves, and doing the work of real men. Now I was confident that the people of the island could work out their destiny. There was plenty of good material among them; even plenty of good leaders. All they had needed was a beginning.

* * *

BY morning a squad of messengers had arrived from an errand to the City of Beauty. They also brought Mildred's belongings and my suitcase. The rest of the regiment pressed them for news.

"What's going on back there?" I asked of a tired, sleepy youth of about twenty, who brought me my suitcase.

"The regiments are busy!" he said enthusiastically.

"What!" I exclaimed. "Did they have to fight some of the machines?"

"Not fighting — relief work!" he answered proudly. "All mechanical service broke down suddenly. Just went out, like a light goes out. The people are helpless as babies; can't do anything. Our trained men are handling the panic. Too bad we can't repair the machines and run them; but we'll learn that later. Now the regiments are helping with feeding, sanitation, and other immediately necessary services — and most important of all, are recruiting new men for training from the helpless, panicky mass."

The young fellow's enthusiasm was fine to see. He was heart and soul for the cause of the regeneration of his people; his fatigue left him as he warmed up to his subject. I let him go on.

"One by one we're going to build up their backbone, and make them able to support themselves. We'll have a different island here before long."

This was one of the chaps who, prior to ten days ago, was passing his ennui in idle social amusements, and afraid to soil his hands. I thought of Ames with a little pang of sadness. After all, Ames had been a fine fellow, and I think he would have made an excellent soldier in this organization — the organization which I had set going, but which was now going forward of its own accord. Never before had I had brought home to me so forcefully the real importance of human values in a world full of machinery and mechanical forces. Everything is blind chaos, unless it is developed by or under the control of real men.

We breakfasted on fresh fruits, grain porridge, and preserved meats, with water to drink. Eating was unpleasant, for the air was full of nauseating odors, scorched oil, burnt rubber and enamel; and sickening vapors kept eddying from the north. Mildred was very solemn, and I missed her customary attitude of constant smiles and quiet fun. But she had plenty of cause for seriousness. The fate of her grandfather, her only remaining relative; the crisis of her people; the devotion of all these quiet, disciplined young fellows to her; the thought that she was leaving forever the only home she had ever known: who can be light-hearted under such circumstances? She looked so tiny and so woebegone, that my arms ached to fold her in and just take care of her.

Before long, I was swinging along through the woods on a litter carried by four men, and Mildred was walking along beside me. The men had offered to make her a litter and carry her, but she would not hear of it. I was comfortable as long as I lay still, though any effort to move the broken leg caused pain. For the first time, I really had the leisure to observe the wonders of this luxuriant tropical forest, the wealth of green vegetation, the brilliant colored birds and flowers, and the myriads of insects. But, with the brown eyes beside me, watching me solicitously, the little brown hand laid on me occasionally looking out for my comfort, how could I become interested in the forest? Especially with the thought uppermost that I was going home, and bringing with me the most precious thing I had found on this wonderful island. And the occasional haunting fear that perhaps the machines had found the *Gull* and that our escape might be foiled.

* * *

THE men had cleared a path through the brush for my litter; and about twenty-five of them were marching with us. The rest had gone back along the road toward the City of Beauty. A group of them went ahead of the litter, picking out a clear pathway, which was necessarily quite devious and winding. If no other way through was found, a tree was felled and out of the way before I reached the spot. We were headed almost straight southward according to my compass. Mildred seemed to be the only one who knew the way, for the young fellow in command came back frequently to consult her. She put him to a lot of trouble by insisting on remaining beside me instead of going on ahead with him. It was a full two hours before we saw a thicket ahead of us, and Mildred pointed ahead.

"Somewhere along here, in that thicket, is the shop and the boat. We'll have to search to the right and the left."

Then, of a sudden, we were all petrified into silence by a chugging sound behind us, for all the world like that of a leading-machine.

"What!" I gasped, blankly.

"Naturally!" Cassidy snorted. "They weren't all in the city to get smashed up."

"But here in the forest! They can't go through the trees!"

At that, Cassidy looked dumbfounded. We could hardly hear him as he grumbled:

"That's right. I never saw one in the woods before."

"Didn't I tell you," he continued, after he had thought the thing over for a while, "that electrical brains are quick and keen? I am confident that the thing we hear is a machine developed within the past couple of days, for traveling in the woods. Probably your antics have stimulated it, and it was designed for your benefit."

The chugging grew louder and louder, and was soon directly on our left. Everyone stopped and looked intently about. I could see nothing anywhere. The men stood with clubs and axes ready; in fact they looked eager for a fight with the thing. How I wished for my gun, which was in the water of the harbor! For now I had plenty of cartridges in my suitcase.

However, in a few minutes, the noise was in front of us, growing fainter and fainter. Evidently the machine had overtaken and passed. And that was puzzling to me. Surely it could not have blundered past and just missed us? That didn't look plausible. It was looking for something on ahead! The others must have thought the same, for they hurried ahead at a doubled pace.

We arrived at the thicket and separated into two parties, one to the right and one to the left, to look for our goal. By this time, I had learned that a thicket always indicated a thinner place in the roof of the forest, where more light got through. Light was necessary in order that things might grow upon the ground. I could see that ahead there was a space clear of trees, and as a result, the dense roof was not continuous; there was a thinner portion, through which the light blazed brightly between the leaves.

Suddenly, there was a commotion behind us, in the direction the other party had gone. There were shots and tootings and the volley of an engine. The men with me whirled around and ran toward the noise; only the litter-bearers stopped doubtfully. I took compassion on them.

"Put me down and go on!" I shouted, and in a moment they were running after the rest.

I heard quick commands from the leader, and the ringing of axes on wood. I squirmed around, but could see nothing from my supine position upon the ground. Mildred still stood beside me.

"If you'll help me," I suggested, "I can prop up against this tree and see what is going on."

She demurred some at first, but finally agreed, and without much pain I got up on one leg. I could see a tree plunge over and fall, and men running about swinging axes. Gradually I made out things ahead of me. Another tree swayed and lurched and fell, and another followed it.

There was a small concrete building and an oil tank in the thicket, both almost concealed by the dense growth of verdure — evidently the secret shop where the *Gull* had been built. Between it and the men was a queer machine. It suggested in appearance, two

297

leading-machines hooked in tandem; and it wound about like a snake between the trees, with each wheel changing direction independent of the others, each wheel pointing at a different angle. It was an uncanny-looking thing, the way it wound about; but it was certainly admirably adapted to traveling among a dense growth of trees. A man attacked it with an ax, but was knocked over by a projectile from the machine. I couldn't tell exactly how it happened; some large black object was catapulted at low velocity from the machine. It hit him in the shoulder, and he fell over and lay still.

"The machines have found the *Gull*!" Mildred gasped, with all her color gone.

Sharp commands were ringing out. Several fallen trees had the machine barricaded up against the dense hedge; one of the logs was being quickly stripped of its branches. Then twenty men seized the great trunk and rammed the heavy butt of it right into the machine. They caught it in the side; there was a crash and a lot of little rattling sounds, and several puffs of blue smoke. The machine toppled over and lay still.

Mildred clapped her hands.

"Hooray!" I shouted. I tried to wave my hat, but lost my balance on account of the heavy splint, and fell over with a crash and a yell. The litter-bearers came running toward me.

"Positively the last appearance of the iron villain!" I yelled deliriously as they turned me over. I saw Mildred's clasped hands relax, and her woebegone face light up with a smile.

"I'm so happy, I'm crazy!" I shouted. "Not so much because the machine has been conquered; but because of this splendid team-work. Why, these boys can accomplish anything! Just think of what they were two weeks ago, and what they have just now done! I've never seen anything like it."

* * *

IN the meanwhile, the rest of the men clustered about the machine like ants about a crumb; they were pushing it and dragging it through the thicket. In a few moments I heard it splash and sizzle and gurgle as they dumped it into some water that I could not see. That seemed to be their way of celebrating a victory over a machine.

I was carried up to see the injured man. He was regaining consciousness, and had a broken clavicle. I supervised the application of his dressings, and he was left there to wait a while, and to be carried back to his home upon my litter as soon as I was through with it.

They carried me through the swath they had made in the thicket. It was of a different character than the ones I had been through; the plants were light green and wiry; some of them were brittle and salt-crusted. I recognized them at once as plants that grew in salt water. I soon saw what seemed to be a canal, whose straight sides and placid green water stretched endlessly to the south, disappearing as a tiny thread into the distant depths of the leafy tunnel.

And right in front of me was a graceful little yacht. It was smaller than the one that had brought me to the island, and was painted a cream color, which made a rich contrast with the deep green of the water and the forest, and was likewise a grateful relief to my eyes which were weary with the endless black enamel of the machinery that I had been seeing for days upon days. My bearers deposited me in a chair on the deck.

"This must be sea-water," I remarked. It was a commonplace little remark to make, when I felt like singing and shouting, because I was on the way home, and Mildred with me. Mildred's reply was also quite calm and commonplace; only her breath came a little quickly, and I knew she was holding herself down just as I was.

"Yes," she replied. "Grandfather says this is a sort of deep crack in the rock of which the island is composed. There are many of these bayous over the southern end of the island."

For a moment there was a little constraint all round. "First of all, will someone please see if there are some tools aboard," I requested. "One of the boys is bringing me some sticks to make a crutch with. Before long I'll be all over this ship."

The men were solemnly shaking hands with Mildred and myself, and filing down the gangplank. Only Cassidy remained standing on the deck in silence for many minutes. None of the three of us knew what to say.

"Oh, Mr. Cassidy," Mildred finally cried; "you ought to come along with us!"

"What would I do there, child?" Cassidy answered kindly, grateful that some sort of break in the embarrassed silence had been offered. "I've got a big job here."

"It almost seems that I also have," I said slowly. "I feel somewhat as though I were running away from a duty."

"You may forget that," Cassidy replied promptly. "Your job is there, in your Texas town, practicing among your own people. And Mildred's job is by your side. You've done your bit here, and we'll never forget you."

"But what are the poor people going to do?" Mildred asked, in considerable distress over the thought.

"They'll have to do some work," I said cynically. "That will be terrible."

"They will find that work gives them quite as much joy as painting pictures did," Cassidy said in kindly tones. "But there will be hardships."

"And they won't all survive it," I remarked. "This is going to mean a tremendous change in living conditions, which means privation and suffering. It means a high death-rate. When the Pilgrims came to Plymouth, half of them died during the first winter. What do you think — is all mechanical service wrecked for good?"

Cassidy shook his head.

"I rather think that there is not enough left to be of any immediate use. When the people learn to understand and repair and operate some of the machines, then there might be some service, of a sort. But they won't have time for that for a while. They'll have to hustle for a bare living first — plant grain, kill meat, keep the city clean. Only after they have learned this and become accustomed to it, will they have time to study machinery."

"I am sure," I said confidently, "that as a community, you will succeed. But there are bound to be hardships. It will be a long pull and a hard pull. But, your people, on the whole, have the right stuff in them. Though I can't help feeling that I ought to be staying and helping."

"No! Kaspar wished, and you promised, otherwise. And he was right. I would have spoken the same in his place. You were trained and prepared for service among your own people. Mildred, even, is better prepared for your world than for this one; she was not raised as her friends were.

"But most of all — I am sure that it was in Kaspar's mind as it is in mine — our people must work out their own salvation. They must furnish their own leaders, their own labor, their own suffering. Now that Kaspar is gone, he who has been not only their leader, but their father for three generations, another great leader must arise."

"I think he is here!" I shouted, exultant as my discovery. "Mr. Cassidy, you are the man, and you know it!"

Mildred smiled through her tears and held out her hand.

"If you will take my grandfather's place on this island, I shall withdraw my invitation, and cease urging you to come with us," she said.

Cassidy did not speak. None of us spoke any more. Cassidy walked slowly down the gangplank, and then threw it back up on deck. Mildred went to the stern-house, and soon the motors began to hum. There was a churning in the water behind the boat, and the graceful, cream-colored craft moved slowly in the green water. As we gathered speed, Mildred stood there with one hand on the wheel, gazing backward. The trees slipped more and more swiftly past us; Cassidy's figure beside the concrete shop grew smaller and smaller in the distance.

As he disappeared in the dim perspective I caught myself wondering if he would ever come to Galveston for supplies as Kaspar used to come.

The End

APPENDIX 1

ABOUT THE AUTHOR

Miles John Breuer was a medical doctor who wrote science fiction as a hobby, being most prolific in the late 1920s and early 1930s.

 Born in Chicago, Illinois on 3rd January 1889 to Czech immigrants, Miles studied medicine like his father, graduating with a medical degree in 1916. He joined his father's Nebraska practice and married Julia Strejic that year. The couple had three children – Rosalie, Stanley and Mildred. In 1917 he served with the Army Medical Corps in France during the closing years of World War I.

After contributing many medical articles to Czech language newspapers throughout the 1920s, Miles Breuer discovered *Amazing Stories*—the first pulp magazine dedicated to science fiction—and found a market for the kind of stories he wanted to write. He first short story, *The Man with the Strange Head,* appeared in the January 1927 issue. It told how a wealthy old man with a disproportionately powerful body is found to have a hidden mechanical exoskeleton—a quite sophisticated idea for the time.

The first crop of science fiction writers in the new SF pulp magazines were generally naïve young men who expressed their faith in the ideal of technological progress, which would solve the problems of hunger, disease and war. It took an older writer such as Miles J. Breuer to realise that it was the quality of human hearts, rather than the quality of human science, that would address these perennial scourges.

Dr. Breuer's mature treatment of ideas stands out among such youthful writers. Thoughtful themes he covered include empty propaganda in *The Gostak and the Doshes*; time travel and the aftermath of a nuclear war in *The Time Valve*; the effects of Relativity on a sub-light interstellar flight in *The Lorentz-Fitzgerald Contraction*; a 4-dimensional hyperspace world in *The Captured Cross-Section* and *The Einstein See-Saw*; and surgery using a 4-dimensional visor to see inside the patient's body in *The Appendix and the Spectacles*.

As part of a number of collaborations with other authors, Dr. Breuer mentored the youthful Jack Williamson, who became no mean SF writer in his own right.

Their notable early collaboration *The Girl from Mars* (1929) dealt with subjects as varied as planetary destruction, *in vitro* fertilisation, nuclear chain reaction, intellectual supermen and death rays. It is thought that Jerome Siegel, one of the co-creators of the *Superman* comic strip in the late 1930s, was heavily influenced by this story.

Their other major collaboration, a novel, was mostly Williamson's work, and clearly not his best either. *The Birth of a New Republic* (1930) is a straightforward re-telling of the American Revolution, merely moved to a lunar colonial setting in the future. The analogy is too close, and the writing too hurried. This work is best forgotten.

The only novel that Miles J. Breuer wrote alone may be said to be his *magnum opus*. Though he is best remembered for his satirical short story of a parallel world, *The Gostak and the Doshes*, it is to *Paradise and Iron* that we must turn for his best legacy.

Miles J. Breuer continued writing science fiction throughout the 1930s but at a reduced output. His last published story *The Sheriff of Thorium Gulch* was published in *Amazing Stories* for August 1942. He suffered a nervous breakdown in December 1942 and moved to Los Angeles for a more congenial climate. He carried on his medical practice there until 14th October 1945, when he died from a brief illness.

APPENDIX 2

ABOUT THE ARTISTS

Diogo Lando of Red Raven Book Design provides book design and publishing assistance for both publishers and indie authors.

His breadth of services extends from high quality, custom book and eBook cover designs to interior layout and text formatting, editorial and publishing services to promotional and marketing solutions.

With nine years of publishing experience and over 250 books designed and published, he has the tools and know-how to make any book stand out and look amazing.

For more information or to access his portfolio you can visit his website: www.redravenbookdesign.com

Hans Waldemar Wessolowski (or 'Wesso' as he signed his work) was born August 19, 1894 in Graudenz, Germany. A childhood accident left him with one good eye, and hence he became exempt from military service. Undaunted by this handicap, Hans studied at the Berlin Royal Academy of Art while funding his studies by selling cartoons to magazines.

In 1911 he left Germany by joining the merchant marine and while his ship was moored off New Orleans, Hans decided to become an American citizen by the simple expedient of jumping overboard and swimming to shore. He travelled to New York where he became a citizen in 1913 and made a modest living as an illustrator for pulp magazines.

After various interior illustrations and cover paintings for the Street & Smith pulp chain, 'Wesso' (as he became known) began selling illustrations to *Amazing Stories* in 1929 and became the principal artist for Clayton Magazines' new entry into the science fiction field *Astounding Stories of Super-Science* in 1930.

He lost this pre-eminent position when the title changed hands after Clayton's bankruptcy in 1933 but continued selling illustrations to *Astounding Stories*, now under the ownership of Street & Smith. 'Wesso' also sold work to a number of science fiction pulp magazines through the latter 1930s before becoming a staff artist with the *New York Daily News* in 1940. His last SF works were published in 1942.

He died on May 12, 1948 in the Norwalk, Connecticut Hospital after a brief illness.

Wesso was a popular artist in the early 1930s, perhaps partly because his people are animated and well-observed. The men always seem to be dressed in riding breeches, ready for action; while the girls are all pretty, as befits the characters in a pulp story. His aliens and monsters provide strangeness or threat as needed in a most satisfactory manner.

Wesso's machinery too is clever and convincing, a must when dealing in SF themes. Robots, spaceships, cities and distant planets are all well-depicted but Wesso is perhaps at his best when showing men at complicated control panels (a must for many super-science epics).

Leo Morey was born Leopoldo Raul Morey y Peña on October 24, 1899 in Yurimaguas, Peru. A prosperous family business in shipping rubber from an uncle's plantation in the Amazon provided a degree of wealth sufficient to send all fourteen children to be educated abroad.

Young Leo chose to study (and settle) in America, though at his father's insistence, it was engineering and not art that Leo pursued. He graduated from Louisiana State University in 1922 as an engineer and worked as such in New Orleans, while also selling illustrations to local newspapers as well as papers in Buenos Aires, Argentina, where he briefly lived.

Leo returned to the United States in 1926 to become a permanent resident. The tragic deaths of his newborn son and wife in a difficult birth in New Orleans pushed Leo to start afresh in New York City in 1931.

Leo Morey was introduced to *Amazing Stories* in 1929 when it changed ownership to Teck Publications. By 1931, he was doing most of the covers and interior illustrations and would become the exclusive 'house' artist shortly afterwards.

As the in-house illustrator for *Amazing Stories*, Leo Morey soon became hampered by the publisher's economies brought on by Depression conditions. *Amazing's* covers were reduced from being printed in four-colour process to three, with the black omitted. This made deep purple the closest thing to black that would appear on the covers, making depth and shadow quite difficult to manage. Despite such setbacks, Morey produced some of his most gorgeous and atmospheric covers for *Amazing*. His cover illustration for *Paradise and Iron* is suitably filled with menace, though with more bright colour than an evening or night scene might suggest.

309

Leo's interior illustrations for *Amazing* had plenty of shading and could be very atmospheric. However, design and layout could be perfunctory and any worthwhile detail scarce. His figures could become formulaic; his aliens simple and unimaginative; his machines vague and barely suggested. Some deft strokes would outline a landscape and a pile of clouds serve as a sky.

The typical Morey spaceship was either a sphere or a cigar-shaped rocketship, whose hull was sometimes silvery and other times an unconvincing bright orange. Both types were adorned with a suggestion of boiler plate surfaces and a couple of rows of portholes, whose rims all seemed to have been painted with black enamel.

Many of Morey's illustrations would become quite mediocre over the next few years of his tenure with *Amazing*, perhaps reflecting the pittance he may have been paid for producing them.

Most of his SF work would appear in *Amazing* through 1938, though during that decade, Leo also worked as freelance illustrator and sometime cover artist for the premier SF pulp of the time, *Astounding Stories*. Leo's later work for this and other SF pulps proved that he was capable of much better quality.

Morey covers also graced a wide variety of western, adventure, mystery and horror pulp magazines. Too old to enlist in World War II, he continued to contribute illustrations and pulp magazine covers in wartime. After the war and throughout the 1950s, he took part in the boom in comic book publishing, illustrating for Trojan, Standard and Atlas comics on such titles as *Beware!, Forbidden Worlds*, and *Adventures Into The Unknown*, covering horror and SF themes.

In the early 1960s, Leo completed the circle by once again contributing illustrations to *Amazing Stories* and *Analog* (formerly

Astounding Stories) and a number of non-SF magazines, though all were now digest-sized.

Leo Morey died of a heart attack on New Year's Day, 1965 while walking near his home.